ISHI'S JOURNEY

FROM THE CENTER TO THE EDGE OF THE WORLD

A Historical Novel about the Last Wild Indian in North America

by James A. Freeman

NATUREGRAPH

Library of Congress Cataloging-in-Publication Data
Freeman, James A., 1956–
Ishi's Journey from the Center to the Edge of the World

ISBN 0-87961-231-2

Cover painting and sketches by Ron Ellison

Third printing, 2002

Printed in USA by Mosaic Press.

Naturegraph Publishers has been publishing books on natural history, Native Americans, and outdoor subjects since 1946. Please write for our free catalog.

Naturegraph Publishers, Inc.
PO Box 1047 • 3543 Indian Creek Rd
Happy Camp, CA 96039
(530) 493-5353
www.naturegraph.com

Dedication

This book is for Mrs. C. W. Lawrance, 97 years young, who is enjoying the twilight of her life, and, especially, for little Kellie Ann Freeman. I wrote the first half of this book while her mother Pat and I waited for Kellie's arrival, and, after she came to us, I finished the second half while Kellie dreamed her naptime dreams. May you grow up healthy and strong, little daughter, and never forget how to dream. Aiku tsub.

I would like to thank Dr. Chris Bursk of Langhorne, Pennsylvania and Ms. Beverly Stoughton of Newtown, Pennsylvania, for their generous assistance in critiquing earlier versions of this manuscript.

Ishi on August 29, 1911

Preface

On August 29, 1911, a thoroughly wild Indian was captured outside a slaughterhouse near Oroville in Northern California. Perhaps captured is the wrong word to use, for, according to reports, he had wandered in a daze onto the cattleyard, half-dead of exposure and hunger. This Yana Indian, of the extinct Yahi tribe, was welcomed into the modern world of the whites by being clapped into jail, in order to ensure that he would not be lynched. The neolithic man spoke neither English nor Spanish, and early attempts to communicate with him were futile. He refused all food and water, preferring instead to curl in the fetal position on the bare pine cot in the shadows of his jailcell. Soon, however, he came under the protection of anthropologists Alfred L. Kroeber and Thomas T. Waterman, who took him to the University of California Medical Center in San Francisco, California, worked with him, became his friends, and recorded all that we know of the now vanished Yahi way of life.

The wild man learned a good number of English words, and the anthropologists learned a fair number of Yahi ones. The world came know this celebrated native man as Ishi, but that was not his real and private name. California Indians do not share their secret names with anyone but family and loved ones. Early on, when asked who he was in Waterman's best choice of dialect, this man from another world replied "Ishi," which means "I am of the people," or "I am a person." For the five years that Ishi lived among the moderns, in a city as fantastic as any science fiction, Ishi made many friends, but he never revealed his true name.

This is the story of Ishi, the man that the world knew and didn't know. The story is told using a fiction writer's techniques, not to play fast and loose with the truth but to deepen it. The excellent anthropologists who studied Ishi during the last years of his life have provided a foundation. They recorded as much as Ishi could give them of his language and history, and photographed him in the performance of his marvelous skills. From their loving observations emerge the outlines of a unique and compelling life story—a story that deserves to be told. This imaginative re-creation of Ishi's life moves beyond the known facts to restore the lost background and human dimensions that the last Yahi people undoubtedly experienced. I have retold Ishi's journey using the tools of a fiction writer because Ishi's story needs a narrative frame in the way a play needs a theater in order to come alive.

For those who wish to know more, both Alfred L. Kroeber and Thomas T. Waterman wrote seminal non-fiction articles about Ishi in the first decades of this century. More recently, Mrs. Theodora Kroeber (Professor Kroeber's second wife) kept Ishi's story alive. Her three non-fiction books are superb. See especially her *Ishi in Two Worlds* (University of California Press, 1961), a thoroughly readable popular classic. Before her death, Mrs. Kroeber compiled, along with Robert Heizer, the best overall source book on Ishi titled *Ishi The Last Yahi* (also University of California Press, 1979). These two books provide extensive bibliographies for readers who want to follow Ishi's clear trail as far as it leads. Her third book, *Ishi, The Last of His Tribe*, was first published by Parnassus Press in 1964. Bantam Books then reissued it.

For original versions of the Northern California Indian myths adapted in this novel, see Edward Sapir's *Yana Texts* and Roland Dixon's *Yana Myths* (printed together in University of California Publications in American Archaeology and Ethnology, vol. 9, no. 1 (1910), pp. 2-236). The First Fire myth comes from Livingston Farrand and Leo Frachtenberg's "Shasta and Athapascan Myths from Oregon" in *The Journal of American Folklore*, vol. 28 (1915). I have adapted it fictively to the Yahi tribe.

The Mary Ashe Miller newspaper account of Ishi's capture and relocation, included in this book, is but one of dozens of newspaper articles about the "Wild Man of Oroville." I have chosen hers from among the many sensationalist journalistic accounts because of Miller's accurate and unbiased style of reporting. Her article first appeared in *The San Francisco Call* on September 6, 1911, a scant week after Ishi walked from one world into another.

Contents

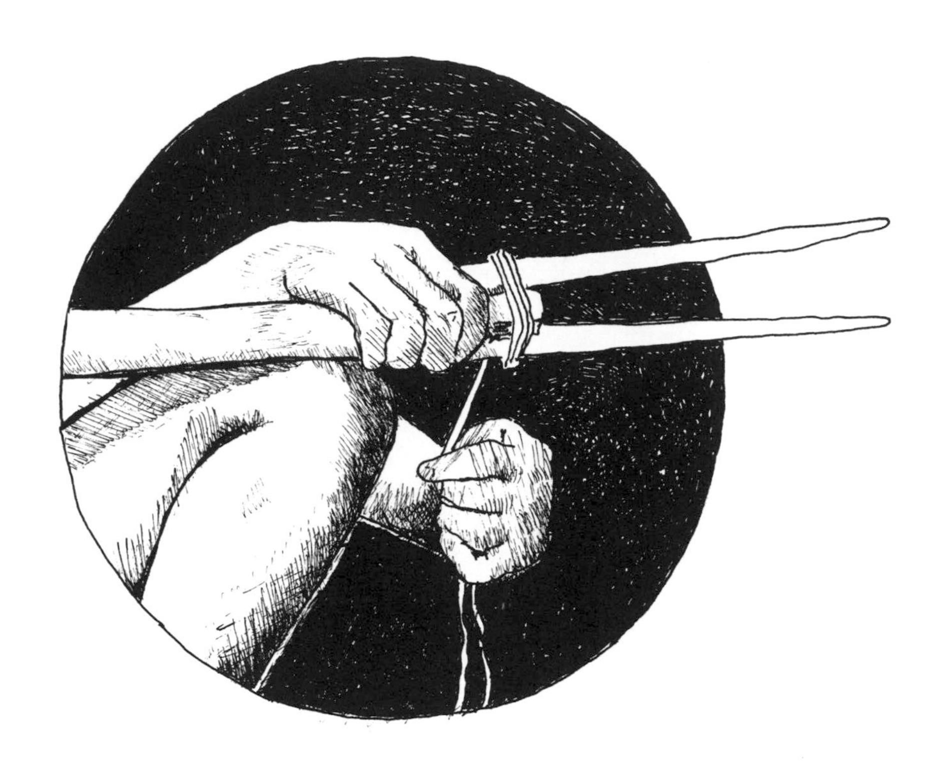

List of Yahi Words*

Ahalamila = a lesser god, subject of the creation gods Jupka and Kaltsuna
aiku tsub = it is well; it is good
aizuna = your own; my own
auna = fire
bahsi = buckeye wood
banya = deer
Coyote = a peer god of Jupka and Kaltsuna and the maker of Fate; he could be a god or a devil at will
daana = baby
Daha = large river; the Sacramento
dambusa = pretty, gentle
dawana = crazy, wild
dadichu = gray squirrel
hansi = many
haxa = yes
hexai-sa! = go away!
hildaga = star
hisi, ishi = man
humoha = hazel wood
Jikula = a lesser god, subject of Jupka and Kaltsuna, and enemy of Ahalamila
Jupka= a creation god; after making mankind he transformed into a butterfly
Kaltsuna = a creation god; later he became a lizard
kuwi = doctor
mahde = sick
majapa = headman, leader

* The first time any of these Yahi words is used in this novel, the word is followed by its English approximate. This Yana vocabulary comes from Edward Sapir's linguistic publications and Theodora Kroeber's non-fiction histories of Ishi's life. Her sources were Professor T. T. Waterman's writings on Ishi and her husband's personal reminiscences.

maliwal = wolf
mani = bow
marimi = woman
mechi-kuwi = demon doctor
moocha = tobacco
nize ah Yahi = I am of the people
Pano = first grizzly bear
Saldu = white man; ghosts
sawa = arrow
sigaga = quail
siwini = pine wood
su! = so! well! ah!
suwa! = thus it is!
tehna = bearcub
tetna = bear
Topuna = son of Ahalamila and his wife, the daughter of the moon
tuihi = sun
U-Tut-Ne = Wood Duck Man
Waganupa = Mt. Lassen in Northern California
wahsui = wild currant
wakara = full moon, moon near full
wami = wild goose
wanasi = hunter; warrior
watgurwa = men's house
wowi = family house
Wowunupo-mu-tetna = Grizzly Bear's Hiding Place (Ishi's last home in the wilderness)
Yahi = the people, human beings created by Jupka and Kaltsuna
yuna = acorn

Part I:
In the Center of the World

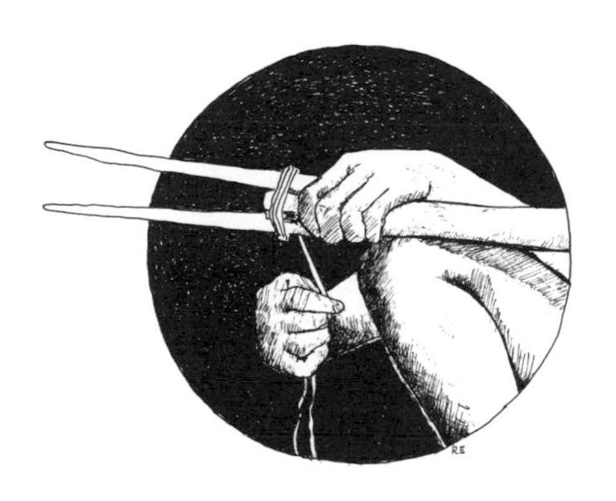

Chapter 1

Ishi lived for five years among the civilized, a living museum unto himself, a museum man among museum men. He died as he wished to, with his friends in the museum house for men. His beloved doctor and the museum men let his spirit go in the old Yahi way. They saw to it that Ishi had those things a Yahi must take from the living world: his own best bow, made in the museum, and five fine arrows; a basket of acorn meal, enough for a five day journey; and his special treasure bundle, filled with his former life. In the bundle were some shreds of his mother's hat from their home at Grizzly Bear's Hiding Place, the shells from his cousin Tushi's necklace, which Ishi had found on the bank of Deer Creek when he searched the old world for her body, the saltwater shells he had found with his new friends at the Edge of the World by San Francisco, and a few favorite pieces of obsidian glass from the Center of the World—Mt. Lassen. When Ishi died, his stone pipe was in his belt, and his pouch was filled with sacred tobacco.

For the ritual five days, my father and I went at dusk to the ocean at the Edge of the World. There we sometimes cried for our friend and scattered a fine powder of acorn meal on the green waves of the ocean, and we said Yahi prayers, but there was no end to my tears and my father saw that he must help me let go of Ishi, my friend for life from another world. He told me what Ishi had said, comforting me as we sat on our windblown bluff above the pale onslaught of waves.

It seemed that it was Ishi himself sitting beside me on the bluff, speaking in his soft pine wood voice through the ocean wind, not my father, the grieving doctor and saddened friend.

It is a five day's journey to the spirit trail, Wolf Boy, and at its end is the Yahi Land of the Dead, where the old ones, the ancestors, live on.

I will meet Tushi there and together we will find the glowing firepit of our lost family. This is how it will be,

> *Maliwal* [wolf]. *My grandfather and grandmother will be there waiting in the land where the dead live, and my elder uncle and mother and father, too. I will never again be apart from my cousin-as-a-sister Tushi, my boy cousin, and my own father. I will never again be apart from the people. Suwa* [It is the way of things], *young wolf.*

I dried my tears, and, with my father, turned away from the lines of green waves coming onshore below us. Together we walked back down the bluff at the Edge of the World to the wet sand below. The sun was almost underneath the earth, on its way to the east and another day's journey over the top of the sky. When the sand was no longer underfoot and we had been walking silently under the trees for some time, we came to the end of Golden Gate Park, where the city lights begin. There, above the last treetops, a bright spring moon shone like a fully-drawn Yahi bow.

* * *

This was how my friendship with Ishi ended, and this was how it really began.

Chapter 2

The last of the Yahi slept warily in Yuna Canyon. Their two, round, earth-covered houses made up the fugitive village. Once there had been many houses.

The boy, Ishi, awakened before the others in the house of men. He wormed himself out of his rabbitskin cocoon, without waking his grandfather, uncle, and boy cousin, and slipped, ghost-quiet, from the watgurwa (men's house). He moved close to the ground, past the house where his mother, grandmother, and girl cousin Tushi were sleeping, then ran into the pine trees beyond the village.

Ishi crawled on all fours under wet bushes, his hands and knees protected by a pine needle carpet, until he came to a wall of rock that led upward to the rim of Yuna Canyon. Once there, hardly breathing quickly, he followed the rim trail uphill a little toward Waganupa (Mt. Lassen), the great volcanic peak, until he came to Black Rock.

His overlook, the Yahi people's place of view, stood many times taller than a man, shiny black and smooth, different from every other rock around it. Ishi knew he was forbidden this point of view until he was a man.

It is time to see what we are hiding from, time to know our enemy, the Saldu.

Using his fingers and toes to hold tight to cracks in its slippery surface, Ishi climbed to the Black Rock overlook. His face rubbed against yellow-green lichen and green moss growing on the side of the rock as he worked his way upward. A waterworn hollow at the top of the rock made a spot for Ishi to sit and watch the rim trail and all around, while no one below could see him.

I will tell no one about coming here. It will be my secret place.

Ishi breathed in and out quickly now. Beyond Black Rock, the Yuna Canyon rim trail snaked across meadows, then up and up toward Waganupa, whose peak was now shrouded in pre-dawn cloud, while its base was surrounded by the flowing white mists of early morning. Two creeks flowed down from Waganupa, Yuna Creek to the north and Banya Creek to the south. Yuna and Banya cut steep canyons through the landscape, with ridges, hills, flats, and meadows in between. This was the world of the Yahi.

Ishi sat on Black Rock, watching the morning mists melt away in the dawn wash. A little at a time, then more and more, he saw east and south, and north and west. He saw for the first time a distant piece of the great Daha Valley his grandfather had told him about, and he saw below the Daha (large river) itself, real for the first time from Yahi legends, curving and bending like a green sinew rope along the valley floor. The brownish hues of the valley spread out even beyond the curves of the distant river, spreading out wide and rambling to the west, until Ishi's vision could not make out distinct shapes. Beyond the valley, he thought he saw the green coastal mountains floating in the white morning haze, but he was not sure.

When the sun had come up fully over snow-covered Waganupa, the focal point of the Yahi world, and the last of the mists had burned away, birds began to call. Quail voices in the underbrush blended with the whisper of Yuna Creek at the bottom of the canyon.

They are all awake now. They will miss me soon.

Ishi's thoughts were scattered by the distant blast of an engine—woo-hooh-hoo, woo-hooh-hoo. He had heard this sound faintly every day of his young life, every day at sunrise and at dusk, for twelve years. Standing on the rock to his full height, he saw the black creature come in sight for the first time. It moved behind the Daha, followed the great river for a short while, and disappeared around a bend, first the smoking head, then the long, snakelike body. Smoke hung in the air long after the black creature was gone.

In my dream, I leave the Center of the World and go to the valley and touch the cold skin of the black creature.

Grandfather says that dreams which return might mean nothing, or they might be power dreams of great importance, which are not understood until we have lived long enough to see their meaning.

Ishi slid down Black Rock carefully, rubbing his elbows and heels against it sometimes to slow his slide. He followed the rim trail downhill, until he slid down the wall of rock that brought him to the bottom of Yuna Canyon, among the buck brush, manzanita, and pines.

Only when Ishi came in sight of the little village did he feel completely safe. He smelled the good smells of woodsmoke and acorns in the air, and, at the village firepit, he saw his mother cooking a basket of acorn mush. He watched the mush boil. It roiled up in little peaks over the hot rocks in the reed cooking basket, and the little mountains popped when they burst, sometimes sending a tiny eruption of reddish mush out and over the lip of the basket, or running down the sides of the tightly woven mesh.

Ishi's grandmother and grandfather sat beside his mother. His uncle, the majapa (leader), and his older boy cousin came to the firepit from the men's house. Tushi, his girl cousin, carried a basket of fresh water from the creek.

Chapter 3

"Tehna-Ishi is back from wandering," said his uncle. "You can see he is a dreamer by reading his eyes. Perhaps he is the only Yahi left with dreams."

Ishi's mother looked proudly at her son. His hair was brushed neatly and tied with a deerskin thong at his neck; his deerskin sash was fresh. He now wore the ear and nose ornaments his grandfather had made for him the past winter when Ishi went from her forever to sleep in the house of men, the watgurwa.

She looked then at Tushi, the pretty little one. Her parents, like Ishi's father and all the others, had been taken by the Saldu. What will her life be like, Ishi's mother wondered. What will all our lives be like in hiding?

Ishi's mother filled smaller baskets with acorn mush from the bigger cooking basket. She served Ishi's uncle first because he was the headman, then she served the old ones, then Ishi's boy cousin, Ishi, and Tushi. Last, she filled her own colored basket.

Everyone waited for the leader. The uncle tested the acorn mush's heat, then dipped his right hand into it hungrily.

It is his sign of approval. It is the ancestors' way.

When the others began to eat and talk, Ishi realized how hungry he was. His first mouthful of the hot, sweet bitterness tasted so good in his mouth that it was almost painful. The basket in his hands warmed his fingers. Ishi heard his mother's soft voice as he ate.

She is still beautiful, though she seems to grow smaller as I grow older. Mother moves in quietness, but she is always here, holding us together, cooking, organizing food stores for the long winter, teaching Tushi the way of the women. I wish she smiled more, though, as in the days of my father.

Ishi listened to the voices of his grandmother and grandfather, watched their lined faces as they told stories of the old ways in the full morning light.

> *Aiku tsub. It is good to have the old ones sing songs, tell stories. They help us forget the Saldu.*

He turned his gaze to their leader, watched him eating, smelling the good smell of acorns. Then his uncle spoke to the little Yahi family.

"Yesterday I saw the leather foot marks of three Saldu by Yuna Creek. And bloodstains and fur where they have killed one of our tehna [bearcubs]."

> *Never have they come so close. It is wrong to kill daana* [baby] *creatures. Dawana.*

"We may have to make a new village soon," Ishi's uncle said. "Suwa! The Saldu must never know that any of the Yahi still live."

When the elder finished speaking, Ishi's boy cousin said: "We can fight these Saldu. Ishi and I are young wanasi [warriors] and are not afraid."

> *He is too bold. He teaches me to shoot the bow and to pray after a good hunt, but he is too bold.*

"Once there were dozens of Yahi families," the leader said, "and other Yana peoples and other Yana worlds, but now we are only seven. The old ones and the women cannot fight. Two wanasi and a majapa cannot fight the Saldu," Ishi's uncle said.

Everyone stopped eating. The leader looked at Ishi's boy cousin, at the shiny black length of his hair and the red toyon berry color of his flushed cheeks.

"The Saldu killed your parents, killed Ishi's father and sister, and killed my wife. They came upon our hiding cave with horses and guns and killed the remaining Yahi people. Only we seven lived under the dead and dying bodies of the lost ones because the Saldu have not the care to burn the dead and release their souls. Do you think two Yahi men and a bearcub boy can keep the Saldu out of Yuna Canyon? The Saldu are thousands in the great valley by the river Daha."

Ishi's cousin did not answer the headman. He went back to eating the acorn mush. Ishi saw that Tushi had taken this all in and was afraid. She fingered the beads of her white shell necklace. Everyone stared at the firepit.

Do not be afraid, little girl cousin. I will protect you.

* * *

Ishi was dreaming. He was with his father in the happy time before he died, in the time when many Yahi families survived together in a bigger village. Then the scene changed to one of horror.

> *Bodies huddled together in the damp cave. Little ones, be quiet. Too late for the people. Outside, the Saldu know we are here. It is too late for the people. Claps of thunder. Little ones screaming. All of us going down in the cave. Some knocked down by the flying stones, their flesh ripped. Old ones screaming too. Smell of blood in the dark. Strange voices outside. They cannot be people. Smell of blood. More Yahi going down. They cannot be animal ones. Women sobbing. Thunder sounds. Flying stones bouncing. Why would the Saldu do this? The people are going down. Yahi blood and twitching bodies on the cave floor. The people going down. Father dead, sister gone. I am running. Splashing through Yuna Creek, rocks stabbing my feet. Thunder noises. Darkness.*

The dream was different than the story Ishi's uncle told; it was different and the same too. Ishi could not tell what was the old story and what might be the new. The dream continued with images of a time yet to come.

> *Dawn breaking over Waganupa mountain hard in my eyes. Sunlight on my skin. Sounds of birds. Gnawing in the*

gut. No food for days. The deer driven away by Saldu. None of the people left anywhere around the creek. The Yahi dead in the Ancestor Cave. Grandmother and Grandfather gone. Mother dead. Tushi and Leader Uncle and Cousin gone. The creek running loud in the dawn light. I must find food soon or die too. Time passing. The creek running down out of the foothills through lava boulders and pines. Banya Creek leading down to the Saldu. I should kill them, but the killing never ends. Better to eat, to live. I have no bow, and no will to kill anymore. The Saldu are too many. I am alone. The people are all gone. Banya Creek wider as the sun climbs.

Chapter 4

Ishi awoke in the watgurwa, then stepped out below an azure sky to see the white peak of Waganupa rising above its jumble of forever-stilled stone waves of black lava. He went to Yuna Creek with a basket for water.

When Ishi returned to the watgurwa, his uncle was stirring, though his cousin and grandfather still slept. Ishi put his basket of water down.

"Majapa, I have dreamed some of the past and some of the future," he said, "and I am afraid. Will you tell me again why my father, Tetna Man, was killed and why the Saldu hunt us until the Yahi are only seven?"

Ishi's uncle, the majapa, sat up and pulled his animal robes about him in the faint smoke and shadows of the house of men.

"I will tell you again the story," the majapa said, "and I will tell you all there is to know this time, for you are now a wanasi and the moon time of our people is wakara [full]. You should know the truth. But then you must forget what the Saldu have done, and must not let it poison you. Haxa, su, it is good to live for the future. It is the only way. Suwa!"

Ishi nodded, and the two others slept on.

"A little while after you were born, Tehna-Ishi, the Saldu came to Big Meadows, far below our Yuna Creek. They took off the women and girls of our neighbors, the Maidu people by the river Daha. The Maidu wanasi secretly took revenge by killing three innocent Saldu who lived on Concow Creek. In return, many Saldu wanasi, led by people killers called Anderson and Good, who are cunning enemies of the Yahi still, came all the way up Yuna Creek, far past the Maidu, believing that we Yahi had committed the murders. Anderson and Good and the Concow Saldu came upon our people at Three Knolls, at dawn as it is now, while the Yahi slept. Saldu Anderson led his revenge wanasi to the top of the

Three Knolls, above Black Rock village. Saldu Good kept his wanasi hidden close beside the downstream entrance to our village, near the only place to ford Yuna Creek."

The majapa paused. He dipped his hands into the water basket and drank. "Have you seen this in your dreams, Tehna-Ishi?"

He knows I dream. Should I tell Uncle of my power dream last night? Should I tell him what I have seen for the Yahi?

Ishi heard the sounds of the women cooking outside at the firepit. "I have not seen that far into the past," he said.

"The Saldu Anderson is a wise killer. He has learned the ways of a wanasi from many hunts against our Yana neighbor cousins, who are all lost ones now. His hunt at Three Knolls at dawn killed over half of the people who remained."

Ishi saw his uncle's face distort with anger in the dim shadows of the men's house. Behind him, brilliant rays of early-morning sunshine coming through the smokehole painted spots of white on the dirt floor.

"As soon as Anderson's wanasi could see to shoot, they fired down again and again on the Black Rock village. When we ran downstream from the Saldu bullets, Good's wanasi cut many of us down. In such a dawana [crazy] time, the people could not think. We had not our salmon spears or bows for animals who walk close to the ground. Many Yahi jumped into Yuna Creek, and the current took them by the Saldu killers. Good's wanasi shot our people in the water until Yuna Creek ran red with their blood. Half and more of our people floated dead down the creek toward the river Daha, and we have never seen those lost ones again. Suwa! The butterfly god Jupka could do nothing; the lizard god Kaltsuna was powerless too against the Saldu, for they are not human and have no faith."

The majapa looked at Ishi with his brown eyes full of anger and sadness.

"Only some fifty Yahi escaped at Black Rock to live on under Waganupa. All of your aunts and uncles died but me, Tehna-Ishi. The Saldu wrecked our village, took the scalps of our people, and stole a little boy who was still alive. All the years you have been alive our upper village has been left overrun, the neglected bodies of our people turning to bones because it is too dangerous to make funeral pyres there. Hexai-sa! The Saldu will never go away to let us free their spirits. They are wandering restless in my dreams still."

"And Tetna, my father?" Ishi asked. "Why did they hate the Grizzly Bear man?"

"The Saldu do not know what they hate. Moons after Black Rock, in the winter, many of our remaining people were starving. Our food stores had been overturned and trampled. Some of the Yahi wanasi raided food from a ranch near Banya Creek Flat. Your father, Tetna, and the other wanasi got away, but Majapa Anderson followed their trail deep into Banya Creek Canyon and found many of our hiding places. Anderson kept making hunts below Waganupa, seeking revenge, learning the secrets of the Center of the World. One day, some twenty moons after Banya Creek, he found your father north of Yuna Creek and trapped Tetna and thirty others, including women and children, in a cave. The Saldu killed all those people. This is how your father became a lost one, Tehna-Ishi. You have seen this in your dreams."

The majapa's voice was low, and now his broad round face was bathed in light.

"You remember the funeral fires, Tehna-Ishi, though you were a little boy. I would not let my brother Grizzly Bear man's spirit stay on the earth. You yourself made his fire with my auna [fire] drill."

Ishi's grandfather stirred in his sleeping robes.

"The last Saldu hunt, the one that left us the only Yahi in the Center of the World here at Tuliyani, was my fault," the majapa said sadly.

"Saldu Anderson? Saldu Good?" Ishi asked.

"No," his uncle said, "even Saldu wanasi grow tired of easy hunts. Four cow men ended the Yahi ways. Four who tend the Saldu cows. I led our hunters to their wowi [house], and there we brought down one of their four-footers with arrows from our bows. We were starving. The cow men had driven away our deer. The cow men, ones named Kingsley, Bogart, and Baker, tracked us on their horses, followed the trail of blood with Saldu dogs, and caught us again in the Yuna Creek caves."

I have dreamed this too. I have lived this and pushed it away into my dreams.

"They killed us with their guns in the darkness. Only we few ran away while the dogs of the Saldu ripped our daana [babies] and young and old ones apart, and Jupka and Kaltsuna could not help. Now we are only seven. For years we have hidden unseen, but I fear they may soon know that the Yahi are alive still."

Ishi's boy cousin awoke and stretched, then his grandfather too.

"The Saldu are very near Tuliyani village, Majapa?" Ishi asked. It was his grandfather who answered.

"They are all around us," his grandfather said. "You have seen this too. It is the wakara moon time for the Yahi people. This too you have seen in your dreams, Ishi, this and more."

"Suwa!" spoke the majapa. "It is better to live what we are given to live. Jupka and Kaltsuna have given us a good morning at the Center of the World. Come, we have things to do."

"Aiku tsub," agreed Ishi's grandfather. "It is so."

I have seen what is to come. Dawana power dream. Dawana things to come.

Chapter 5

Moons passed over the Yahi village of Tuliyani, the place on Yuna Creek where bears hide, and no Saldu gold seekers found them. In mid-summer, the seven moved north at night, for four nights, until they came under the moon to the great looming shadow of Waganupa, whose snows give life to the coursing Yuna and Banya creeks and to all the animals and humans around. Five of the seven built a summer village, for Ishi's grandfather and grandmother were worn from the journey. The two young wanasi, Ishi and his cousin, went out to hunt each morning for deer, rabbit, and quail. Each evening they fished with the harpoon and net, while Tushi and Ishi's mother cooked, wove new baskets, and cared for the majapa and the old ones. The seven survivors of the people lived well at the center of the Center of the World. The young three thrived in the cooler air, deeper shade, and abundant game at the base of Waganupa, with its mists and swirling cool clouds, far above the scorching dry heat of the canyons and great valley below. For a time, life continued to be good for the people.

Then the fall snows returned to the rich land of pine trees, streams, lava rocks, and pumice boulders around Waganupa, and it was time to hide the summer village and take the food stores of sun-dried venison and sun-dried rainbow trout down to Yuna Creek Canyon, where the water gushed cold white, swollen with water from above. It was time to return to Tuliyani to gather acorns and to winter near where the bears hide.

The winter of 1872 was a hard, cruel one. White men like Indian killers Robert Anderson, Hiram Good, and Sim Moak, living with their hired help in strong wooden houses, came close to leaving the foothills around Mt. Lassen permanently for the warmer climes of Tehama and Red Bluff in the Sacramento Valley.

That fall the Yana foothills around Mt. Lassen had frozen hard at night making the deciduous trees flame in brilliant reds and yellows, while the evergreens had glistened in white coats of ice until the morning sun had stripped them each day. The winter storms then came down hard over the Siskiyou Mountains from the northwest and from the Pacific Ocean, over the coastal mountains, dumping deep snows on Mt. Shasta and Mt. Lassen, and swirling lighter snows, dry and powdery, on the valley floor. The storms came remorselessly, one after another.

That winter touched everyone in Northern California, white and red alike. Almost warm in his sturdy cabin, the pioneer rancher W. S. Segraves waited out the Yana winter in Twenty Mile Hollow, only two miles from Hiram Good's ranch in Acorn Hollow. He hadn't a clue that he still shared his white woods with wild Indians.

The Yahi's summer village, now abandoned at the base of Waganupa, lay under twenty feet of drifting snow. For the seven Yahi, the winter of 1872 was nearly the end.

Starving, with no voice for prayers or songs, Ishi and his family huddled in the men's and women's houses at Tuliyani village, trying desperately to keep their fires lit through the wind and ice storms.

> *Cousin and I must find food for us. It is the way of the wanasi, though Majapa will not tell us to go through the frozen meadows and snow. Suwa!*

"Majapa Uncle," Ishi said in the watgurwa, "may Cousin and I hunt one of the Saldu four footers this day?"

His uncle, grandfather, and older cousin looked at Ishi in the pale yellow flicker of the firelight.

"They will track you in the snow and find us here," the majapa answered.

"Haxa," Ishi's grandfather agreed. "They will kill us all."

> *In my dream, it was springtime when they found us. We will survive this and other winters, but only if we can hunt soon.*

"Uncle," Ishi urged, "Mother and Tushi grow mahde [weak] and we have not enough food. We must do something soon."

The majapa looked around the watgurwa at the faces of the Yahi men. A bitter draft circled in from the smokehole.

"Aiku tsub," said the majapa, "the little bearcub boy grows to be a bear like his father Tetna. It is so, we must do something, but I am the majapa and I say what we are now forced to do. We will give our lives to the butterfly god Jupka and the lizard god Kaltsuna and hope that Coyote guides us well. It is the way."

"Let us go to the house of women," Ishi's uncle continued. "We must not keep this dawana secret from the marimi [women], for they must know what good or bad magic Coyote may bring us. Perhaps the young cousins may not have to walk the ancestors' star path east until long after the majapa goes."

"Suwa!" Ishi's grandfather said, and the four men pulled their deerskin robes tight and went to the women's house as light snow kissed their faces and melted on their warmer skin.

Later, in the swirling white, leaving light moccasin prints in the snow behind them, the entire Yahi nation moved down Twenty Mile Hollow, five of them carrying bows.

"What kind of mahde dawana majapa would ask me to leave our warm shelter—and dressed as a man, too?" Ishi's grandmother demanded.

Ishi looked ahead to the majapa.

> *It is not good for a woman to anger the leader, but Grandmother speaks a question we all want to know.*

Ishi's uncle turned around, snow all over the shoulders of his deerskin robe, and answered patiently.

"Dear old dambusa woman, you know that five is the sacred number of the people, and we have only four wanasi left, and you among women look most like a man in old age, now more to with the snow falling in your face, so you must be our fifth wanasi. You must carry a bow so the Saldu know the significance of what we do and that Coyote and Jupka and Kaltsuna guide us."

The people walked the rest of the way in silence.

We will not die in winter. Majapa does what he must do. We must hope Coyote does not want to be a mechi-kuwi [demon doctor]. *I have promised to take care of Tushi, but the gods must choose to take care of all of us.*

Chapter 6

W. S. Segraves had no idea, that cold night in the harsh winter of 1872, that he would be visited by five Yahi wanasi, each armed only with a strung Yahi bow but with no quiver or arrows, and with a grown Yahi woman and a girl trailing behind. He came to his front window when he heard a soft crunching in the snow outside his cabin door. He saw, first, five snow-covered Indians standing side by side, each holding out a bow like an offering, then two more pairs of eyes in the moonlight behind. Jeezus! Segraves thought, I'm twenty miles from town. Jeezus Damn!

He grabbed his whale oil lamp and his .56 caliber Spencer rifle, put on his heavy leather vaquero coat, and opened the door.

The shivering Indians looked comical in the moonlight and the pale flickering orange from the cabin fire inside. The five men lined up straighter with much formality: two brown-faced boys trying to look like fierce men, a middle-aged, round-faced Yahi with clear, unblinking eyes, and two lined old men, one rather squat, soft, and dumpy looking. But Segraves did not laugh. He knew what five Yahi wanasi could do, even those as weak and worn as these.

They stood, staring at each other silently in the moonlight and firelight. Long, tense moments passed. The middle-aged woman, shivering behind the line of warriors, slipped to her knees and was helped up by the Yahi girl waiting there too. A nighthawk cried. The snow kept falling, swirling in the orange-white light.

Then, with even more formality, the warrior leader began a long guttural speech, unintelligible to W. S. Segraves, but impassioned in its delivery. When the speech was over, each man stepped forward, one by one, and presented Segraves with a bow by laying it at his feet. Segraves saw in the light from his cabin that one of the Yahi men was really a woman, which confused him even more. What could they want? Was it food? Was this offering a trick?

Thoroughly puzzled about what to do, Segraves pulled his coat around him, pointed his Spencer rifle at the Yahi leader, and motioned for the four Yahi men and the one false wanasi to pick up their bows. This done, he herded them at rifle point, all seven of them now, on the two mile trek in deep snow to Hiram Good's ranch at Acorn Hollow. Jeezus! thought Segraves. What in holy hell gives?

Hiram Good, being a sensible man, was not at home. He had retreated to the relative warmth of the town at Red Bluff, leaving his hired men to mind the Acorn Hollow ranch until early spring. When the island nation of seven Yahi marched ceremoniously up to Good's main house, herded at gunpoint by W. S. Segraves under the moonlight, there was no one to whom Segraves could present his peace-offering captives.

The seven natives, shivering in the snowfall under the guns of Good's hired hands, stood silent for a long time. Then their leader gave his formal, unintelligible and impassioned speech again, and again the four Yahi men and one impostor wanasi laid their bows gently at Segraves' feet for all of Good's men to see.

They mean to give up their livelihood, Segraves thought, they mean to give themselves up to me.

"Can we spend the night here with ya?" Segraves asked. "Can we bed down til the mornin comes and I can take these savages back to Twenty Mile Hollow?"

One of Good's hired men spoke. "Sure you can stay with us, but the goddamn Mill Creek thievers have got to die."

Ishi and his family could not understand the hired man's words, but the tone of his voice made some feeling of danger clear to them all.

> *Mahde Saldu. No good will come of the majapa's offering. The first Saldu means us no harm but these others are dawana Saldu.*

"Isn't that right boys?" the leader of Good's hired men asked. "All but the girl savages have to die or these damn Mill Creeks will steal us blind."

The white men grunted approval there in the frigid night air, under the Yana moonlight.

Ishi looked to his uncle, the majapa, to his grandfather and cousin shivering in the awkward surrender line. His grandmother, still dressed like a Yahi man, huddled together with Tushi and his mother behind the men. He saw the majapa's breath come out in white clouds, hanging for seconds in the midnight Yana stillness.

We will not die in winter. We must run.

One of the hired men went to the barn, and returned moments later with a block and tackle and a hemp rope. He threw the rope and wood block over the thick lower branch of a madrone tree in front of Good's house.

The snow began to fall again, lightly at first, then with more white fury.

"The hell you're going to hang the Mill Creeks," exploded Segraves. "They're mine to do with as I please!"

He pointed his Spencer at the ranch hand who had spoken, then ran its sight across Good's men, stopping for a second each time the barrel lined up with a man's face. The snow fell harder.

"Go on," Segraves yelled and motioned to the Yahi headman, "get the hell out!"

The majapa understood well what was happening, though he did not know the words.

"Hexai-sa!" he said to his family. "Run away!"

Ishi's grandfather touched Ishi's shoulder, and with that sign Ishi bolted to Tushi, took her hand, and they all melted away into the whitening forest, leaving only the majapa.

"Whatever you want, Mr. Segraves," the head ranch hand said gruffly. "Whatever you want."

The Yahi leader pulled off his thick, black bearskin robe and laid it at Segraves' feet. Then he gathered quickly the five Yahi bows, and he, too, was gone.

W. S. Segraves stood holding several white men, his neighbor's employees, at gunpoint in the heavy snowfall. Christ, he thought, now I've got hell to pay. He saw several huge snowflakes kiss the black barrel of his rifle and melt away.

* * *

In 1872, the Yahi people retreated deeper into the Center of the World, sharing their Yana gorges, caves, and the impassable forest undergrowth only with the animals: bear, elk, deer, rabbit, fox, lizard, and snake. They found a new hide-out in an abandoned grizzly bear's den on Deer Creek, which they called Wowunupo-mu-tetna. There their retreat and secret life of hiding took them twenty-five years further into the future than Geronimo's Apaches and thirty-five years further than the Sioux nation that defeated Custer.

From 1872 to 1884, Ishi's people disappeared to all outsiders, completely concealed and silent. None of the whites' horses or stock were hunted, no cabins were rifled, no grain was stolen; no Yahi footprint was found; no ashes, no wisp of smoke from a Yahi firepit was discovered; not one arrow shaft or lost salmon spear point or milkweed rope snare was found in a meadow to prove that Segraves and Good's men were right that the savage Mill Creeks lived on.

W. S. Segraves never saw a Yana native again, but in the years that followed he knew more and more what it meant for the last of the Yahi able to bend the bow to lay down, in sacred number, their only weapons, their only means of staying alive in the old and good way.

Chapter 7

The hidden ones passed their waking and sleeping moments in the old and sacred way. Silently, they fished with the harpoon and the net, hunted with the bow and arrow, and set snares. The men took on the women's work and the women, the men's. They all gathered acorns in the blazing colors of Yana autumns, enough, if possible, to get them through a winter like the one that nearly ended them, but no winter so harsh ever came again. The people ate green clover in the springtime and brodiaea bulbs in early summer, and in the heat of midsummer they returned to the great mountain Waganupa—taking the four nights' journey silently, concealed by darkness—so that the seven could live in the cooler air and deeper shade of the volcano and hunt its more abundant game. Ishi grew taller between the trips to the center of the Center of the World and Tushi grew more like a marimi. They were more like a brother and sister than cousins, and even might have married, if not for the strict Yahi incest taboos.

For most of those twelve ghost years, the Yahi lived at Grizzly Bear's Hiding Place in their small houses: the watgurwa, the women's house, and sometimes a communal family house. All were camouflaged so that from the Yuna Canyon rim, the only direction from which a white man could see them, the bent pine and alder branches that covered them looked exactly like the work of nature.

Ishi's small family kept their storage houses, which were filled with drying frames, baskets of dried meat, fish, and acorns, eating baskets, tools, and hides, disguised in the same way. Sometimes the three younger cousins and the majapa traveled for miles by leaping from boulder to boulder, hunting or fishing along Yuna and Banya creeks for food for the aging ones, their bare brown feet leaving go prints; sometimes they walked in the water when the current was slow. The majapa taught the others to obliterate any footprints outside of Wowunupo, to cover them with dead oak leaves. Ishi and Tushi and their cousin walked trails that went under the thick buck brush and manzanita chaparral. Often they crawled on all fours like the lizard god Kaltsuna. The Coyote god smiled on them, for they disappeared completely from white history for those twelve years.

The Yahi never chopped wood or broke branches, because the Saldu settlers moved ever nearer into the Yana hills below Waganupa, the great mountain the whites called Mt. Lassen. They kept their fires so small that the smoke dissipated through the brush and never sent a dark beacon through the sweet-smelling bay tree canopy above their fires, and Ishi and his family covered every firepit with broken rock as soon as the fire went out.

The three young ones grew into strong adults climbing up and down the steep cliffs of Yuna Canyon on milkweed fiber ropes of their own making, safely screened by the red madrone trees that overhung the canyon rim. They got down to the creek for a swim or to fill a water basket more quickly on the rope, and the footpath stayed less used that way, more like the runways of rabbits.

For twelve years, the little Yahi nation had everything it needed in the Center of the World, and the only reminder of the whites was the twice-a-day whistle blast of the black creature far down in the great Daha Valley. The faint blast scattered quail, stopped the tapping of woodpeckers, and made Ishi's heart race.

The people lived this good life as it had been for centuries, but with more urgency now. The majapa told them constantly to be on guard. The seasons melted together peacefully and the moons tracked overhead, and under them the Yahi wore capes of deerskin and wildcat, and robes of bearskin. Through the watgurwa smokehole at night the stars passed overhead as the Yahi slept warily under robes of rabbitskin.

When the old ones, Ishi's grandmother and grandfather, became to feeble to walk, the others cared for them until the old Yahi man and then his wife died two winters apart. The remaining five built their funeral pyres of carefully dried wood. Each time, Ishi used the majapa's fire drill to start the tinder and then stoked it into a full red blaze that sent showers of sparks up into the night sky below the white stars and freed his grandparents to walk the star path east above Waganupa to where his ancestors lived on.

Chapter 8

For five days, after each death, Ishi and his family mourned their loss. They burned their hair short in mourning, as was the Yahi custom, and said prayers while the lost ones each made their five day journey on the star path to the firepit of their ancestors, glowing deep in the night sky above Waganupa. Each night of their journeys, Ishi's dreams troubled him.

At the end of their second mourning, Ishi climbed Black Rock just before dusk, heard again the black creature's far off cry as it made its snakelike way, this time south, behind the green band of the river Daha. This time he saw more of the black smoke pour from the creature's head and hang in the air longer after the creature was gone down the valley, and this time its call seemed more plaintive and sad to Ishi.

Now we are only five. Suwa! It is the wakara moon time for the Yahi. Mother and Majapa Uncle are getting older. We have no daana to preserve the people, and the old ways are fading. Hexai sa! Saldu. Hexai sa!

Ishi watched the last of the light fade from crimson to pink to gray above the blur of haze on the distant valley floor. The colored twilight glistened off a curve of the Daha at the end of his eyesight. He watched the black creature's faint trail of smoke finally disappear into the night.

My dream is of the land of the Saldu at the Edge of the World. Soon there will be not enough Yahi hunters and not enough Yana game.

When Ishi moved to break his solitude, to slide down the Black Rock for home, a tiny gray lizard scooted by him over the rough stone and disappeared.

By 1884, the twelve years of complete Yahi concealment deep in the Center of the World were coming to an end. The Yana hills below Mt. Lassen were changing, filling up with permanent white settlers. The gold rush all but over, the new settlers came for new land, for opportunity. Cattle ranches, saw mills, and towns, connected by roads instead of trails, spread far upstream into the Yuna and Banya canyons. There were no more wild Indians to drive out, or so it seemed.

By the end of the long hiding, Ishi's uncle knew that Coyote was changing the world again, letting the Saldu in, for the animal ones were being driven away in greater numbers. The five natives clung to their way of life, but the majapa knew their world would shrink further still, and he grew tired. He remained the leader of Wowunupo, but he trusted more and more to Ishi and his boy cousin to go farther out of the Center of the World for food. The majapa wished now that Tushi, who had blossomed into a striking woman, could have a child with Ishi, but in his dreams Jupka and Kaltsuna reminded him this could never be so. He watched Tushi sit, the long fringe of her deerskin skirt forming a circle of brown on the forest floor. New to womanhood, she was the Yahi's only hope, yet only Ishi's boy cousin could rightfully marry Tushi.

So it was that by 1884 Ishi and his older boy cousin began to raid for food. Once again, the whites in the Yana foothills noticed a calf or sheep missing, or a storehouse emptied of its flour and barley, but strangely with none of the canned goods touched. Once again, the old legends were revived in dusty saloons in towns like Vina, Tehama, and Red Bluff. The inconvenience of a few white cattlemen—who, during the roundups of the years following 1884, found their storehouses deep in the hills pilfered of barley for their horses and flour for their flapjacks—became tall tales of bloodthirsty savages in the woods. Ironically, the outrage over stolen foodstuffs grew far greater over frontier whiskey than the occasional missing calf or steer. The desperate acts of the younger Yahi, trying, usually at the end of long winters, to steal enough food to keep the people alive, became the argument of the day. Some believed the Yana Indians had all been exterminated years before, or had surely long since died. Others, like Anderson, Good, Segraves, and another white settler named Norvall, suspected otherwise.

Chapter 9

Mr. Norvall had settled on lower Dry Creek, had built his oak and fir cabin there because, in his words, he wanted to get the hell away from everybody. So Norvall was surely startled when, hurrying back from his outhouse one cold, clear April morning in 1885, he heard someone moving inside his cabin.

Holy god, Norvall thought, I've got my gun in there. He felt the blood beat in his neck. Warily moving closer to his cabin to investigate, Mr. Norvall stopped and stared open-mouthed as first one brown Indian, then four others rapidly climbed out his cabin's lone window.

> *A Yahi wanasi should never have to hunt the Saldu's food even though the majapa says it is safer than using our arrows to bring down the Saldu's four footers. It is dawana to bring the old ones, Mother and Uncle, when Tushi and the wanasi hunt the Saldu house. It is too risky. Here the smell is of good siwini* [pine], *but this one smells musty like a bear's den. Hexai-sa! We must go quickly.*

Open-mouthed and miles from any other whites on his lower Dry Creek settlement, Norvall tried to yell, but no sound would come from his throat. Ishi felt the sudden presence of another watching, and froze ahead of the others in his family.

"Majapa," Ishi whispered, "stay still."

Behind him with the four others, Ishi's uncle hissed, "Run, younger ones, leave us here and go!"

> *I will not leave the old ones to the Saldu.*

Ishi felt his heart race, motioned to Tushi and the others with his open hands to stay still.

> *It is in Coyote's paws. The Coyote god will decide what is to become of us.*

Norvall, the brave pioneer, had never been so frightened in his life. He stood staring incredulously at the five wild Indians, his breath coming in rapid, shallow pants, his mouth still unable to issue any sound. His throat felt full of feathers.

Not expecting to be confronted, finding themselves caught, and unsure whether there were other whites with guns nearby or whether they could make it together across the wide cleared yard to the tree line, the desperate Yahi family bunched up quietly against the rough cabin wall, leaving the next move up to Norvall.

Norvall's breath now came easier, but he, too, was unsure of what to do. What the hell is a body to do, he thought. If I move, they may bolt. Can I capture any of them with no gun? Norvall looked at the Indians with a clear head for the first time, pondering what to do.

Up close, the savages didn't look so threatening. The first one stood expressionless in front of the others, as if to shield them. Norvall saw the light brown-red of this Indian's skin, his wide forehead and fine aquiline nose, his black hair short and fire-singed, and his clear, deerlike eyes. This one is probably in his mid-twenties, Norvall guessed. He looks like a man with the heart of a wild animal.

> *He looks at me. This Saldu looks at me as if I am from the Spirit World.*

Pioneer Norvall's voice came back to him. "Why do you take my things?" he asked the group of five.

No answer came from the Indians at the cabin wall. Norvall heard mountain quail calling to each other behind him. He looked at the middle-aged Indian standing next to the first, saw again a wide forehead, black hair burned short, and deep, wide-set brown eyes. But this one's eyes were cloudier and he was thin to the point of emaciation, shoulders slumped. The older man wore one of Norvall's old leather jackets. He looked Norvall back in the eyes, then spoke a quick rush of wild sounds.

"Tetna-Ishi, take your cousins and run!"

Ishi and the others stayed frozen still.

This Saldu has no weapon. Perhaps he will let us go.

"Majapa Uncle," Ishi said, "we are five and he is one. Let us give this Saldu his robes and go."

In my dreams, it is spring when the Yahi walk the ancestor path. It is early spring as now.

Ishi's mother spoke too. "It is true, Majapa. We have found and taken no food nor any of the shiny containers. Perhaps we can give back the Saldu robes and go in peace."

The quail called again in the distant fir and pines. A ra raa. A ra raa. Then there was silence.

"Aiku tsub," the Yahi leader agreed. "We will try."

The majapa stepped forward out of the shadow of the cabin and took off his pilfered cowhide jacket. Then he laid it on the ground.

"Tushi, dambusa one, take off the Saldu coverings."

Norvall heard the Indians talking clearly enough, but he could not understand their speech. He saw a striking young woman step forward out of the shadows. Again, the same deep, clear eyes as the young man's looked at him, brown and doelike. Without a word, the graceful Yana undid one of Norvall's blue coveralls, then stepped out of it. He saw that she had two others on underneath. The woman, looking younger still because of her close-burned jet black hair, unbuttoned and took off another blue coverall. Norvall's heart quickened.

The quail shrieked again. A ra raa. A ra raa.

The Saldu looks at Tushi with man hunger in his eyes. I will kill him with my hands if he touches her.

"Hurry on, young dambusa one," the Yahi majapa said.

Tushi's cheeks flushed red as she slipped off Norvall's last denim coverall, leaving only her winter deerskin dress following her small curves. With the modern clothes off, Norvall saw that she too was rail-thin, in need of steady food, but she was beautifully wild and unlike any creature he had ever seen.

Then the older woman was in the morning light, her round face a map of fine lines from years of weather and from near starvation. She had on Norvall's shabbiest cloth overcoat. Why in God's name don't they have any of my canned goods? Norvall wondered. It was clear to him that the Indians were in urgent need of food.

In my dreams, it is early spring when the Yahi die, spring as now.

The older Indian woman, bent in sad submission in contrast to the young woman beside her, moved to pull off her dirty and torn overcoat.

"No," Norvall said.

He raised his right hand, white palm open.

"You keep the clothes."

Then, seeing that none of the five Indians had understood him, Norvall pantomimed, clutching his jacket around him.

Another young male Indian, still in the cold morning shadows, clutched a red cloth work shirt to his chest. This one also carried Norvall's spoiled food garbage tied tight in a burlap sack.

"Uncle," Ishi's boy cousin, now a man, said. "The Saldu is a good Saldu. Jupka had made it so."

"Aiku tsub," the majapa answered. The bright light of morning was on his face, but he did not feel warm. Now we are at the mercy of one Saldu who does not wish to kill us, he thought. Once the Yana peoples lived free and well and alone in the world.

"Let us go," the leader said.

In five quick movements, the Yahi family were across the wide clearing, the bent woman still wearing Norvall's tattered overcoat, the second young man still clutching the red shirt and burlap garbage bag.

Norvall watched them silently vanish from the sunshine of his clearing into the shadows of the nearby pine forest. He saw the first young Indian disappear last, but his mind was on the striking young woman and the curve of her buckskin dress.

There was near silence around his cabin. Only a light breeze blew through the trees. At his feet, Norvall saw a little gray skink lizard flash away. He shook his head, then went inside his fir and oak hewn cabin to escape the cold. When he shut the door, the mountain quail called each other again.

* * *

Settler Norvall never saw a wild Indian again in the Yana hills or anywhere else. But when he returned from the town of Red Bluff one day in the early fall of 1885, stocked with provisions, he saw that his cabin had been entered. There on his rough-hewn table sat a colorful Yahi cooking basket, with a small orange butterfly and a small gray lizard design woven in with colored reeds.

Chapter 10

The seasons changed again and again in the Yana foothills. The sun kept rising over jagged Waganupa in the east and the Yana moon kept cycling over the little Wowunupo village, but no more Yahi were seen. Ishi's family stayed closer and closer to Grizzly Bear's Hiding Place on Banya Creek, except for the difficult and dangerous expedition every summer to the great mountain to find relief from the breathless heat of the canyons. White settlers lived all along the Lassen trail by now, but no one ever saw the ghostlike Yahi on their secret night journeys to the center of the Center of the World. Their old leader taught the remaining Yahi to elude the white man at all costs. He taught them to lie face down in the brush along their trails, sometimes even covering themselves with dirt and stones, when whites rode near on their tall animals. The majapa taught his band to hold their breath under water in Banya Creek, to cling to boulders in the cold current, and to come up silently for a quick moment to breathe and disappear like a frog again. He showed the younger ones how to hide behind the tumbling white waterfalls of Banya Creek if they knew a white man was near. The Yahi lived as wary, frightened deer in their home at the Center of the World.

Each step to a tighter circle of retreat around Wowunupo was a surrender of another piece of sacred heartland, of oak stand, of basaltic rock upcropping, of green meadow land, of salmon fishing place, of upland hunting ground. There remained to the people, when they last put their baskets down, only two adjacent tracts of land to the south of Banya Creek Canyon, which were theirs for the long hiding from 1885 to 1908. Each strip of Yahi land was less than a half mile wide and under three miles long; in this way the natives lived above and below where Banya and Sulphur creeks came together, only a few miles from the Speegle Ranch on Sulphur Creek. None of the nearby white men ever glimpsed Ishi or the others. No one but the Yahi ever entered the thickets of Banya Canyon: the thick alder, manzanita, pepperwood, and buck brush were surer protection than remoteness itself. Ishi, Tushi, and their cousin could sneak all the way to the creek's edge with baskets for water or snares for game under nature's screen of laurel and the tangle of brown and green chaparral.

Still, the rumors of savages yet alive in the Yana foothills persisted. Years had come and gone since the Five Bows parley and Norvall's odd cultural exchange, but tongues still wagged in the many bars of the white towns along the Sacramento River. A bloodthirsty Indian-hunting expedition of white ranchers from Chico found the site of the legendary Kingsley Cave massacre mysteriously empty of the bones of the many Yahi bodies they expected to find. Rumors raced again.

Elijah Graham hated wild Indians, though he had never seen one. He spread the story around Red Bluff that he "was gonna to get him some damn Injuns," bought an extra sack of flour, and headed back up country for his hill cabin. Most of the nearby cattlemen and miners doubted that there were any redmen left in the hills, sure that the robbing and pilfering over the years was not done by Indians, but men like Graham wouldn't leave the vendetta alone.

* * *

The two Yahi wanasi came to Graham's cabin, as always, at the end of winter, when their family of five had little or nothing to eat, when the old ones, especially, grew gaunt and silent.

"Tetna's son," Ishi's man cousin said, "there is no auna light in this one's watgurwa. This Saldu in not at home."

Ishi looked at his cousin's face in the light of the wakara moon. His cousin, too, would make a good mate for Tushi, Ishi thought. Ishi wished it could be so. He wished even stronger that Tushi could be his own, that the people could live on.

"Haxa. It is so. The Saldu has left his watgurwa alone."

The two crept silently to Elijah Graham's hill cabin under the cold Yana moon. Ishi and his man cousin, now a brother to him, found the plank door unbolted and entered the cabin, smelling its dank Saldu smells.

Su. It is too easy. Perhaps Coyote plays his tricks on us. Perhaps I am only afraid because it is early spring again, the time of my vision.

* * *

Down in Red Bluff, where Graham had returned to wait out the hard winter, he was bragging.

In the tavern smoke and smell of cattlemen, Graham, warm from drinking whiskey, watched some overweight and worn-out girls that had been brought up from San Francisco grind lifelessly through their cancan dance above the sawdust-covered saloon floor.

"I showed 'em bastards," Graham shouted down the bar over the wild player piano music. "I done mixed a brew a half part rat poisin and half a part wheat flour and marked it plain as day for any civilized man ta see. Left the door damn near wide open!"

He swallowed a burning gulp of his three dollar whiskey and kept talking to the stranger next to him, who tried to keep watching the somewhat high-stepping girls.

"I done set a trap for 'em ignorant savages, and tomorra I am gonna see if they took my bait."

His neighbor at the bar looked at Graham's liquor distorted face. "Ya goddamn fool," the stranger said, "there ain't no wild Indians round here, an many's the white man can't read no written poison warning like yours."

The stranger on his nearby barstool saw Graham's face grow even uglier. "Best to just shut up and watch the girlee show," he said.

"You'll see," Graham blustered. "I'm gonna poisin me a goddamn Injun sure as I'm gonna bed down with a San Franciscee city woman tonight."

"Another?" the bartender asked Graham.

"Hell yes!"

Elijah Graham awoke with a wicked hangover in a Red Bluff whorehouse the next morning. But by nightfall, he had made it up country to his hill cabin to find his poisoned flour gone. Sweet damn! he thought, as he settled in for the night.

* * *

After eating a little warm mush by a small fire, making their hidden night camp on the way back to Wowunupo and falling warily to sleep, Ishi awoke suddenly from his dream in the last of the moonlight.

> *It is this spring and then another! I must wake my brother-cousin and we must go!*

"Come," Ishi called to the sleeping wanasi, lying there beside him, on the frozen ground, in a cocoon of fur traveling robes. "Wake up!"

There was only the call of a nighthawk hunting and the sound of an owl.

> *He sleeps deeply. He has eaten well for the first time in many days, and my friend is dreaming. Perhaps his soul has left his body for a time; it will return when I awaken him.*

"Suwa, cousin hisi," Ishi said. "It is time to go. Soon Sun's face will be over Waganupa."

His friend lay still.

> *Aii-ya! He does not breathe!*

Ishi shook his friend's arm. The only other true Yahi wanasi lay still in his shroud of fur robes on the ground.

> *My dream has come.*

Ishi knelt with both arms wrapped around his cousin-brother, crying in the pale forest dawn. The sun stung his eyes, his breath came out in frigid clouds in the cold air, and Ishi did not know what he did next.

He walked the thick forest in a trance of mourning, the full weight of his grief on his back. Ishi walked through the day until the sun was long since gone and the wakara moon made the night world almost as bright as day.

He stumbled, fell onto the forest underground. Then Ishi came back to himself. He saw that much time had passed, that it was night, and that he was no longer anywhere near the Saldu's cabin with its unbolted door. He was on the trail down Banya Canyon, carrying his cousin-as-a-brother.

Ishi stood up, settled his friend's weight on his back as it had been before he fell, and he walked on again. He heard a coyote bay nearby. The eerie call hung in the dark trees under the strong glow of the moon. Deer moved wakefully in the brush.

Where do my footsteps take me? Where do Majapa's lessons teach me to go?

In his half-waking state, Ishi walked on. Somewhere in the night, a mountain lion crossed the trail ahead of him, a rabbit hanging floppy eared and bloody from its mouth.

When the wakara moon was gone again and dawn had come, Ishi arrived at the Ancestor Cave, and he knew that this was where his feet had been taking him. He went inside the shadowed cave, and brushed off the smooth stone slab he remembered from his elders' teaching. Quietly, he brought his friend there, and laid him on the clean, flat stone on the floor of the cave. He rolled stones across the cave entrance so no animals could enter, and then he was in near darkness.

There, alone, Ishi performed the sacred rites he had learned in the watgurwa. He had never performed a Yahi burial, but the majapa had taught him well. Ishi could not risk the proper funeral pyre outside—it could bring the Saldu to the last four people—but he could help his friend's journey on the star path by releasing his soul inside the old sacred place for the entombment of the ancestors' cremated remains.

In the darkness, using his auna drill, Ishi made the fire, building it high. He breathed the smoke of his brother, and threw sacred tobacco and pine resin from his treasure bundle into the flames.

When the fire had turned to ash and was cold, Ishi lifted the stone slab to one side, laid his brother's ashes and bones in the rock-lined burial hollow with the ancestors, and slid the cool stone slab back into place.

In darkness still, he had no sense of time, nor had he eaten or slept since his brother had eaten too much of the Saldu's poison. It was night again when Ishi left the Ancestor Cave, replaced the boulders in the entrance for the final time, and started home for Wowunupo. He bathed away impurities in the icy waters of the creek before going down the trail to Tushi and the others. In the chill of the rushing water, Ishi heard a nighthawk's hunting cry above him.

> *The majapa says it is well to guard a lost one's body during his five days' journey to be with his family in the night sky above and beyond Waganupa, but I am afraid to leave the other ones too long. It is only the two old ones, Tushi, and I. My brother will walk the stars alone. He is strong. Suwa!*

Chapter 11

Back at Wowunupo, Ishi's uncle had said nothing about his wanasi for two days. He thought of them each minute, and, silently, with Tushi and Ishi's old mother, he counted each hour they were away. Meanwhile, they went about the everyday tasks of life at their tiny village high above Banya Creek on a hidden ledge in the canyon wall. The majapa knew his two wanasi's desperate hunt for food was taking too long, but he said nothing to the Yahi women. In this way, silently, the three natives lived with their fears.

When the sun had risen twice over white-covered Waganupa and had twice gone down under the western edge of the earth, leaving its orange and blood-red afterglow to fade slowly over the Daha Valley, their leader spoke.

"Coyote plays tricks on us again. Aizuna wanasi are gone too long," the majapa said to the two women at the family house firepit. "I am going after them with the dawn."

Ishi's mother answered. "And what of us, Majapa?" she asked, motioning to Tushi. "These Saldu are everywhere in the world, but my son and his brother-cousin are strong. What would become of the marimi if you are taken from us?"

"Jupka and Kaltsuna will watch over you."

World weary, cold, and hungry, Ishi's mother looked at her lost husband's brother in the pale firelight. This man who had been so vital, as strong as her own Tetna man, had grown gaunt and hollow with the long years of hiding, had grown gaunt with concern.

"I fear for them too," Ishi's mother said. "I fear for my own son, my Tehna-Ishi. Soon may come the ending time of the people. You are our majapa. You are all we have."

The leader looked at Tushi, who listened silently at the fire's edge. She has grown far into womanhood, he thought. Her brown eyes dance with the firelight, but her days hold too much sadness.

She has come to her prime at the wakara ending time. For her, there may be no little daana ones, he thought.

"I will wait until tomorrow's sun is high. If our wanasi do not come home, then I will go after them," the leader said finally.

In the morning, a cold mist hung in Banya Canyon. Ishi's uncle went to fish again in the gushing creek, and Tushi climbed down as close to the canyon trail as Ishi's old mother would allow, listening for the missing ones, wanting with all her heart.

It was near midday when Tushi heard the soft beat of bare, running feet on earth. Her heart leapt. The men must be coming down the trail in the shifting gray fog. Tushi waited, breathing quickly, and in a moment a single head appeared briefly through an opening in the thick chaparral. She saw Ishi's drawn face.

Just that second in the hazy light was long enough for Tushi to see that her cousin was alone. She put a hand over her mouth and made no sound. Ishi's long mane of black hair was gone, burned off close to his head, showing that someone loved by him had died, and across Ishi's face were painted the wide black stripes of mourning.

Tushi ran to Ishi, her buckskin dress catching in the manzanita bushes, caught up with him, but she dared say nothing. Instead, she waited for Ishi to speak.

"Our majapa?" Ishi asked flatly.

"Fishing at Banya Creek," Tushi answered, "waiting for you two."

Ishi motioned for her to climb back up to the little village. She watched him disappear in the fog, then turned to Wowunupo. The sun, shining ghostly above the cold mists around the creek, could not make it fully through.

Ishi ran the faint trail to the creek. The majapa was there fishing, anxious and uneasy. His greeting words froze on his lips.

"Where is our wanasi?"

"In the Ancestor Cave," Ishi said.

"And his spirit?"

"I have done what I could do," Ishi answered. "My brother's spirit is released. He lies with the Ancestors. I have bathed and said the purification prayer."

The majapa's lined hands shook so much that he had trouble taking his carry pouch from his milkweed rope belt. From his flat palm, Ishi's uncle, the last Yahi tribal leader, blew a pinch of sacred tobacco over Ishi, saying prayers while his body shook with grief.

> *Hexai-sa! The majapa wants to make any lingering spirits from the Spirit World go away. He wants to protect me from going over to the other side. Elder Uncle tries to keep from crying. See how his old hands shake.*

One after another, the majapa blew five pinches of the sacred tobacco down the way he knew his lost one's spirit would be journeying to the Land of the Dead. He said and then repeated prayers for the dead. When this was done, and only when his pouch was put away again, did the majapa speak directly to Ishi. He looked at his only wanasi with haunted brown eyes stung with grief.

> *The leader looks as if he may let his spirit die.*

"Come home with me," Ishi's uncle said sadly. "Come home with me, son of my brother."

The majapa searched Ishi with those wounded eyes. The younger man's eyes were red around his wide brown irises; he was drawn, pale, and thin from the long winter and from grief.

"We will mourn, my son, for I do not know what you and I shall do without our brother wanasi," the elder said.

"But for now you must go to your mother and Tushi and their food basket. You have not eaten for three suns, nor slept. Eat some of your mother's good acorn mush, then tell us your story. Tonight you must sleep. Tomorrow your heart will lighten a little."

Our old leader is wise. See how he tries not to cry as he speaks. He is brave, but his spirit is dying. These Saldu have killed it. It is our ending time as I have dreamed it. Coyote visits me at night to bring me bad dreams, not to lighten my heart with hope.

When Ishi's mother grew so tired of crying and wailing that she could cry no more, Ishi ate a little of the cold mush Tushi gave him and told the story. At the end of telling, Ishi said to his three remaining family: "My soul came back to my body and I saw I was carrying my brother wanasi in Banya Canyon, and I was no longer afraid. The Ancestor Spirits must have come to me. I did as they wished me to do in the old ways."

"I made the fire over the burial place and said the prayers Elder Uncle and Grandfather taught me in the old watgurwa, and made sure our brother's bow and arrows, his pouch and treasure bundle, and some acorn meal were with him for his journey. I may not have done all as Kaltsuna and Jupka would have it done. Perhaps it was wrong to enter Ancestor Cave. I wished to hide our wanasi's fire from the Saldu...It is not easy to be wise alone."

Ishi's uncle was crying softly now, not trying to hide his grief from the women. The tears tracked down his wrinkled face and fell from his lower cheeks.

"Aiku tsub. You are wise beyond all that I have taught you, my brother Tetna's son. I should not have sent our wanasi to the Saldu lands for food, it is better to starve here in the Center of the World. Soon our friend will be at the night campfire of our people, and in the stars above great Waganupa there will be bears to fight; there will be Yana mountains and tall pine trees; and there will be those who taught our wanasi to bend a bow and to run and jump when he was but a boy. Aiku tsub. I tell you it is so."

Haxa. The majapa is truly wise. What will we do if he chooses to walk the star path?

The four Yahi in Wowunupo mourned. They never again spoke their wanasi's private name, calling him instead "our lost friend," or "the lost one." Ishi never told the story of the Saldu's poisoned flour again, but sometimes in the days to come he wished he had eaten more of it that terrible night.

It was Tushi who changed the talk to remembering the lost one as he was in life. Soon the others spoke no more of his death but talked only of their friend as a hunter of elk at Waganupa, as the strong swimmer of Yuna and Banya creeks' currents, as the one who liked to lie awake all night under the summer stars in the thin mountain air, telling hunting stories. None of the people ever saw Tushi crying, but Ishi was sure she did cry in those long days after, alone, in the shadows of the little den of Grizzly Bear's Hiding Place. One day when her mourning was over and the old ones were busy at their work, Ishi slipped a small piece of his cousin-brother's fur robe into Tushi's hand. He had been saving the small fragment of traveling robe to remember the lost one by. Ishi saw Tushi wipe the back of her dambusa hand shyly across her wet eyes.

* * *

For all their advances, for all of their feeling that they owned and mastered the new California land, the white settlers knew little of their surroundings. Sometimes men from New York City and Philadelphia were not stewards of the land. One of them, an easterner transplanted to a played-out gold mine east of Chico, was even less sensitive than the rest. Giving up on his mine at the head of Rock Creek, the settler grew aimless. Frustrated and angry, he left his campfire burning one June day and started back for the bars of Chico. His fire was hungry. It almost ate up the last four people of an older, some say wiser, race.

* * *

The spring of the year the Yahi lost their hunter turned over to early summer in the Yana foothills below Waganupa. The ground and thick chaparral covering the hills grew dry. The four fugitives had decided for the first time to summer in Banya Canyon, since they felt that the trip to the cool of the great white mountain could no longer be risked.

Now they faced a new and unforeseen danger. Smoke poured over the southern rim of Banya Canyon, moving northward like some strange, acrid summer fog bank, enveloping the Yana forest, sending long trailing bands of darkness upward among the trees. Ishi's nose burned with the acrid smell. His mouth tasted smoke.

Soon the flames may come over the canyon wall and up to Wowunupo. The world is burning.

Ishi gave up his fishing, and set down his thin two-pronged harpoon. He had seen no large trout in the shadowed pools of Banya Creek. He climbed up the northern rim of the canyon. Fire was visible a few miles below to the south, sputtering across the top of Rock Creek Canyon, occasionally igniting whole stands of green pines, turning them into minute-long red flares and then bare black skeletons.

The sun hung in the air, far over to the west, a disc of faintly pulsing gold-red, and the wind blew hot from the south, almost unbreathably dry.

It is alive. Dawana auna is alive.

Ishi watched the inchoate gray smoke flow northward toward his people, obscuring everything behind the fireline. When sunset came in the west in a rush of crimson above the great Daha Valley, Ishi climbed down to Wowunupo to plan with his majapa uncle. He thought he saw a quick flash of summer lightning against the black outline of Waganupa in the east.

In the morning, the sunlight could not make its way through the smoke to Wowunupo. Ishi awoke in the family house before the two old ones and Tushi, and he left them still sleeping in their cocoons of light summer robes as he went out of the shadows of the old bear's den. He climbed down to the creek to splash his face with clean water and to fish again with his hickory harpoon.

The majapa's spirit grows tired. He will not give up our village to run to another unless the fire is upon Wowunupo. Perhaps this wanasi will have to become a majapa to save

Mother, Tushi, and the old one. Mahde. It is bad to think such thoughts.

Ishi heard soft footfalls behind him. It was Tushi coming to him at Banya Creek.

"I have come to you in a new way," Tushi said. Her voice was lower, more throaty than Ishi had heard before.

"Our majapa will not leave this home," she said. "Your old mother has lost too much already too. They may choose to step off Waganupa onto the star path."

Ishi looked at Tushi directly, at her black hair still burned close with mourning, at the strange light in her woman's eyes. She looked somehow different.

The thick smell of smoke was around them.

"I have come to make love with you, wanasi Ishi," she said. "I have learned of the ways long ago when I was a girl in the women's house. I have come to you while the old ones still sleep."

Ishi felt small flames of sensation run through him, felt his face flush red. He put down his fishing harpoon.

"It is forbidden," he said.

Behind him, the creek ran.

Tushi stepped closer to him.

"We must live in this world, Tetna-Ishi. You are our only wanasi man, and I am the only dambusa woman of the people. Perhaps we can make a daana Yahi. Perhaps our people can live on longer in the Center of the World."

Tushi moved closer still.

Ishi felt her breasts against his chest, felt her warm soft mouth press against his lips, smelled the smell of smoke in Tushi's hair.

She pulled his flushed face down to hers, then moved her hands between his legs, touching softly.

"It is right," Tushi said quietly.

Ishi felt her lithe curves against him, her brown body warm under the thin deerskin dress. His whole body was growing hot, his skin on fire. He moved his lips to hers again. They stood in the smoky air, male and female, the last of their race, their mouths joined, hands grasping, exploring while the water ran behind them and their whole world burned.

It is forbidden.

Ishi heard thunder roar high up on Waganupa.

"Lie with me," Tushi said, her voice deep and inviting.

Ishi's whole body trembled and shook. A sudden flash of lightning showed him Tushi's beautiful face in a moment of blue-white light.

It is against the way.

"Come to me Ishi. We will lie down by the creek."

Another flash of lightning close by.

She is beautiful. Her eyes.

Lightning split the bark from a sugarpine on the canyon rim above them.

"We cannot be as lovers," Ishi said. He looked at her, felt her breath warm on his face.

Deep brown eyes.

"We will be the ending people," Tushi said, her voice turning sad. "Please make love with me. We are the only ones left."

Ishi wanted this beautiful Yahi woman full in a man's desire, full in desperation for the survival of his people. He held her lithe body close to his, while her hands traced his back.

Then raindrops fell around them—a few drops at first, then sudden hammering drops of water lashing down out of the dark sky.

They stood holding each other tightly, the rain advancing all around them. Ishi's face ran with water. He saw water soak Tushi's hair close to her head, saw cool water run down her face and mix with new tears.

"I love you, dambusa marimi. I will always love you, but we cannot be as husband and wife. Coyote has made it so."

Her deer eyes watch me in the rain.

"Maybe someday we can lie as one in the Spirit World," Ishi said.

Tushi looked him back strong. "I will wait for you in the stars, Tetna-Ishi."

Lightning lit the two natives, man and woman, in the sudden rain, bathed them for a second in blue-white light and just as quickly went away. When the half-darkness of the smoke-filled morning rushed back, a little skink lizard hunkered down lower on its island rock in the rushing water.

* * *

Thirteen more years passed for the four Yahi living according to the old ways, as they hid from the white settlers and ranchers all around Banya Creek Canyon. Every year, more and more of the Yana forest came down to clear the way for houses and white settlements. The old ones, Ishi's uncle and mother, grew feebler and nearer their time to die. Ishi and Tushi grew middle aged, and, though they sometimes looked privately at each other in the Wowunupo firelight, neither of the two close ones ever spoke of their storm again.

Chapter 12

In the late fall, in November, Ishi worked hard to spear as many running salmon as he could in Banya Creek. The four remaining Yahi depended on the dried and smoked red flesh to help them survive winter. Ishi watched the nearby still pool for flashes of silver, his two-pronged harpoon poised, his bare feet on the cool surface of his favorite Wowunupo fishing rock. The year was 1908.

Long into the afternoon, Ishi fished. Once in a flash of silver over black rocks, he saw a large salmon swim into the pool. With a quick throw, Ishi harpooned it. He brought it to his rock, cleared the harpoon, and watched the big ocean fish, which had traveled so far to swim the cold, clear water of Banya Creek to spawn. The salmon flopped around, trying to thrash its way back into the water, back to life and purpose.

Haxa. You are aizuna fish. You are like the people.
Thank you salmon for giving Tushi and the old ones food.

When the fish stopped its wild flipping and its gill covers moved slower and its bright scales began to lose their shine and dry out, Ishi put his harpoon down. He watched the fish gasp a few last times, then finally lie still.

Ishi saw a splash of color in his side vision. Another floated by. Then a storm of orange butterflies encircled him, floating and diving all around him as they rode the air currents up the creek. He marveled at the bright monarchs as they flew upward just a few feet over the fast moving water. Some of them wobbled, gave up their petal-like dance for a second, then flitted upward just before striking the water. What were they doing alive so late in fall, Ishi wondered. Was Jupka, the butterfly god, playing tricks on him?

Beautifully, slowly, one butterfly quivered and fell to the dead salmon. Ishi saw it light on the still fish, its brilliant orange color perched on dull silver, its wings opening and closing. He watched it build its strength for a time, and then the solitary butterfly launched itself upward into the rising cloud of orange. Ishi's slow heart pulsed its song.

Jupka has come to me. If the old ones die, if Tushi is taken from me, I will never be alone.

Ishi lay face down on the cool rock at the water's edge, letting his hands hang limp in the colder water. He closed his eyes. When he opened them, he saw his reflection in the still pool. Ishi's eyes were like his elder uncle's, sunk deep in their sockets and inward looking, not the eyes of a Yahi wanasi. Their clear forest brown had clouded a little. Ishi saw a face thinner and nearly as lined as his mother's or the majapa's. He saw the face of a nearly old man and, behind it, splashes of orange flight.

Tetna-Ishi has become an old tetna, older than my own father when the Saldu took him.

The one remaining wanasi felt unaccountably tired. He closed his eyes again, left his hands dabbling the still water, and fell into sleep. Ishi slept there, face down on his rock, in the weak afternoon sunlight of November, and as he slept he dreamed.

In his dream, Ishi traveled into the low-slanting plumes of a blood-red sunset, became part of it, moved down the river Daha, brilliant as a curved rope of fire, and onward to the great gathering of waters where rivers ultimately flow. He came to the Edge of the World.

At the end of everything known, it was as the lost ones, Ishi's grandfather and grandmother, had said long before. The red-burning sun dove over the Edge of the World into the great outer ocean, making it boil white and green, sending its strong waves again and again up and down the shore.

In his dream, Ishi also plunged into the outer ocean that surrounds the world, following the red sun down and under the earth's belly. Ishi traveled with the sun as it tracked along a straight broad road on the underside of the flat world from west to east, a trip that took all of one night and brought light to strange lands of darkness.

Then he rose up with the sun over the top of the flat world again, long plumes of golden red streaming up until the top of the earth was all alight. Ishi and the sun now walked the day sky road from the east behind Waganupa and continued toward the gathering place of rivers in the west.

He awoke to the distant shrill blasts of the black creature steaming south down in the Daha Valley. Ishi opened his eyes and pulled his hands from the cold water, blurring his reflection with the sudden ripples. He sat up. The butterflies were gone. The sun was nearly down. He had slept for several hours, and he knew that the others must be hungry. Ishi saw that his salmon lay stiff and lifeless on the rock.

The last Yahi fisherman stood, and picked up his two-pronged fishing spear.

> *Enough dawana dreams. Tushi and the old ones are hungry. Sun will soon drop into Outer Ocean, yet I am still here. I will try to catch one more good salmon before dark.*

* * *

Alf Lafferty and Ed Duensing were both young men, born a little too late for the harsh romantic lure of the California gold fields of the 1840s, 50s, 60s, and 70s. They came west in the first years of the new century to escape the crushing sprawl of New York City, to find work in the new promised land: Northern California. Both came into the new country along the Peter Lassen trail, passing south in the shadow of the snow-capped volcano, newly named Mt. Lassen, avoiding its jagged lava outcroppings, the fragmented remains of the great exploded volcano the ancient Indians had called Tehama. From a high vantage point, the young men also marveled to see huge, white-angled Mt. Shasta for the first time, far off in a blur of haze to the north.

The two settled in the town of Chico, and later found work in Oroville at the Oro Light and Power Company. Lafferty and Duensing were to clear brush and to help survey a flume line that would carry water to a power plant from a proposed dam site at the junction of Deer and Sulphur creeks. November 9, 1908 found the two junior engineers walking back upstream from their ditch surveying work on Deer Creek to the main engineers' camp at the Speegle homestead on Sulphur Creek. The two novices were dog-tired from clearing thick brush from a ledge above the south bank of Deer Creek. They walked quietly up the trail along Deer Creek just before sunset, too tired for talk.

* * *

Ishi watched the slow pool for movement. He no longer thought of the mysterious butterflies or his new power dream. He saw another large salmon swim into the pool with a quick flash of silver. Just as quickly, with a sudden, accurate throw, Ishi speared the big fish. He brought it up, gasping, onto his gray rock and cleared his harpoon while the stranded fish flopped at his bare feet.

Then, more suddenly than the flash of salmon, Ishi saw two white men standing below him on the sandbank of the creek. The two whites stood wide-eyed, only a few yards away, staring as if they had seen a ghost.

> *Never have Saldu come so near to Wowunupo! Never have they moved so quietly into the middle of the world! I smelled nothing, heard nothing. I was thinking only of salmon for the others!*

Ishi raised his harpoon, and poised it to throw.

"Hexai-sa! Go away! Hexai-sa!" Ishi shouted at them, threatening with his two-pronged spear. The two young easterners turned and ran into the dense brush, their heavy boots leaving deep marks in the soft sand. Ishi heard them crashing away in the thick green manzanita and laurel, heard their curses and shouts when their heavy flannel shirts and denim pants snagged in branches.

> *Are these Saldu everywhere? What is it they do in the siwini woods and the Center of the World?*

Wanasi Ishi waited long after the sounds of running men died away, but no others came along Banya Creek and the two frightened ones did not return. He hid his harpoon and gathered the two lifeless fish. It was just dark when he climbed the canyon wall to the ledge at Wowunupo.

The last four Yahi made no fire that night in the family house at Grizzly Bear's Hiding Place.

Chapter 13

Back at their survey camp on the Speegle ranch, Alf Lafferty and Ed Duensing were wide awake under a full Yana moon. They told their wild Indian story over and over again around the warm Speegle fireplace. They told it long into the night while a nighthawk hunted and Sulphur Creek rushed endlessly by. The other engineers and the Speegle family sat or stood drinking brandy, doubting the two city boys' tale. The two were tenderfeet, new to God's country; they had been deceived by the play of evening shadows; they had heard too many sheepherder's tales.

J. M. Apperson, the engineering survey party's guide, listened closely. Several times he stopped the young men's excited babble to ask questions. Where on Deer Creek had they seen the wild man with the harpoon? Did he run? How did he speak? What color was his skin?

Merle Apperson knew the Yana foothills well. Inheritor of the legends of men like Good and Anderson, and later Segraves, Kingsley, Norvall, and Graham, he thought it possible that there were wild Indians living on Deer Creek. The idea excited him. It put new life into the Yana wilderness, into the sounds of night outside the main house; made it palpable for him again. It made the wilderness almost a taste again in his mouth, the way it had been when he had first seen the looming peaks of Lassen and Shasta when he came north from San Francisco years before.

* * *

In the bear's den at Wowunupo, only a few miles away, Ishi and his ancient majapa made plans in the dark. The four fugitives had heard the alarming activity at the Speegle place and at the mouth of Sulphur Creek for several days, but never had they expected to be seen. With their leader an old man who could no longer walk well, and Ishi's mother bedridden and near to the Spirit World, the band had decided before that they could do nothing but watch the forest for Saldu and keep out of sight. Now, in the face of this newer and more terrible danger, Ishi and his uncle talked over a desperate plan while Tushi and Ishi's mother listened in fear. In the event of discovery at Wowunupo, they agreed, the four would split up. Tushi would try to escape with the majapa, who could still walk a little, while Ishi would remain with his bedridden mother in the house-den. In the meantime, the four secret Yahi would lie still, hoping to elude the Saldu. The four stayed up the whole night while the same nighthawk that had flown over the Saldu now hunted the moonlit skies above the people. None of the Yahi moved to clean or smoke Ishi's two good salmon. They were all quite hungry but dared not risk even the smallest fire.

* * *

When the morning sun came up on November 10, Merle Apperson got up early and woke Charley Herrick, a cattleman who had come along to help the power company engineers. Herrick complained loudly of a late night, of too much to drink and too little sleep, but he got up begrudgingly to "go hunt imaginary Indians."

By eight o'clock in the morning, Merle Apperson and Charley Herrick had worked down the south side of Deer Creek. They had turned away from the stream after a mile or more and were working their way back up through thick chaparral, this time on the southern rim of the steep canyon, Herrick voicing his profound disbelief in wild Indians all the way. Ishi heard them coming.

As soon as it was light, he had gone part way down the steep trail from Wowunupo to the creek in order to keep a lookout. He had not waited long when he heard the heavy clump of shod feet coming uphill along the hidden Yahi trail. His ash bow drawn, Ishi waited, his pulse hammering loud in his head.

Apperson came gasping into view, Herrick jabbering breathlessly behind him. Apperson's battered green felt hat fell to the rocky trail, and he bent to scoop it up.

Hexai-sa! I should kill them. I should kill these mechikuwi Saldu now before they find my family. But killing Saldu has never kept them from killing the people. Killing can never bring an end to killing.

A quail called in the brush. Ra-raa-ra. Ra-raa-ra.

Ishi trained the flight of his arrow next to Merle Apperson's head when the white man stood back up, holding his lucky hat. Apperson saw nothing, but he heard the sudden twang of Ishi's bowstring, felt a sudden terrifying rush of air, the whisk of arrow quill feathers piercing the still air next to his cheek.

"Sweet Jesus!" Herrick yelled as Apperson stumbled back onto him, and the two slid back down the steep creek trail.

Ishi heard them crashing downward through the manzanita and buck brush as they fled away from his little village. He walked to the spot where Apperson had appeared, and saw that the Saldu had dropped his felt hat again in the panic. Ishi kicked it aside into the dew-covered brush along the trail.

> *Hexai-sa multiplying Saldu. Let us be the ending ones here in peace at the Center of the World. Let us live here in the old ways until we are no more, until my dreams swallow me.*

The quail called again in the faint morning breeze, looking for its covey. Ra-raa-ra. Ra-raa-ra.

Hearing nothing more, Ishi climbed back up to Wowunupo.

* * *

The four remaining people stayed hidden in their family house-den, waiting, praying in the faint, musty, long-enduring odor of bear. Outside, not far away, Apperson and Herrick had rejoined the crew of the survey party, and were telling the second wild tale of an encounter with savages in as many days. The crew had already begun work that morning, chopping the area surveyed for the flume out of the brush along the south bank of Deer Creek, using the very same ledge that Wowunupo village was built on. When the engineers and cattlemen heard serious-minded Apperson's story and Herrick's stammerings about his newfound faith in wild Indians, they gave up cutting the thick chaparral growth and turned upstream to search for Yana Indians.

In the bear-cave house, Ishi and the majapa were hurriedly planning. There was dread on the women's faces.

"Go to the big pine in our village clearing," Ishi's uncle said. "We must have a warning if the Saldu come near. Climb only high enough to free your ears and eyes. Kaltsuna will protect you."

Ishi reappeared through the reed screen at the mouth of the den in a moment. "Haxa," he said to the Yahi leader, "I think the dawana Saldu may be on Wowunupo shelf. I see nothing of them, but hear the sound of devil knives cutting through our brush."

Tushi hugged Ishi's old mother where she sat, covered with animal robes and blankets, near the entrance to the den. "How near are they?" she asked.

Ishi looked at his majapa. "They are in the thick brush. I do not know how close. We have never had our enemies here."

The elder spoke again. "Perhaps these Saldu will dig somewhere else. They may give up and use their shiny knives some other place."

Neither of the two Yahi men spoke about what they knew. They did not want to frighten the two women any more than they already were. Already, Ishi's ancient mother cowered under her robes. Ishi saw Tushi shaking.

Coyote plays tricks on us. These Saldu can only dig their water ditch on our ledge. If they are not digging, perhaps the morning ones are back to search for our village. Suwa!

Ishi spoke to the majapa, his voice calm, trying to hide its urgency. "I am going up the big siwini tree again."

In the pungent middle branches, Ishi heard gruff Saldu voices, grumbling and grunting just outside Wowunupo village.

Su! These devils have found one of our trails. They move so quickly!

Ishi's heart pounded.

We may yet escape. Haxa. My dream says it is spring-time when the people are no more.

He felt the presence of heavy moving bodies in the scrub brush below the madrone and pines. Twigs snapped in the still morning. Suddenly, a distorted, puffing Saldu face appeared through the manzanita near the Yahi's storeroom, near the path to the center of the village and Ishi's pine.

Ishi slid to the ground, branches scratching his face and hands. His feet struck the ground seconds before the Saldu dragged himself completely out of the brush and stood up. Ishi ran to the cave-house, blood pounding in his head, his thoughts confused and racing.

He came to the reed screen and yelled in a rush of words: "Run, run, you and Elder Uncle! Run like sigaga [quail]. Saldu! Saldu are coming!"

He broke through the screen into the house-den. There was no time to carry his crippled mother into the brush outside. Ishi threw the rest of their sleeping robes over her, and urged Tushi and his old leader out of the den. Ishi watched them leave together, saw Tushi's eyes, the beautiful, wide, frightened eyes of a deer, for a second in the shadows. Then she too was gone.

Ishi swung himself far up into another big pine at the outside of their clearing, where he could still see the mouth of the family house and watch over his mother's hiding place. From between the tangle of branches, blood pulsing in his neck, he saw Tushi with the majapa leaning heavily on her arm. As quickly as she could, she was leading the old, hobbling wanasi toward the steep creek trail.

His two cherished ones went out of sight, sliding down the rocky drop-off just at the instant the Saldu from the brush came into the open clearing. The white man stood in the open circle, his face flushed from exertion. He yelled out something in a tone of surprise to the men behind him, who were still struggling out of the thick brush. Ishi saw only patches of what went on from his high vantage point. Pine branches blocked much of his view as he heard other excited Saldu voices come into the clearing, exclaiming, calling, talking strange words to each other.

The Saldu were all over the village. Ishi caught glimpses of them running from shelter to shelter in the dappled forest light of late morning. He recognized the Saldu who had come part way up the creek trail that very morning. This white man, Merle Apperson, found the Wowunupo cave-den, and yelled to the others.

Ishi saw only the outer edge of the family-den through the thick branches, but he heard the Saldu taking baskets and food from shelves inside Grizzly Bear's Hiding Place. Then one of the Saldu shouted excitedly again, and Ishi knew they had discovered his old mother beneath her cover of robes and rabbitskin blankets.

Below him in the cave-den, Ishi knew his mother would lie as still as she could, frozen as a frightened fawn, taking on the hiding look of inanimate nature, but perhaps trembling too. He felt sick to his stomach, but he was poised above, ready to jump to her aid if necessary.

> *If she cries out or if any Saldu touches Mother, I will jump down and fight as many of them as I can. Suwa! They will see what it is to fight with a Yahi wanasi!*

Ishi heard the familiar Saldu, the one who had worn the green felt hat, speak softly to his mother in the cave. He heard the Saldu's strange words through the rustle of the breeze in the branches until, through the rush of nonsense, one word came close to sense. He heard the white man ask, "Malo?" Then came his old mother's answer: "Mahde." This Saldu had seen her bandaged legs; he knew she was sick and crippled. Still more Saldu came into the den to look, but the sympathetic one, perhaps moved by the sight of her frightened face and swollen legs wrapped in strips of buckskin, seemed to be ordering them outside.

Ishi heard much talk among the Saldu; he thought they quarreled. In the end, the kinder white man seemed to convince the others to look elsewhere in the village, to leave Ishi's mother alone. He heard this Saldu, the one he had shot at earlier, ask his mother some words about water, and assumed that he was giving her a drink. Then the white man from the creek trail came out of the house-den, put down the old woman's blankets and capes at the entrance, and left Ishi's sight. Those whites who stayed in the cave's mouth paid no more attention to his mother, who lay helpless as they carried baskets and clothes outside. Ishi, ashamed to be hiding and watching their home being defiled, caught glimpses of the other Saldu going through the other shelters, taking the things the Yahi needed to survive. He saw them tear into his work shelter of pepperwood boughs. One Saldu in a bright red shirt fingered his sacred stone tools. Another white man broke into the women's hut, then came out, holding up Tushi's unfinished buckskin dress to show the others.

> *Hexai-sa. These dawana Saldu care nothing for the ways of Jupka and Kaltsuna. They will enter even the women's house, these demons. It is well that Tushi and Elder Uncle got away. The good Saldu will not let them touch my mother, but when will they go away? Hexai-sa!*

Ishi watched, his heart sick, as the survey crew and the Speegle cattlemen ransacked Wowunupo. He wanted to go to his mother, to find Tushi and the majapa, but, instead, he had to watch as the whites gathered all the people's precious things. The Saldu brought acorns and dried salmon in baskets from the storage shelter into the clearing. In the cook house, beside a small stone hearth, they found a fire drill and Yahi cooking utensils. In the other shelters, the invaders found Ishi's arrow-flaking tools, a deer snare, his bow, arrows, quivers, another two-pronged spear, more baskets, some moccasins, tanned hides, and the majapa's wildcat pelt robe. By the end of morning, Ishi's heart beat more slowly, but he grew sicker as he watched the white men gather all their important possessions, even their little remaining food, and for some callous reason get ready to take it with them as souvenirs. Only the Saldu who was kind to Ishi's crippled mother refused to rifle the sad, little village.

Chapter 14

History notes that J. M. Apperson was against the looting at Wowunupo. Others in the Oro Light and Power Company survey party reported that their guide, Apperson, wanted to carry the sick, old woman back to the Speegle ranch, where she could be tended to, but the cattlemen in the party would not allow it. One of the surveyors, Robert Hackley, later wrote to Professor Waterman, an anthropologist at the University of California at Berkeley, to say that the grave blame for driving the Yana Indians from their home did not belong wholly with the surveyors. As Hackley told it, the cattlemen were angry over small thefts of food by the Indians from years prior, and they demanded all of the four Yahi's life-sustaining tools as payment for past insults. It was much on Apperson's mind that a terrible wrong was being done. He suggested leaving some gift or token behind as a friendly gesture to any remaining wild Indians, but he had nothing suitable in his pockets that fateful day, and none of the other whites would offer anything. Apperson argued with the others. He pleaded with the armed ranch hands to leave the Indians' food behind, or to return with food from the Speegle homestead, but he lost his case.

Watching helpless from his vantage point, hidden in the dense branches of his high pine tree, Ishi heard the Saldu's gruff voices, but he did not understand their strange and graceless words. Ishi felt through intuition that the white man of the creek trail arrow, the man who had most reason to seek revenge, meant no harm to his people. He knew this instinctively as he heard this white man's voice rise and fall differently from the others.

When the last of the demon voices trailed off in the pale green and brown chaparral, and Ishi heard the last leather-booted steps pound out of hearing, he shinned to the ground. Ishi's feet felt funny, tingly, as he ran across the pine needle carpet to his mother.

Neither of them spoke for fear of being heard as Ishi gathered her small weight up in his arms, and carried her to his work hollow in the brush, his place for chipping obsidian and, more recently,

Saldu glass arrow-points. The two Yahi, ancient mother and middle-aged son, sat among the litter of black stone and green glass chips, their breath coming quickly.

> *Su! Will the devils come back to finish my dream? Or will they wait for spring, as I have seen?*

Ishi listened and looked for a moment more, then carried his mother across the bare shale rock clearing into the thick laurel and madrone trees growing on the rock ledge high above Banya Creek. There, well-hidden, he put his mother down and spoke.

"You are not hurt? They did not harm you, dambusa marimi?"

"The Saldu did not touch me. I am in no pain," she answered. "Where are my dambusa one and the majapa?"

> *These mechi-kuwi! If these Saldu had walked only fifteen feet one way or another on our ledge, they might never have seen our hidden homes. Coyote has no more love for the people!*

"They are safe," Ishi said, looking away from his mother's cloudy eyes. "I saw them slide down the tetna trail to the creek."

"Aiku tsub," his mother said. "Let those rude ones go far away. After one or two suns, we will all return to our firepit at Grizzly Bear's Hiding Place."

"One Saldu with a human face—one who uncovered me—wanted to carry me, I think, to a Saldu village, but the others fought him. Not all Saldu are mahde kuwi, Tetna-Ishi."

"I should go after our family," Ishi urged, but his mother, wary, disagreed.

"Stay with your old mother for a while, my only wanasi. We must be sure the dawana Saldu have truly gone."

Apprehensive, restless with a strong protective urge to find his cousin-as-a-sister Tushi and his elder uncle, Ishi fought his instinct.

Suwa! I must not let Mother know how much has been taken by the Saldu.

For long minutes, Ishi and his mother talked among the forest undergrowth, the pungent laurel, and the red madrone trees. The old woman lay down where the early afternoon sun dappled the ground, leaned her head against the trunk of a feathery chamise bush, and stretched out on a carpet of soft leaves and twigs. She said she was comfortable.

When Ishi was sure that the outsiders were finally gone, and not playing tricks, he stood up, ready to leave.

"Marimi, I will look to see if our family has returned. I will get some things from the bear-den wowi," Ishi said.

Ishi hurried to Wowunupo, hoping that Tushi and the majapa might have returned already, and hoping to find anything the whites had overlooked, perhaps a bow and a basket of water, perhaps some dried food or a fur blanket. He kept close to the brush line at first, out of sight, until he was doubly sure no Saldu had returned. No one was in the little village.

He stood by the big lookout pine at the middle of the clearing, looking. Their shelters were not torn down or harmed, but Ishi felt an eerie emptiness, the quietness of an abandoned home.

Have they taken everything?

The reed screen cover of the storehouse stood ajar; inside the tree bough shelves were empty. Ishi walked to the family cave house, searched in its cool shadows, but the den was nearly empty. His mother's sacred treasure bundle had been overlooked on its shelf at the back of the cave along with a few small baskets. Ishi gathered these things, and went outside into the afternoon sunlight to the smokehouse, then to the watgurwa. With each place he checked, he slowly understood more and more. The emptiness was palpable: the four remaining people did not have enough left to survive.

Gone were Ishi's bow, arrows, and otterskin quiver. Gone were his spear, fire drill, stone knives, and arrow-point flakers and chisels. Gone were Tushi's kitchen tools, and, more distressing, virtually all of their food. Ishi, his heart empty, searched the little village from end to end, and crawled through the brush tunnels leading away from it, hoping to find Tushi's cougar and raccoon fur cape or their bearskin blanket, anything the whites might have dropped as they carried off their stolen souvenirs. He found nothing.

He took the small water basket and the small baskets of berries and seeds he had found in the bear's den house and went back to his mother. The wrinkled old Yahi woman sat up when he returned to her hiding place, and smiled at her son.

"Our family has not come back yet," Ishi reported, nor have the Saldu mechi-kuwi returned."

Ishi's mother did not ask him why he had not brought the mended and ragged rabbitskin sleeping blankets, nor why he had not brought his good bow, and Ishi withheld the truth. Instead, he made a softer bed of bent tree boughs and ferns for his mother, and together they waited for the night.

If I could find Tushi and Elder Uncle! Su! If I could know the running ones are safe!

Ishi sat anxiously by his mother as the night grew colder. He had no way to make even a small fire. Ishi thought of what to do, of what his own dead father, Tetna Man, or his elder uncle, out somewhere in the cold, dark tangle of trees, racing creeks, and wilderness, would tell him to do. Ishi's mother, exhausted and disoriented, fell into an uneasy sleep soon after sunset. Wide awake, Ishi stared into the moonlit canyon long into the night, torn between the urge to search for the two loved running ones and the need to stay with his mother.

Coyote hurts his own chosen people while Jupka and Kaltsuna stand beside watching. I do not understand...

When the morning came with a white hoar frost covering the bushes and the dense fern swale, Ishi was still awake, trying to stay warm. He left his mother still sleeping and went back to Wowunupo to see whether the two running ones had returned.

As he neared the clearing on the ledge at Wowunupo, Ishi's pulse raced in his neck. There were sounds of movement in the village. He crawled on his hands and knees over the cold ground to a clump of manzanita at the edge of the clearing, listening, watching. Could Tushi and the majapa be back safely?

Inside the bare village, Merle Apperson, accompanied by Charley Herrick, was doing what his conscience had told him to do. He too had passed a restless night thinking under the nearly full moon, and now he had come back with the dawn to the Indian camp to try to make things right. He had hoped to help the wizened old woman from the afternoon before, to carry her out to civilization with Herrick's reluctant help. He swore aloud when the two shivering men found the village obviously empty.

"Damn," Herrick agreed half-heartedly, "the fisherman or another Mill Creek has carried her off."

Ishi's gut sank when he saw the two whites from his hiding place. The sight of the familiar Saldu not only meant that his family was still lost but also that whites would no doubt come again and again to Grizzly Bear's Hiding Place. He knew that the two Saldu were looking for his mother as they tramped around making dark footprints in the shining frost. He sensed that they wanted to help her, but even these almost-human Saldu could not understand the Yahi way. They would never understand.

The two men searched the village thoroughly while Ishi watched. They covered the surrounding brush and the length of the rock ledge in the new morning light, looking for footprints or other clues in the disappearing frost. Apperson, never a quitter and as good a woodsman as any of the local settlers, came close to Ishi's hiding bush. His leather coat brushed the manzanita Ishi crouched behind, but he saw no faint movement, heard no whisper of Ishi's shallow breath. Ishi's wide nostrils smelled the strong odor of cow as the white man walked past. His mouth tasted of danger.

The hard frost had melted before Apperson and Herrick gave up the search; Ishi still shivered in the chaparral. When they were finally ready to leave for the comfort of the fire at the Speegle ranch, Apperson stopped again at the cave house entrance. He reached into a deep pocket of his cowhide coat, and pulled out a small black pocketknife and a tiny bundle of tobacco. He placed them at the mouth of the Yahi's family house. Then the two trudged away disappointed, their booted footsteps echoing in the trees.

When the two whites had been gone for a safe interval, Ishi came into the clearing at Wowunupo. He stared at the bright metal knife and the small burlap tobacco bag, then turned away and was gone.

Part II:
The Journey

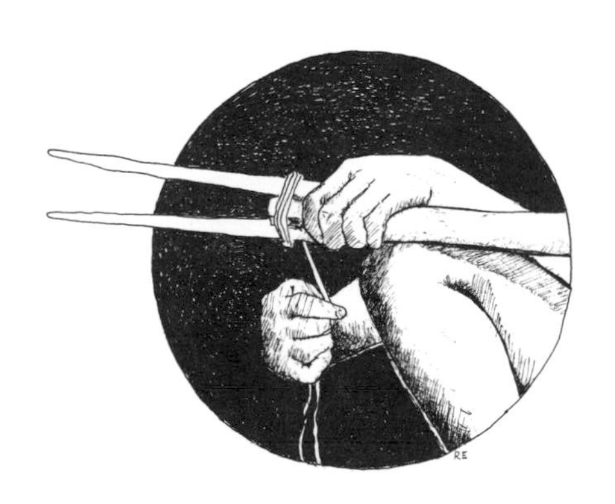

Chapter 15

Back with his mother, Ishi saw that the white covering had left the slate green manzanita leaves and the feathery chamise bushes. It was full morning now, but still cold. Ishi's urge to search for the two running ones was an ache that would not go away. The sun of a new morning only made their absence clearer, more biting, poignant.

Ishi's mother's mind was jumbled, but she could feel. She sensed that her son was in anguish over whether to stay with her or search for the two others. She dared not think the thought that she knew was also on her son's troubled mind. The old woman ignored the few berries her son had saved from the day before. She drank only a little water from their sealed reed basket.

Long minutes passed between the two of them, and Ishi did not have to say that their running ones had not come back to Wowunupo. Nor did he speak of the two Saldu's return or their well-intentioned but ridiculous offering. The truth passed between them without words.

"Go. Please go to Tushi and the majapa," his mother said finally.

When Ishi began to speak his protest, his mother raised a gnarled finger to her mouth to dismiss her son's objection. Ishi touched his mother's creased face. She smiled back at him. Then he was gone.

He did not use the old bear trail down to the creek, because the whites knew of it; instead, Ishi picked his way through the brush as quickly as he could while still staying silent, until he came to the creek below the trail. What he saw and heard there worried him: Banya Creek was now running high and muddy, carrying the cold rains off Mt. Lassen from several days before. Ishi looked across the rushing creek, his wide eyes searching the thick tangle of green and brown brush on the opposite shore. He saw no sign of his aged uncle or Tushi.

Clearly, there was no place for his two cherished ones to have hidden on the Wowunupo side of Banya Creek. There, the canyon wall and bank of the creek were too steep and now, as Ishi looked carefully for any footprints or broken branches, nearly all of that creek bank was flooded with deep reverse eddies and swirling pools of muddied water.

> *The majapa did not have his walking sticks. There was no time. Suwa! How could he have walked the alder log crossing?*

Ishi moved quickly upstream on the Wowunupo side of Banya Creek, his moccasined feet in the chilly flooding waters, looking for signs.

> *Coyote, please protect them. Let us live out our lives in the old, sacred way. When we are gone along the star path above Waganupa to our ancestors, then will be the time for you to play your best tricks on the Saldu world.*

Ishi's heart beat faster as he moved upstream toward their alder log crossing. His mouth was dry with fear, his thoughts tumbled from worry and lack of sleep.

Ishi saw something bright ahead of him, half buried in the mud at the bottom of a silty pool where water and sand eddied in circles from out of the creek's main current. He knelt at the flood-pool to see what it was, cupping and fanning his hands in the cold water to clear away the silt. Ishi's heart pounded in his throat. He saw a length of deerskin cord on which were strung two white shell beads and a broken fragment of a larger yellow bead.

> *Tushi's necklace! Mechi-kuwi Coyote no longer loves his people!*

Forgetting his mother, forgetting the Saldu, forgetting everything, Ishi picked up the broken necklace, then ran up the bank to the wet alder log, losing a moccasin in the water. He tore the remaining one from his foot and threw it into the swirling creek. He crossed the treacherous log on his stomach, using his bare feet and hands to grip the slippery wood. His belly against the alder log was sick with dread. Across the creek, Ishi ran to his fishing cache in the brush along the bank. His mind spun with thoughts. The hollow place was as it had been. Tushi and the majapa were not there. There was no sound in the late morning wilderness but water and wind and sometimes the solitary call of quail.

Ishi hurried back across the creek to the pool where he had found the flickering beads. He looked up and down the creek bank there for prints or a piece of clothing, but, with each new unsuccessful search, Ishi's hopes grew dimmer. He returned to where the bear trail met the creek. There, a little way up on the steep path, he saw faint but unmistakable foot marks, where Tushi and the majapa had stumbled and slid down the final, steepest part of the path.

He continued to search above and below the log crossing and in the heavy brush along the bank, a new urgency in his efforts, but Ishi saw no sign of a foot, or of a hand, no fragment of robe, dress, or hair on a thorny branch or sharp rock. Here the Banya Creek crossing point was as barren as the village above. The story told by Tushi's beads was clear to Ishi, but he did not want to believe it. He stood barefoot and shivering in the water, watching it spray high and terrible over the slippery log crossing.

> *If Coyote laughs at Mother and me, perhaps Jupka and Kaltsuna will again come to love the people and return our running ones to us. Butterfly God and God of Lizards, let it be so!*

Ishi ended his thoughts with a prayer that the Yahi ending people, at least, be allowed to pass away together to the stars in the old and sacred way. California Indians were known for being stoic, almost fatalistic, but Ishi could not stand this cruel helplessness. He dove into the icy water of Banya Creek to search for the bodies of his loved ones.

The last Yahi wanasi felt his breath taken away by the numbing cold of the current. Every pore on his body startled awake. His sleepless daze disappeared instantly. Ishi found a large, spinning madrone branch in the current and held strongly to it to brace against the force of the water which buffeted and numbed him as it poured down the canyon from the November rains and sleet on Waganupa far above.

Ishi searched the bottom of the creek with his feet, dragging them over smooth and sharp rocks, feeling for Tushi and the majapa. In a sudden swirl of violent water, the madrone branch was torn from his grasp. Ishi's feet left the stream's bottom, and the turbulent waters knocked him hard against a boulder in midstream. His head cracked hard against the unyielding stone, exploding with pain. His mind ran awash with scattered impressions and flashes of confused thought. He tasted blood in his mouth from where he had cut his tongue. A trickle of blood ran down from each of his wide nostrils. The cold flood then forced him into a whirlpool, where he spun sickeningly around and around.

> *Come take me, Coyote. Wait till I drown and wash up on the bank. Then come to me in the winter when you are most hungry and tear at my flesh with your Saldu friends. Work me down to a litter of bones. Come take your own grandson, Coyote. Come eat your Tetna-Ishi!*

Ishi was nearly ready to give in to the cold waters, but the small hope that Tushi and the majapa were still alive kept him swimming, face above the broiling water, until his head began to clear. Ishi was carried downstream by some new force, feet first, floating uneasily on his back, carried in the roar and power of cold white water farther and farther downstream, until he spun headfirst onto his belly and swam with all his remaining strength and hope to the bank of the creek. He was on the Wowunupo side of Banya Creek, far below the sandy fishing spot where he had been seen by the Saldu two days earlier.

Ishi lay half-conscious, panting hard like some frightened animal that had been chased and was now hiding, his brown hands clinging to the cold rocks, the taste of blood still in his mouth, his strength and purpose slowly returning. When he could move, he pulled himself upright, shivering, and began to make his way up the creek toward the alder log. At first, it seemed impossible to fight the flooding water, and there was not enough trail exposed to walk along the steep bank, but he knew what he had to do. Wanasi Ishi, man of nature, gained the measure of the swift downstream water. He used his knowledge of the creek bed, stayed out of the strong-flowing current and deep pools, and did not give in again to panic. He searched for the bodies of his loved ones, bracing himself against boulders, diving swiftly to the bottom of slow pools where a sacred Yahi body could lodge, doing as his elder uncle and grandfather might have taught him in the watgurwa of long ago.

When Ishi came again to the alder log crossing, his heart held little hope for his dambusa Tushi and his wise majapa. He had searched well, covering the water pockets and rough places full of colored rocks and the shallow, clearer pools from the alder log all the way back downstream to where Banya Canyon began to open out toward the great river. He had found nothing, heard nothing but the roar of water and now a lonesome sigaga calling, Ra raa ra, Ra raa ra, Ra raa ra.

> *Su! Am I meant to follow the running ones below Banya Canyon where the water widens, where the Saldu wowi begin? Is this what my new dream tells me? Am I to go soon as far as the river Daha after our family? Jupka, send me your butterfly sign.*

Ishi saw no splash of color as he had seen two days before. Even the quail call died away, leaving him trembling beside the incessant roar of the water in the deep green shade of the canyon walls and the forest.

Ishi dove back into the water.

> *I shall go then to the Daha where the black creature lives! I shall follow Tushi's beads where they take me.*

Tumbling down with the force of the white water again, trying to keep his face up out of the white spray, Ishi thought of his mother, alone above the creek, hiding, unable to move.

I have been gone from her since morning. Sun is moving down in the Daha Valley.

It was the remembrance of his mother that pulled him back from his desperate search. Ishi reluctantly turned and swam to the rocky bank, and pulled himself heavily from the water.

On his way to his mother, Ishi crossed warily over to his fishing hollow to get an old reed basket. He recrossed the creek slowly to his mother's side, filled the leaky basket with water, and climbed steadily upward through the thick brush toward their hiding place. He avoided the dangerous bear trail up from the creek. Bruised in his body and in his heart, Ishi came to his mother. She looked up at him quietly, every expectation clear in her milky brown eyes, but she asked no questions.

Chapter 16

Though crippled and disheartened beyond tears, Ishi's mother had not been idle during the long hours he had been away. She had crawled around near her chamise bush, dug up some late fall bulbs and shoots with a stone, and sifted ripe seed from the nearby grasses.

Now the two remaining people sat together for a moment not speaking, the truth between them in the cool, late afternoon air. The old Yahi woman broke the silence, holding out a wizened hand cupped full of seeds to Ishi.

"You must eat them my son, eat all of them. I have been tasting good seeds and bulbs all day."

Ishi took her small offering, tasted the seeds' tongue-prickling taste. He knew his mother had not eaten at all. When his mouth was clear, he told her of his search.

"Dambusa marimi, I have looked well all this day for our running ones, but the Saldu must have driven them farther away. I have not found them, nor their trail, but Elder Uncle will know what to do. Aiku tsub."

Then the words came easier to mother and son. They said to each other that the dear running ones would make their way back to Wowunupo before very many suns; they agreed that the wise majapa and intelligent Tushi had found another hiding place because of the flooding creek or the nearby Saldu surveyors. All the while, Ishi caught himself almost believing their hopeful conclusions. He did not tell his mother about Tushi's shell beads that he had found.

Their second night away from Grizzly Bear's Hiding Place, the cold came again, but it was not life-threatening. Ishi's mother slept, or at least pretended to sleep for his benefit, her tattered clothes pulled around her, her bound legs covered with slate-green manzanita leaves. Ishi sat looking into the darkness of Banya Canyon below them, into the darkness of his soul. Again they dared no fire, and, when the moon crept up, an owl began to punctuate Ishi's thoughts. All around him, the bay trees and tall pines glowed like dull apparitions, frost already forming on their low branches and reflecting whitely in the pale moonlight. For the second night, Ishi did not sleep.

In the hard dawn light, Ishi left his mother again, this time while she still slept, white frost covering the leaves over her legs as if she were half buried. He crept silently all the way to Sulphur Creek, near the Speegle ranch where he knew the whites were camped. Ishi saw none of the Saldu, but he came close enough to the dam worksite at the confluence of Sulphur and Deer creeks to see their metal-headed axes and shiny metal shovels leaning against a rough-hewn pine fence.

Ishi, his heart sick, went again to Banya Creek's steep banks. He searched the creek waters and both banks from far above the alder log crossing all the way down to the end of the canyon below it. He looked in the places he and Tushi had gone together often: places where Tushi, were she alive, would know to return in order to be found. Ishi also searched the steep, old bear trail up to Wowunupo shelf, looking for more tracks or signs of the running ones. He searched carefully, but in vain, along the ridge top until he knew he should return to his frail mother's side. Beautiful Tushi, the woman who should have been his marimi, the mother of his daana tehna-ishi, and the majapa, his sacred elder uncle, his father's own blood brother, were not in any of the places Ishi searched. The two most loved ones, half of the ending Yahi nation of four, had vanished without a trace.

* * *

Suns kept coming in the mornings and moons at night, but neither Ishi nor his mother kept track of days. Ishi must have slept during those first days after the forced dispersal of his family's village, but he was not conscious of where or when. He worked to keep himself and his mother alive, and he went to search for the lost ones at each new dawn while his mother slept or rested.

When the high waters had passed, Ishi dared to carry his mother down the sheer canyon side and across the fateful alder log to his fishing hollow on the opposite bank of Banya Creek. After this momentous trip of several hours, the two remaining Yahi were more comfortable than on Wowunupo ledge. Here was water, his fish nets, some fish lines and hooks, a few scraps of baskets and mats, a stone fish scraper, and a chipped black obsidian knife carved long before from the rock glass near the summit of Waganupa. This was all the people had to begin again.

More suns came, more moons at night, but Ishi did not give up his search for the two running ones. Each dawn he continued to look for them, and later each morning he came back, unsuccessful, to the little fishing shelter camp to perform the tasks that kept them alive. There was just enough food on days when the weather held good: overripe berries, nuts, and late salmon runs up the creek. After Banya's high water passed, Ishi had little trouble catching smaller salmon and trout with his recovered net and his hook and line. Sometimes he even fished as his elder uncle had taught him, by moving his hands in swimming motions in the water until, sometimes, a fish swam into them as though they were the inviting shadows of other fish.

Middle-aged Ishi knew the watgurwa lessons of his youth well. He only needed a young Yahi boy, some promise of the future, to teach them to, to perpetuate the old and sacred cycle of Yahi life. Ishi made the sacred fire as his elder uncle had taught him, and as his majapa had in turn been taught by those of the people before him, those with a history of over 3,000 years in California.

Ishi made an auna drill bed, fashioning it from a small slab of cedar he found by the creek, then gouging a socket and groove in it. For the drill itself, he cut a stick of oak, working it carefully as his old mother watched expectantly. The bed and drill were not a very good match at first. Ishi worked long and weary hours just to get the spark the two Yahi needed to stay alive. Finally, the shreds of frayed milkweed tinder which lay in the groove caught fire; Ishi held the faint burning tinder in his cupped hands over a small bed of dried grass, and blew softly in his hands until the fire spread and singed his skin. He set his new fire down on the dry ground, a tumble of yellow flame and faint smoke, that sacred gift from long ago when Coyote first got fire. Then he added small, dried chips of pepperwood and manzanita until the pale orange flames became a sure red blaze.

In some strange way, it was their fire that brought Ishi back to the living. In that blur of days following the invasion of Wowunupo, he had been strong only for his mother and the small hope of finding Tushi and his uncle. Now that the two survivors had fire, Ishi again felt the possibility that the ending people had a chance to endure longer in the Yana homeland.

Ishi's mother, too, was heartened by the fire. She nursed it during the day when Ishi was away or when he slept in their fishing shelter hideaway. The two of them, aging mother and only son, cooperated as naturally as twilight and late afternoon sun, never allowing the fire to grow dim or cold until Ishi had time to make a proper fire drill, straightened and hardened by the new fire itself.

They had no proper cooking baskets. Instead, they cooked in their one water basket until Ishi could prepare some resin to waterproof a larger basket. Ishi caught more salmon and steelhead than they could eat. He set up a frame and hung the extra fish in crude strips to dry and save for the fast-approaching winter. His broken knife was little help, so the fish strips were more torn than properly cut.

In those industrious days before the winter of 1908–09, Ishi gathered old summer acorns, digging them up from below dry leaves and dirt where they had fallen and been buried months before. He kept the ones that were not rotten, and ground the dry acorns into meal with rocks from Banya Creek. In the older days, the acorn harvests had brought together two or more of the Yana tribes to practice a ritual done with humble ceremony and perfectly molded, smooth grinding stones. Ishi's mother cooked the coarse, unevenly ground meal slowly, as she had done for two generations, making it into a hot mush that took away their chill and hunger pangs.

Hunter Ishi set out his snares and nets and gathered the skins and feathers of even the smallest birds and animals he caught. His mother kept busy fitting the small skins together. They had no needle, but she punched lines of matching holes in the skins with a jagged piece of buck's antler bone and laced the fragments together with milkweed string. What began as a patched neck ruff grew to cover her bent shoulders. Before the snows came, Ishi's mother had sewn herself a full cape, the upper part of mixed feathers, the bottom half of squirrel and fox. Still, each morning as the warm cape grew, Ishi went out to look for the two running ones. Each day he returned, having found nothing, but neither having been seen by the many whites around Deer Creek Canyon.

Broken-hearted, Ishi and his mother did these and many other practical things to survive, and in doing these tasks, they kept their minds from being consumed by the numbing fate surrounding them. Ishi's feeble mother still could not walk, but she worked hard to keep the two of them centered on the daily tasks of survival, never complaining or letting her private demons come into the light of their new firepit. She and Ishi talked about his fishing, about the small creatures of the deep woods making their winter burrows and nests by the creek, not unlike themselves, and about the late big V lines of ducks and geese passing loudly in the skies above.

The last two people used the ancient sayings in speaking to each other, almost as softly as one speaking privately to oneself. When a meal was finished, Ishi echoed the majapa's old words to his mother: "The acorn mush is fresh and good at your cooking firepit, my mother..." His mother often answered in the old way, her phrases caressing his wounded spirit: "There is a grown son who hunts well for us, a brave wanasi, a great hunter..."

The vegetable-dyed baskets they ate from were either old and frayed, like the basket Ishi had saved from his fishing shelter, or new grass ones woven hastily together and partially decorated by the feeble old Yahi woman whose eyesight had dimmed over the long, good years at Tuliyani village and the longer, harder years of hiding at Wowunupo. Ishi's mother served their hot acorn mush with a wide stick of bay tree wood which Ishi had hollowed out at the end with his broken knife.

As each new sun traveled its long road up, over, across, and then below the flat earth, spreading light and then darkness behind jagged Waganupa, Ishi thought only of the moment. He moved as if in a sleep, not daring to think back to their recent pain nor forward to the time of their inevitable ending in the heart of this good and sacred country. He lived as a man whose spirit had gone hunting in the deep night to find meaning in the harsh life they lived and in the cruel tricks Coyote had played on them by sending pale killers into their very homes. He waited for his divine spark to come back to him from the deep woods with the daybreak, needing his spirit and the meaning it brought back out of the darkness to go on living. Ishi felt sometimes that his own father's spirit or the butterfly god's directed him to use his hands and mind in order to keep his mother and himself alive. Only when the weather turned colder yet did Ishi begin to think more clearly, more like a Yahi wanasi, noticing all around him, planning his attack on the future.

> *Dambusa mother studies me closely from her bed of leaves and new cape of frost each morning as I leave to search, and each day when I return with no signs. She pretends to sleep when I go, but I know she sees. Suwa! Even the blind see when their hearts long to see. Mother thinks always of the two running ones, wishes only to talk of them. It is well to think always of dambusa Tushi and Elder Uncle, to keep their memories and hope for them alive, but I cannot speak of them now. I cannot bear to hear our lips speak aloud that our dear ones' bodies are cold white victims of the creek or that the Saldu have shot them and left their bodies for a bear or mountain lion. Haxa, I cannot face this. Wanasi Ishi is as a tehna-ishi again.*

His mind becoming more his again, Ishi went to their new fire and burned off his bristly black hair closer to his scalp, as it had grown wild in the lost days of new hiding across Banya Creek from Wowunupo. Mixing charcoal from old coals around the firepit with pine pitch, Ishi repainted the dark mourning stripes on his hollow brown cheeks. Ishi's mother watched him renew his ritual mourning, all the while breaking apart inside her soul. Still, she said nothing of their missing family and she tried hard to hide her tears from Ishi's view.

One cold early morning, Ishi recrossed the alder log, as usual, to go down Banya Creek to the pool where he had found Tushi's favorite beads. Now, as he stood by the swift-flowing water, he fumbled for her beads, and found them in the soft moleskin treasure bundle he kept around his neck at all times since the ransacking of the village. Holding the shell beads close in his worn hand, Ishi said an old prayer and blew some sacred tobacco upward, then downward, then to the east toward Waganupa, north toward the other great peak of Mt. Shasta, west to where the sun travels at twilight, and then south to where the black creature traveled noisily each day before sunset. For a strange moment, Ishi thought he heard his elder uncle's deep voice calling to him like an owl. Whoo hoo hoo...

Then came the higher, clearer call of Tushi's beautiful voice, calling from the thick chaparral. Flika, flika, flik, flika!

Ishi ran in the direction of the calls, his moccasined feet breaking through the thin skin of ice on puddles along the creek trails, until he heard a covey of mountain quail flush wildly into the thick bushes ahead of him. One startled quail whizzed just by Ishi's right cheek, its pea-sized heart pounding, its stubby wings beating the air in wild, zig-zag flight.

He is afraid as I have been, animal and man. Rest little bird. Your home will be yours again.

The pell-mell fan of many wings in the creekside brush faded, and Ishi guessed his mind had been playing tricks on him, but he was not sure. He stood perfectly still, frozen as a wary forest deer, and in minutes the dispersed quail began to call to each other. Ra raa ra. Ra raa ra, the language of lost birds came through the cold.

In the calls of the lost, Ishi thought he heard again the majapa and Tushi, owl and flicker, among the creekside woods. He searched wildly for footprints, for a bush stripped of its berry foods. He searched again the Banya woods, the thick brush of the canyon walls, behind boulders in the frigid creek, in each hidden cave on the walls of Banya Canyon. He found no sign of the running ones.

In the cold days to come, whenever Ishi saw red skinned buzzards circling above their canyon, he searched until he found the dead animal carcass they sought to feed upon. He checked every cougar's kill, ever bear's or fox's, to see that the forest hunters were not eating the carrion of his loved ones.

* * *

Ishi and his mother settled into an uneasy rhythm of life, always wary of the Saldu around them, always half-conscious of their unnatural and solitary life without their family, until the last harvest moon faded and the cold rains and sleet came. The first of the winter moons came with a light snowfall. More snows came and the forest started to fill up with white. Ishi began to stay in the drafty fishing shelter to tend to his mother instead of crossing the winter creek, staying close to keep her warm and safe. He piled wet earth before it froze against the little branch-built shelter to protect it better from wind and snow.

Her new cape of mixed feathers and skins pulled tightly around her, Ishi's mother sat close to the new fire watching her son. "Do you no longer cross the creek, my son?" she asked directly, her eyes steadily on his.

Ishi shook his head, and looked away.

"Haxa. I cannot find our family. It is no good."

Understanding flashed in her eyes—3,000 years of accumulated intuition, 3,000 years of harmony lost in forty years of change.

Ishi's mother spoke very softly now.

"The running ones are not here, my wanasi, or you would have found them long ago."

His heart in his throat, Ishi came to her, cold earth on his bare hands. He felt her soft arms around him, as it was when he was a child, felt again that same safe, warm feeling of love between mother and child. They cried together in their shelter, white swirls of snow falling outside to the ground. These were good tears, long and difficult in coming, held-in, lonely grief that had to get out. In the whitening forest, they spoke again of Tushi and Elder Uncle, although they never used their living names, but called them instead the lost ones.

Ishi's mother spoke quietly in his ear, softer even than the snowfall outside but strong and sure and soothing too, as when she was a young dambusa marimi, a new wife to Tetna Man, impetuous and brave, and Ishi was a squalling babe with red-brown cheeks, hands, and fingers, swaddled in the softest Yahi deerskins of other, better times.

"The lost ones may have a hard time putting their feet on the spirit trail, but our majapa is wise and our beautiful one has had visions. Together they will find the right path and walk the stars above Waganupa, the red glow from its crater warming their feet. Their spirits are wandering now, but one day soon they will know the way to the ancestors' eastern village in the night sky. Perhaps there we will soon meet them and Coyote will choose you be Tushi's husband in the hildaga [star] life where all things are possible that are not possible here. Perhaps someday, my good wanasi, you will have a child in the stars, and children from other tribes and nations will look up on clear spring nights to see him playing, leaving white star streaks flashing in the blackness when he runs."

Ishi's mind raced. He felt more alive than he had for as long as he could remember, felt the skin over his whole body tingle. He looked outside at the whitening world, at the heavier, fast-falling pace of the snow. His mother, her warm arms around him, felt him looking outward.

"Now that there is no smell of flowers or ripe berries, it will be easier for our lost ones to leave this world. There are no birds singing to call them back from where they have to go. This is the way, Ishi. I know you have dreamed of their spirits calling lost, but we must let them find the right path on their own. Aiku tsub. We cannot tempt them back to the living when they are meant for a better way."

The last two Yahi huddled now in the pale twilight, holding each other tightly, listening to the soft kiss of snowflakes on the interwoven branches above.

* * *

It was a winter of heavy snow as 1908 passed into 1909, but the snow lay still and perfect as a blanket on the Yana land because the winter wind was kinder than Ishi could remember. Some days the sun shone bright and they were comfortable in their hiding place; they ate Ishi's good dried fish and kept their fire going, almost smokeless, days and nights in their little earth-covered home.

One sun-drenched, white afternoon, the two talked together almost jokingly over the fire while Ishi skinned a squirrel.

"You look like a true hunter again," his mother observed.

"Haxa! Ishi grinned, "I am a great hunter of squirrel-bears."

"It is not what you hunt, my son, it is how you hunt it. Su! You have the eyes of your father again, full of light. You are in his image, and I am no longer afraid for your spirit."

Ishi smiled at his mother as she spoke these warm words. He missed, in his rising warm feeling at her compliments, that his mother was making her peace with this world of snow and coming renewal. He saw only the deep tenderness in her brown eyes, clouded but alive and young again for this moment. He heard his mother's voice, soft and strong, as he had heard it all those years ago when she nursed him at her breasts. It was a gift when he needed one most.

In the dawn of that mild January morning of 1909, Ishi got up to gather branches for their new fire. The sun was not yet lighting their shelter, but red flickers of firelight reflected off its woven branches onto Ishi's mother's wrinkled face. She slept soundly, her eyelids closed, her soft lips curved in a smile. Curled up like a daana in her swaddling cape, with one small hand cradled closely against her cheek, she looked to Ishi as peacefully asleep as she had ever been in those many good years long before the world changed. Ishi suddenly noticed on her usually bare wrist the old, worn grass bracelet his mother always kept secreted in her treasure bundle. Then Ishi knew.

The faded, old bracelet was his father's gift to his bride-to-be. Ishi's mother finally slept in complete peace. She had left the man she loved most among the living, her Tehna-Ishi, for the man she loved most in the night stars, Ishi's father.

Chapter 17

Most people's spirits are severely tested at one or two passage points in the short journey of their lives: sometimes the terrible loss of a loved one or some other stinging grief will obliterate all sense of time, even our will to live out the rest of the journey. In January of 1909, in the dead of winter, Ishi came to such a point of timeless vertigo. He was utterly and unalterably alone, the last of his race.

Ishi moved as an injured animal moves, perhaps as one of the last of the Northern California lynx must have moved, having chewed off one of its own legs to escape some settler's trap, trailing blood in the snow, finding some reason to keep stumbling forward, leaving that important part of itself behind. Ishi carried his mother in a daze, the white trees a blur around him, his moccasined feet crunching softly in the dry snow. Had he been more clear-headed, he might have been surprised at how light his mother's body was on his back as he stumbled along the powder-covered path to the burial cave of his ancestors.

There, outside the sacred cave, Ishi made the cleansing funeral fire for his mother, using the auna drill they had fashioned together. When the fire had consumed his mother's frail body and died away, Ishi buried her cremated remains inside the cave along with some small treasures: her sweetgrass bracelet, her digging stick, and a small basket of acorn meal. Ishi slowly breathed the lingering smell of the smoke that had sent his mother's soul upward along the star path to the ones gone before and to her husband, Tetna Man, leaving her son alone on the earth.

When the old ritual was done and the stone slab back in its proper place over the Yahi bones in the sacred cave, Ishi went outside into the stabbing brilliance of afternoon light reflected off shining snow. He put a hand to his eyes, as if shielding them from some white-hot star that had fallen too close to earth.

Ishi, eyes stinging, stumbled through the white-covered land, driven only by some primal instinct. He did not return to

Wowunupo ledge or to their fishing shelter. He had no home to return to, for it is family that makes a home. Instead, his feet took him over an invisible, snow obscured trail toward Black Rock and his childhood village of Tuliyani, places he had not seen through the long years of hiding.

The last Yahi man walked the afternoon into muted forest twilight as he came nearer the old place of memories. He did not take care to avoid any Saldu who might have hunted him. Ishi would have welcomed death if he had been conscious enough to think realistically about his fate. Once, his hunter's awareness brought him back to sharp lucidity when he heard some large forest creature breaking through the brush toward him, but Ishi did not stray from the path of his memory or hide. He kept walking, putting one moccasined foot in front of the other, as the headlong crashing came closer and closer. Perhaps a bear, awakened early from its long sleep and angry, would take him down in restitution, maul him and leave his ripped body open for coyotes to feast on under the winter moonlight until his earthly body became a litter of clean, white bones. Ishi did not care. The frantic charge of the creature in the woods was on him. Out of the tangle of brush and trees came a tawny flash of buckskin across the trail. The big buck, too, was running from something it did not understand, leaving a momentary strong smell of wild animal fear in Ishi's nostrils. Then it was gone, just as suddenly as it came, crashing away through frozen alder, bay, and madrone trees. Then there was silence in the Yana forest.

Ishi came to his old overlook at Black Rock in near darkness, and climbed upward the old way by memory. When he pulled himself up onto the top of the lookout, panting like a deer that had run hard in cold, still air, Ishi could still see the distant landmarks in the final wan hues of twilight. To the west lay the familiar scene of the great Daha Valley and the big river running through it, the coastal mountains behind, all blending in the fast-approaching darkness. When he turned east, though, toward the great mountain, Ishi saw the final alpine glow linger on the tall upper slopes of the volcano, just as he had seen the light play there before, many times as a young man, long after winter sunsets. This was where his mother, the two lost running ones, and the lost ones before them had entered into the night sky, had stepped into immortality, each one becoming a glowing star to forever shine in the blackness of the night.

For many hours Ishi could not sleep there on the high rock, though his body was exhausted and his mind numb. The biting cold air and the rough rock under his back kept him awake, eyes open, watching the hundreds of stars dance in the clear night sky. Once, a shrieking white band of light flashed momentarily across his sight, and another band blazed across the first, until both shooting star tracks faded to nothingness in the east.

In the darkest hour before dawn, Ishi finally drifted into sleep. His eyelids and muscles twitched as he lay high on Black Rock, above his childhood home.

> *Cold. Cold water. I am swimming up Yuna Creek as when I was a boy, but I need no air. Nize ah Yahi, but I am a fish man too, swimming, swimming ever upstream as salmon man does. Suwa! Saldu are all around, above me on the creek's banks. I see their dark, water-distorted shadows above, hear the water hissing where they shoot their small metal stones all around me. Hexai-sa! Saldu. I am fish man, swimming strong up Yuna Creek's current. You dawana mechi-kuwi can never harm me. Only grizzly tetna or a Yahi wanasi can catch me. But I was the last wanasi before I became fish man. Suwa! I am swimming past your shadows upstream to where I hear Tushi's fish song calling me through the rush of water singing over stone. I am swimming strong to Waganupa's snows where Tushi's song calls me, where Yuna Creek is born out of the great mountain's snows. Su! You and no one can catch me, Saldu shadows. I am fish man. I am swimming strong upstream through the cold rushing water. I am on my way to join the others, to swim upward, even through ice fields, up and off the great mountain and into the water sky*

beyond. There is nothing you can do to stop me. Even if you dam up my Yuna Creek, I will become eagle man and fly up above you on to Waganupa and beyond. I hear Tushi's water song. Suwa! I swim through the cold to her.

The lonesome, high pitched sound of a quail calling stirred Ishi. When he opened his eyes, the full morning sun blinded him. Everywhere around Black Rock and below on the forest floor around old Tuliyani village, the brilliant sunlight reflected off an endless blanket of white. Even Ishi's tattered robes glinted with sunlit frost. He was cold and hungry, but he was still among the living creatures in the Yana foothills. As Ishi sat up stiffly, he saw, in the corner of his vision, a tiny skink lizard flash out of sight behind a rock. He moved to the edge of Black Rock's shelf to study the tiny, splay-toed marks of the lizard's path.

Kaltsuna sends his son to me even in the winter. Perhaps the lizard and the butterfly have not forgotten me.

When Ishi touched his bare fingers to the tiny trail of prints, he felt the sting of frost, and then the prints he touched melted into white. Ishi knew what to do. He would climb the great volcano and step off into the sky.

Chapter 18

In 1908 and 1909, even in the fast disappearing old west, news traveled quickly. Newspapers, like the backwater *Oroville Register* and the bigger Bay Area papers like the *San Francisco Call* and the *San Francisco Examiner*, were desperate for any sensational story that would sell their papers. The story of the discovery of a genuine Indian village, one that had recently been inhabited by wild Indians, made excellent copy and delighted headline makers. Like a winter virus, the startling revelation spread through the bars and homes of Northern California, touching off more than a few heated conversations and more than one fight. Reactions varied. Some couldn't care less that a tribe of aboriginal people had survived against all odds or logic into the twentieth century, had lived and might be living still a stone-age, hidden life in the backyard of modern and industrious Americans. More commonly, at least in the north of the state, the theme was outrage, even anger that the thieving, murderous Mill Creeks were back. In the smoke of the bars of Oroville, Chico, Tehama, Red Bluff, Redding, and Old Shasta, over the sawdust covered floors, drunken men boasted about what they would do to one of the possibly real savages, and shouted threats through the hurdy gurdy music and the heavy-stepping sound of cancan girls' feet on the stage boards. There was no shortage of volunteers to go on Indian hunting parties in the winter of 1908 and 1909, but those bloodthirsty groups made their pacts at night, after work, with whiskey-bolstered resolve, and, in the light of morning, there were jobs to go to, and reason almost always prevailed. Fierce Indian hunters like Anderson and Good had long since given up the "glory" of killing Indians. First, there were no more Yahi to kill; second, Anderson and Good had years before come to the conclusion that one-sided massacres were not much fun.

Cattle ranchers, surveyors, engineers, loggers, railroad workers, thieves, and gamblers were not the only ones to read the latest news in the papers. Down in the Bay Area at the University of California at Berkeley, established late in the nineteenth century as the first of the universities of California, educated men and women read the stories with a different reaction. In particular, the vital and young anthropologists Thomas T. Waterman and Alfred L. Kroeber read the news excitedly. There in the *San Francisco Call* and the *Examiner* were the words that would change their lives indelibly.

For months, Waterman and Kroeber corresponded with the surveyors who had ransacked Ishi's home at Wowunupo-mu-tetna, pressing for details, hoping for any sign of a live Yahi who might be discovered as the survey work for the new dam continued. Perhaps, the anthropologists reasoned, the middle-aged Indian who had brandished his harpoon on Deer Creek might reappear, in desperate need of food and tools with which to get it. Perhaps the old, bandaged Yahi woman the surveyors described or another wild Mill Creek might still be alive, they hoped. Unfortunately, there was no more news. Weeks passed and then months without any sign of the resurrected and elusive Yana Indians. Waterman and Kroeber had the passion of youth and a deep, almost mystical, interest in all things California Indian, so they did not give up the quest. They wrote, with increasing urgency, to anyone who might have any information about the dispersed inhabitants of the Yahi village, lest this window back into the time of primitive man close forever. But there was no news. The trail seemed to have ended.

* * *

On a cool October morning in the year after the break-up of Wowunupo village, Waterman awoke to the sounds of quail calling and to the babbling and inarticulate riffles of nearby Deer Creek. His camping companions, the engineer G. W. Hunt and Merle Apperson's son, were already up and about the tasks of cooking breakfast. Although Waterman, university researcher and educator, had little in common with his newly acquainted mini search party, he had grown to like Hunt and the Apperson boy in the two weeks they had spent combing Deer Creek Canyon. He heard a hiss and pop as Hunt fried eggs in a cast iron skillet over the fire, heard young Apperson teasing the skilled, older man. Waterman had grown to admire Hunt's machine-like efficiency and to appreciate

Apperson's folksy and sometimes obscene backwoods humor. Waterman crawled out of the cocoon of his university-owned sleeping bag, and stood fully upright in his red longjohns to stretch out the kinks from a night of sleeping on the ground. He felt the morning light on him as he stretched; his brown eyes focused first on his companions, then on the green and brown chaparral all around them. He hoped this would be the day.

Waterman and Kroeber still had real hopes of finding a living Yahi, and when it became clear that a comprehensive search could not be initiated through the mail using local Tehama and Lassen county citizens, Waterman had volunteered to search the faint trails around Deer Creek himself. He took his charge quite seriously, and he knew that Kroeber's hopes went with him into the fast disappearing wilderness. Unfortunately, his quest was failing.

It is true that the young professor and his party found a lot of evidence of Indian occupation at and near Grizzly Bear's Hiding Place on Deer Creek. Hunt, Apperson, Jr., and Waterman could find Yahi artifacts at will, but they could not turn up a trace of living Indians. Those small, ghostly dwellings at Wowunupo looked exactly as they had when Apperson, Sr. had visited them the morning after their discovery a year before. Since those fateful two days, no one had occupied the shelters centered around a grizzly bear's den high on the canyon ledge above Deer Creek.

In their remaining week, Waterman and his companions searched with increasing urgency, for a second winter was coming on since the forced dispersal of the village, and the sickly native woman described by the Deer and Sulphur Creek surveyors and cattlemen could hardly survive another winter without the tools and shelter of the village, even if she had somehow miraculously survived the first. The searchers rose early every day and returned late every evening to their own camp near Wowunupo, but they found no evidence to suggest that any Yahi Indians were yet alive in the twentieth century. Yes, Waterman returned to the university anthropological museum with many striking photographs of the primitive village and some evidence of the hidden Yahi way of life in the wilds below Mt. Lassen, but Waterman and Kroeber had to admit that the mission had mostly failed. True, Hunt had gleaned some new ideas about roads and dam sites in the deep woods, but the mystery of the aboriginal people remained.

After the invasion of Wowunupo, neither Ishi nor anyone else ever saw Tushi or the majapa again. The ending one, Ishi, son of Tetna Man, was convinced that his people had not survived. Although his cousin-as-a-sister had run one way and Ishi another, he knew that had Coyote not chosen death for her, he and Tushi, with their common knowledge of familiar places, would have found each other quickly, within hours, certainly within days. Ishi sensed that the majapa and Tushi had drowned at the treacherous and slippery Banya Creek crossing. If they had somehow survived the high water, some other violent death had met them soon thereafter, perhaps at the hands of the Saldu killers or by the claws of a bear or cougar. Otherwise, Ishi knew he would have found some sign of their bodies during all his desperate searching. So he reasoned, and so it wounded him deep down in his heart, and so it was.

* * *

In Berkeley, inside the Kroeber's small house on Parker Street, Thomas Waterman and Mr. and Mrs. Kroeber were talking over dinner, looking at the new black and white prints from Waterman's Deer Creek negatives, sharing the fellowship of good friends and good food. Outside the warm house, the city lights of Berkeley and Oakland sparkled, and, across the wide, dark bay, the distant yellow glow of San Francisco shimmered. Through the narrow mouth of the San Francisco Bay and over the Marin hills, fingers of fog reached toward the confluence of the Northern California rivers and the lit-up cities around the bay, just as they did nearly every evening. On this cold November night in 1909, the Golden Gate Bridge would have already been swallowed by the advancing fog bank, had the famous bridge been there. Foghorns moaned across the big expanse of salt water, warning any unwary ships of the night, but the small party on Parker Street did not hear their cries. Instead, the three sat close together around the small dining room table, sharing icons and photographs of another world, one not so far away. Mrs. Kroeber, intelligent, young and pretty, was fascinated by the slightly blurry prints. Her hazel eyes stared at one print in particular until she called to her husband, who had taken his plate to their small bright kitchen.

"Honey, come here. There are monarch butterflies all over the frame of this Indian house!"

Professor Kroeber hurried back to his wife's side, and Professor Waterman crowded around her chair too.

"These were taken last month, in October?" Mrs. Kroeber asked incredulously.

"Yes," Waterman answered. "Way past the monarch season."

"Damn strange," Alfred Kroeber said. His hand traced his wife's neck as they all stared at the softly-focused photograph. "Damn strange."

There before them, clear in black and white, was pictured the ruined skeleton of a Yahi shelter, and hundreds of butterflies, caught frozen in time, clung to the bare skeleton of wood.

Chapter 19

The late winter snow was deeper where Ishi camped at the base of towering white Waganupa. He had made the long hike on will alone, sometimes struggling through snow up to his hips, sometimes falling suddenly through the thin crust of surface ice into the deeper dry snow below, fighting his way out using only his hands and windmilling arms. Near death from freezing, he had come at last to the mountain at the center of the Center of the World. Ishi's will to end the long living story of the people, to jump literally off into the eastern star path, had brought him to the great volcanic mountain, but now it was clear to him that he could not make the difficult climb to the peak. From his pathetic, drafty shelter of pine boughs and bark, gathered hastily and set up directly on the snow of the already angled slope, Ishi had not seen Waganupa's summit for days. The white peak was lost in heavy, swirling gray clouds. Besides the danger of exposure to the threatening weather, Ishi was weak, depressed, and starving.

> *Leader Uncle taught us many moons ago, at Tuliyani, that a Yahi wanasi has one four footer friend if he is near death. If a Yahi is starving and has no bow and is too weak to fish, he may kill and eat the mountain marmot. The majapa taught us that this is the old and sacred rule because the marmot is so easy to kill. Four footer marmot who lives in the ground will give himself to me, for it is the way. Suwa! I will catch him as he sleeps in his burrow.*

After much digging through the snow with sharp volcanic rocks in his hands, Ishi found the mouth of a marmot burrow, very near to his makeshift mountain camp. He dug the frozen ground with the stones until, seeing a hibernating mass of brownish fur curled restfully in a ball, he stopped digging and said a prayer. Then Ishi struck the sleeping creature, gutted it as best he could with an obsidian rock, and ate the warm meat. He sat still in his pine bough lean-to, lost in thought for long hours before darkness fell, sometimes saying the old prayers, sometimes half-singing the old songs. Then he slept fitfully.

Aizuna Tetna-Ishi, Tushi's voice calls distantly, come higher up Waganupa toward the stars. Sigaga, sigaga, Leader Uncle and I are quail calling down to you from above. Come up the mountain to where there are hot springs and caves, and you will be warm.

In the cold overcast of morning, the hunger sickness had left his body, and his mind had cleared a little. Ishi left his shelter, and stood stooped and gaunt outside, looking up at the swirling gray. He pulled his tattered traveling robe tighter around him.

Ishi climbed through the long morning, lost in cloud, his feet on bluish ice and black rocks. The day grew colder and colder. The slope grew steeper, and the cold air hurt his lungs. Ishi stood winded, his breath coming out in cool blasts that hung in the air for seconds before they disappeared. Then in front of him on the snowy slope, in a dark jumble of volcanic rock, he saw the shadowy opening of a cave.

Sigaga, sigaga, my lost quail ones, is this where you call me from?

Inside, the cave was nearly pitch black and rank with old animal smells. But it was also warm and dry.

"Tushi! Majapa!" Ishi called, but only his echo answered him, ringing long in the small cavern, growing softer and softer until the sound died away.

Ishi's throat felt scratchy: he had not used his voice much since his dambusa mother's ashes had floated up into the sky. His breath came easier in the warm cave, and Ishi removed his makeshift robe, shaking the condensation and melting ice off. Using some dry twigs and punky wood he found on the cave floor, Ishi made a fire. It took a long time to produce sparks, but, when the fire caught, a soft orange light filled the cave and lit up its volcanic walls. He saw that he was not the first person to use this new home. Someone, perhaps one of the Pit River people, had long ago fashioned a bed of large pine boughs hauled up from below the treeline and set up neatly at the back of the cave. Fed and warm for the first time in many days, Ishi considered waiting before making the rest of his climb, waiting before giving up his life to Coyote God and the stars, before climbing up to the firepit of his lost family.

His decision to stay made, Ishi went out of the cave to gather up light pumice rocks to blockade the cave's entrance. Outside, what little daylight there had been was fading. The small, rough black boulders littered the icy slope of Waganupa; they scratched his hands as he piled them in the cave mouth. Feeling the cold penetrating his body, he crawled through the opening, now smaller, for his robe.

Hexai-sa! Something is behind me!

Ishi spun around, a blazing branch from the fire in his hand. Huge yellow eyes stared unblinking at him from the entrance. Then the eyes were almost upon him as the mountain lion rushed forward. He felt her huge front paw strike him, her claws raking the side of his arm. He saw the flash of white incisor teeth in the firelight, and, in an unplanned instant, Ishi shoved the flaming stick into the cougar's gaping mouth. The angry cat bit down on the burning branch, her twisting shape eerily outlined on the cave walls and roof, and, with a roar of fear and pain, she leaped away.

When she was gone, Ishi wearily crawled out the narrow mouth of the lava cave to see his wounds in the pale afterglow of the alpine twilight. The mountain lion was nowhere around. He cleaned the deep scratches on his arm as well as he could, using dry snow he melted slowly in his hands. He took some sacred tobacco from the bundle on his hemp belt and poulticed the throbbing cuts. Ishi's eyes swept the frozen incline above him and then below: the half-darkness revealed only glowing ice and, here and there, scattered boulders of black pumice poking up out of the white surface. He saw no cougar tracks. To the west, the last of the unearthly, muted colors of the setting sun faded behind the distant coastal mountains. Ishi saw Shasta Bally and the Yolla Bollies for the first time in years, black silhouettes in the pastel northwestern light. His head was spinning, high on Waganupa. To the north, the white peak of Mt. Shasta dominated all around it.

Up there, the Achomawi people once prayed to their spirit mountain. Now there are none living in the shadows of Waliwa Shasta. Below, the mechi-kuwi Saldu are hidden everywhere among the folds of this vast world, and Coyote has allowed it to be so. Dawana god spins the world, spins my head. I must go inside my little watgurwa in Waganupa's side.

The blood he had lost added to Ishi's weakness. He struggled to pull two lava rocks into the small passageway at the opening of the lava cave, until the mouth was nearly sealed from within. His new fire still glowed orange and yellow in the cave, and, just as Ishi had been taught as a child, the volcanic mountain was warm beneath its outer surface. As he made his way to the old pine bed at the back of the shelter, Ishi did not care whether that warmth came from hidden gods, who had retreated inside Waganupa after Jupka and Kaltsuna made the world, or whether his was the false warmth of one who is freezing to death. He only needed sleep, craved sleep, and so he slept.

The fire died down until it was only a bed of red coals glowing on the rocky lava floor. World-weary Ishi slept on, his eyelids fluttering.

A ra raa, a ra raa, my dear lost one Tushi is calling. Raa ra raa, raa ra raa, raa ra raa, Elder Uncle calls plainly too. Aiku tsub. My lost ones are sigaga spirits calling me higher. A ra raa, raa ra raa, their voices are strong. Su! The dear ones are not far away!

Ishi awakened suddenly and jumped to his feet, pulling on his torn robe. His hands tore at the rocks plugging the mouth of his cave. He felt a rush of cold air as several of the rocks fell away. Then he heard the close calling of Tushi and the majapa again. Ishi plunged outside into the icy night.

Outside, on the white-covered slope of Waganupa, Ishi answered the calls. "Ra ra raa, raa ra raa!" he yelled. His frantic voice echoed down the great mountain, growing softer and softer until the sound was gone, but no answer came. Only the thousands of white-hot stars danced overhead, making small, shimmering dots of light in the dark. Hearing no answer, Ishi raced up the steep mountainside. His bare feet slipped on the ice, and his bare hands bled from grasping rough pumice rocks to keep from plunging down the ice fields to his death. He called and called, climbing ever upward as fast as he could move. When still no reply came from his lost family, his desperate calls turned to sobs, and then to plaintive prayers that the Yahi gods still lived and cared about his world.

Ishi climbed upward through this steep land of ice, rock, and sulfur smells and steam vents, moving more and more slowly as his strength waned and the air grew thinner, until it was nearly dawn. He called out weakly from time to time, but he heard only the wind moaning over the ice fields, so high up that there were no trees to temper it. He saw no sign of his loved ones or of the mountain lion whose cave he had taken. Ishi saw only the fading stars in the late winter sky.

When he turned back, Ishi was near the volcano's summit, where he had hoped to hurl himself off into the sky, but the peak had formed a gray pre-dawn shroud around itself. He did not have the strength to live well or to die. Far below him, over the foothills and the great Daha Valley to the west, Ishi saw a blanket of white fog covering the world completely in the gathering new light. Only the spirit mountain Shasta, to the north, tore up through the pale, shifting cover of white.

Stiff with cold and the rigorousness of the long downhill hike, still sobbing gently from the emotional pain of his brief closeness to the spirits of Tushi and his uncle, Ishi came to the mouth of the cave just as the sun rose behind the clouded peak of Waganupa. Once inside the tiny cavern, he pulled some of the loose lava rocks into place and made his way to the back of the cave where he fell, unconscious, onto the old pine bough bed. The bearcub boy, Ishi, now a broken man of forty-nine years, slept the sleep of the dead.

* * *

The spring of 1909 came thankfully early to the great Daha Valley and to the Yana foothills, spreading like the fingers of a hand reaching down from Waganupa toward the valley. It came in with warm rain and blustery winds which blew down off the big volcano. The spring rains melted the softer snows at the base of the mountain: the meadows around Yuna and Banya creeks began to flood, warming the frozen ground, replenishing the soils through nature's constant dance of minerals and elements. The creeks at the Center of the World gushed with high, racing waters. Each new morning, the sun's plumed headdress of intense yellow lit the sky and warmed the ice high on the sacred volcano.

Ishi looked out of the mouth of his cougar's den. As he chewed a rind of stale, dried salmon skin and flesh, he felt the rush of warmer air pouring around his face into the musty cave. Coming up on the warm breeze from the Yana foothills below, he thought he smelled the sweet smell of new grass and clover.

> *Su, su! I am back to myself again. I am alive in the world.*

He pulled away the remaining rocks from his blockade. Then, gathering himself for the awakening, he crawled outside the lava cave. Blinded by the searing brightness of the sun's rays reflecting off the snow and ice, Ishi lay down on the melting surface, shielding his eyes with his hands. Like a blind Indian Oedipus, his mind wandered far while he saw nothing but the darkness of light. The morning sun warmed him, blessed him, touched him with soft eagle feathers from its great, far-away headdress of feathers and plumes that lit up the world.

> *I am of the people! I am alive.*

Ishi's eyes adjusted to the brightness, while the new sun warmed his light brown skin, which had lost its red hues in the long weeks of darkness. He sat up slowly, his head reeling with vertigo. When his mind had cleared a little, he rubbed his stiff legs, his knees, and his elbows.

> *I am as stiff as an old tetna at the end of his winter's sleep. Bay leaves and sweating, as in the sweathouse at Tuliyani, are what I need. But aizuna Tuliyani is empty. Its wowi are empty, as are those at Wowunupo.*

Ishi looked below him, saw the emerging green of the forest in the clear light, and heard babbling riffles of water flowing over stone somewhere far off below.

> *Su. This tired world is renewing itself again. How long have I floated in darkness? Su. I must heal myself if I am to be strong enough to climb up to the star path.*

In this time of renewal, when life was beginning again all around him, Ishi was confused by what to do next. As his mind emerged from the long, semi-conscious days of hiding, Ishi regained his resolve to take his own life, to join his lost Yahi family in the stars. But, at the same time, the warm sunlight felt good on his skin, and he suddenly felt very hungry, felt the pangs of his body wanting to cling to life.

Ishi sat on an outcropping of reddish black pumice in the angled ice, transfixed by high-altitude vertigo and indecision, his eyes half-focused on the distant treeline below the den of sleeping. Something moved in the trees. He saw a tawny-colored flow of motion.

First he saw a sleek, full-grown cougar amble out of a stand of dwarf pine trees below his vantage point, and then, wobbly legged and uncertain, a little tan cougar cub followed its mother up onto the open mountainside. Ishi's haggard face broke into a smile. The cub's huge paws and large ears and head seemed all out of proportion, even from where Ishi sat. His smile changed to a huge grin as he watched the little cub trip over its own stubby legs, and saw the baby cougar's mother come back and impatiently pick her offspring up in her mouth by the scruff of its neck.

The two wild mountain creatures, the mother still gingerly carrying her cub in her mouth, came up on the soggy ice toward the last wild man. As they came nearer, Ishi saw that the mother cougar's paws were wet from the rivulets of water trickling down the ice. There were no trees between them now, only an open field of ice separating animal and man.

Aiku tsub. She does not see me!

The smile faded from Ishi's face and his facial muscles tightened as he saw the big cat turn directly toward him. He saw a dark burn scar on the mountain lion's mouth and suddenly felt again the ache of his own scars in the flesh of his arm. Looking to the cave mouth, Ishi calculated whether he had enough time to bolt to the opening and block it from inside before the cougar arrived. He felt the huge yellow eyes on him again.

The cub growled a miniature growl from its mother's mouth. She set her cub down on the ice, then sat back tall on her haunches, tilting her head quizzically to one side, watching this strange, tattered brown human with her liquid yellow eyes.

"Su!" Ishi said. "Are you the dambusa one who tried to tear off my arm? Are we friends now that you have a daana cub? Nize ah Yahi."

The sleek mother cougar rolled her head even further to the side, while her baby nipped at her front paws, growling softly. The big tan mountain lion purred softly.

"We were not always friends," Ishi said from his rock retreat, the strength of his voice surprising him. "Su. It was not always so, lion of Waganupa. You, too, wanted this cave. Were there no other cougars for you to take your long sleep with? Dawana majapa Ishi took your shelter, when the last of the people, above all others, should have understood. Why did this ending hisi not let you have your cave? What is it that I do here?"

The mother cougar picked up her cub gently and stood, ready to move, on all fours. Ishi stood on his stiff legs, too, waiting. Then she turned and walked slowly down the ice slope toward the dwarf pine trees, lugging her flesh and blood, her short future. She stopped once before she reached the treeline, and looked back quizzically at the native man.

Ishi walked to the cave when she and her cub had disappeared into the small green trees, and he looked inside the cave as if he had never seen it until this day. When his eyes adjusted to the darkness, Ishi saw pine nut husks and the caps of acorns spread all over the lava floor. He did not remember eating them. He searched, but found no more food in the cave.

He went to the rickety tree bough bed.

> *Suwa! This is where I have slept? Why did the son of Tetna Man not sleep as my dambusa mother slept, without ever again waking to walk the earth? Why?*

Ishi lay down on the makeshift bed. The brittle pine branches creaked, even from Ishi's frail weight. He lay on his back in the near darkness, his fire having extinguished itself long before, and stared at the ceiling of the cave. In the weak, indirect light from outside, Ishi saw, for the first time, tiny mineral deposits above his face. The cave roof, he now saw, was covered with small green stalactites, some as tiny as the tips of his fingers, others the length of one of his hands. He became aware, too, of the sound of drops of water falling every few minutes. My time is short, he thought, but the time of lava caves and spring thaws is endless. Then he remembered.

> *It was the wakara lost ones who kept me from sleeping forever, as mother slept. It was the sigaga voices of Tushi and the majapa that held me to this life.*

Images of his crazy winter climb up Waganupa flashed before his mind's eye: the uphill world of rocks, ice, and cold darkness; the voices of the dear ones calling him upward; the freezing retreat back down to the cavern. Ishi sat up. His head was swimming. He tried to stand, but the ceiling and stalactites were too low, too near his face.

Su! This is why I walk as tetna walks, like a four footer and not a Yahi man. Wanasi Ishi shall sleep no more in darkness. He will live whatever life is left as a man. Aiku tsub.

With newfound determination, Ishi walked over the rough lava floor to the cave entrance and pulled away the remaining rocks. He went back to the old ashes of his firepit, kicked them about, and set stones over the fireplace. He picked up the pine nut and acorn husks, and threw them outside on the melting ice. When he was finished, there was no evidence that he had wintered in the warm cave. Everything was as it had been.

Mother puma of Waganupa will see that this wowi is empty, she and her dambusa cub. Auna will not be made again in this place in the warm belly of the Center of the World. Suwa!

Outside, in the brilliant sunlight, Ishi walked stiffly downhill over the slushy ice field to the trees. He heard the ancient babbling language of water on rock grow louder as he hiked downward through the stubby green pines, over black volcanic rocks covered with phosphorous green lichen. He came to swift Manzanita Creek below Waganupa. Ishi washed his hands, face, and neck in the cold water, and drank the sweet melted snow of Waganupa, snow he might have walked over only weeks before. Then, suddenly, he sensed something watching him.

Downstream from where he bathed, in the shadows of a thick stand of alder trees, the cougar had nudged her baby out of the water and onto the rocks by the stream. The cub's fur was water-drenched, making it seem even smaller and more vulnerable. Its mother watched Ishi, cocking her big head again in curiosity. He saw her pink nostrils expanding in and out as she breathed. The frozen moment broke then, and, picking her baby up by the scruff of its wet neck, the mountain lion disappeared in several quick, liquid bounds. Ishi heard only the sounds of the breeze and water running.

Go in peace, marimi puma. Your home is yours again. We have understood each other here on the great white mountain. Aiku tsub. May Coyote God watch over your little cub.

The last Yahi man felt stabs of hunger in his gut. He was lightheaded from the long fasting. He knew he must eat soon or die. Ishi forded the racing creek, his bones aching in the cold, then started down the steep mountainside toward the Yana foothills where the people had prospered for thousands of years.

Su, I must find strength once again, enough to carry me home. I will go through the old world one last time. I will try to find the lost ones' bodies, if they are there, to perform the sacred rites. I shall listen one last time for the sigaga voices of Tushi and the majapa to see if they no longer call out to me, no longer need me. Then it will be time to walk the bright hildaga path.

Chapter 20

In the lower elevations, the spring of 1909 had taken full hold of the Yana lands. Ishi spent his first night away from the Waganupa cave at the border of Upper Meadow, where he, Tushi, and their boy cousin had played as children. Before dark came to the lush meadow, Ishi ate sweet, wild onion bulbs and some new clover. He slept a dreamless, restful sleep. When he awoke at dawn, with the bright sun rising behind the mountain, he felt much less lame and stiff. Ishi remembered coming here—just as he was now—moons ago to search for his lost ones, but, just as then, the sweeping green meadow had no spirit presence and held no Yahi bones. Yellow marigolds shone everywhere in the marsh like little suns against a darker green background. Ishi recalled scenes from his youth when he and the pretty one, Tushi, used to run barefoot in this meadow, laughing, stepping sometimes on the soft bright marigolds, their feet sinking into the cool, black sludge of this same boggy meadow. They would stop, lie on their backs on the wet humus, and wave the soles of their feet at each other, soles painted yellow and green and black from the flowers, grass, and soggy earth. And they would laugh, as Ishi laughed now in his mind's eye.

The vibrant yellow of the flowers and the rush of warm nostalgia turned Ishi's thoughts to the old places and old times of his childhood. He decided to go to Yuna Canyon, to follow Yuna Creek one final time to Three Knolls, to Black Rock, to Round Meadow, and to Tuliyani village, to make one last search for the bodies of his elder uncle and Tushi. Not only was Ishi driven to make every last conceivable attempt to free their souls by performing the sacred burial rites, but he was also only too aware of the ancient and powerful Yahi belief that the soul of a dead one, lingering on too long in the Land of the Living, was in an unhappy and lonely limbo. His elder uncle had long ago taught him that any lost Yahi, caught between the sky Land of the Dead and the Yana Land of the Living, would assume an animal's voice and call out to his or her loved ones still living to join their family in the sky. Ishi had heard the voices repeatedly, and, in spite of the danger to himself, he wanted with all his heart to release his people from their uneasy limbo. He did not care if they took him to the Land of the Dead with them.

As the spring progressed, Ishi went to the fateful place at Three Knolls and to his lookout at Black Rock, where he again watched and heard the black serpent come up the Daha Valley each dawn and steam back down each dusk. Ishi followed the curves of Yuna Creek through Round Meadow to Tuliyani. He found the village long-abandoned and its structures nearly erased from sight by the tireless workings of nature. The remains of their shelters, storehouses, and drying frames could only be distinguished from the dense plant growth by Ishi's trained eyes. Nature, Coyote's mistress, was claiming back the loaned Yana lands. At the rushing creek, near his childhood village, Ishi heard beavers at work, building and rebuilding their dam, trying to slow down the flow of water, to slow down the flow of mortal time. In his weeks of searching his past for the lost ones, Ishi saw only his cousins the animals on the living land. Baby deer, rabbits, and foxes played in the late spring meadows of Yuna Creek Canyon.

One morning, Ishi flushed a covey of mountain quail at his feet. The adults burst ahead in a whirring explosion of wings, landing some ten yards in front of Ishi. Immediately, two of the mother quail began their broken-wing dance of deception. When he saw the two wild birds, each dragging its extended wing around in a pantomimed circle, Ishi looked at his feet. A broil of tiny white and gray quail chicks swarmed around his feet in the thick, tall green grass.

> *When the people left this good Yuna Canyon, Elder Uncle asked Coyote to cover the trails of the Yahi with earth so the Saldu could not follow us. Majapa asked that the Saldu's feet tangle in this high brush and grass. Haxa su. This wish is being granted. The trails of my people are almost gone, and this Yuna land is becoming as it was in the beginning when Jupka and Kaltsuna made the world. The Saldu in this canyon will live as uneasy strangers in*

nature's home. Suwa! Wakara Tetna-Ishi prays that the canyon will soon forget that the Saldu were ever here.

The summer came hot and dry over Yuna Canyon, turning the tall green grasses yellow, drying out the manzanita-covered cliffs, scorching verdure and wild onions in the meadows. As the heat moons settled in with a vengeance, Ishi's newfound strength, gained from the renewing time of spring clover and spring salmon, began to fade. He wore only a breechclout that long summer. Ishi's reddish brown skin turned darker copper, then nearly black-brown. The skin of his weathered face felt leathery when he touched it. He could feel his skull, the hollows of his cheekbones, bone-hard below his skin.

He had searched all the old Yahi places by July of 1909. Restless, always moving his tiny camps lest the Saldu discover him, Ishi grew tired of the oppressive heat, of the oppressive fate, around him. He decided, finally, to give up his futile search in the old lands. Ishi hiked, hungry and weak in the sun's heat, up the thick stands of pine above the Three Knolls area. There, in the better shade and safer hiding, Ishi lived as well as he could until the heat moons passed and the harvest moons hung in the sky above Waganupa. Then, before the heavy snows of winter covered the Yana hills in a shroud of white, Ishi gave up his camp at Three Knolls. He crossed over the difficult ridge to Banya Canyon, where thick stands of trees were now aflame in reds and yellows. Ishi, now clothed in his tattered animal robe, took the familiar way down Banya Canyon to his ancestors' burial cave. There, near the bones of the Yahi who had vanished from the Land of the Living, Ishi felt again what it means to be utterly alone. When he crossed over to the other life, Ishi knew it would be as if the Yahi people had never been in the world. He removed the heavy stones at the mouth of Ancestor Cave, stones he had placed there himself, and settled into the dank cave of the dead to wait out the passing of the fall and the coming of the winter.

* * *

The winter of 1909 passed into 1910 as Ishi prayed and slept long hours. His dreams haunted him. He ate what little food he could find outside the cave of his ancestors. When the first signs of spring came and the sun's journey to bring light grew longer, Ishi decided to follow Banya Creek down to Wowunupo. One early spring day, he said a final prayer for his dead mother and boy cousin and all who had gone before. He slowly replaced the stones at the mouth of the Ancestor Cave and set off in his torn robe for his former home.

He walked the disappearing trail down into Banya Canyon and came to the rushing creek. A short way down the trail, the sounds of coursing water and spray all around him, Ishi came to the old alder tree crossing over Banya Creek. He found his old fishing shelter, the place he and his mother had made a temporary home over a year before. The shelter was weather-beaten but untouched by Saldu hands. Ishi made a fire there, then heated stones and poured water from the creek out of his cupped hands onto the hot rocks to make a sweatbath of sorts. When his naked skin broke into its first beads of sweat, Ishi stood up, his head spinning momentarily, and ran to the fast-flowing creek. Ishi dove in, feeling the icy grip of the water close around him, and tried to swim upstream against the current. This new effort left him breathless and shivering. He was barely able to pull himself up out of the water onto the same flat rock where he had been spearing salmon that fateful evening so many moons before when the two Saldu had surprised him. Panting, Ishi lay on the rock in Banya Creek. He remembered being startled before at the aged and weary reflection of his own face on this same pool of water. He dared not look to see his face reflected now. Instead, he lay naked on the cool rock, the spring sun's rays warming him and soothing his aching joints, drying his bristly hair.

For a few weeks, Ishi camped in his old fishing shelter by the sounds of running water. He waited for this new springtime to take full hold of the Banya lands. When the sun came strong and warm every day through the webbed roof of his shelter and he felt stronger, Ishi gathered his few possessions, and tied them with milkweed rope to the deerskin belt he wore around his waist. He rolled up his battered traveling robe and tied it, too, around his waist, using it to secure his fire drill and other tools by covering up the deerskin belt they were tied to.

Ishi walked upstream to the old village of his parents and grandparents, Gahma. He saw at once that this ancient village, a green crescent strip of earth curving out into Banya Creek, was nearly as it was when the Yahi people had first been given this land at the Center of the World. As Ishi walked through the village of his ancestors, he saw that the old tree bough houses had fallen in on themselves. The animals of the Yana wilderness had dug and rooted near the old firepit and where the food shelters had once stood. Here and there, Saldu explorers had littered Gahma village with shattered glass bottles and tin cans. During the weeks Ishi spent camped at Gahma in the spring of 1910, he picked up and cleared away all of the white men's debris, restoring the small curve of rich land to its natural state. It was his way of saying goodbye.

When the summer came hot and dry again to the Center of the World, holding only the promise of more searing heat for several moons to come, Ishi left his camp at Gahma. He gathered his few belongings and walked again under the green and brown canopy of overhanging branches that shaded Banya Creek. He moved downstream along the creek bank until he came to the place which marked the beginning of the end of his own strange life. Ishi turned away from the creek's whispering to climb up the steep Banya Canyon wall toward Wowunupo, where he and his cousin-as-a-sister Tushi had fallen in love, each for the first and only time in their life of endings.

He climbed more slowly than he had as a younger man, stopping for breath at the very spot under the pine tree where he had shot off Apperson's hat. Moving on again, Ishi pulled himself from dry manzanita bush to manzanita bush on all fours. He was winded when he reached the familiar level shelf of rock and earth that had been his loved ones' home for so many years.

In the village of long hiding, nature had changed what once was. Ishi saw bright magenta splashes of poison oak growing all through the clearing and around his old, familiar gray pine lookout tree. The salmon and deer meat drying frames had fallen flat on the ground. The storehouse roof had collapsed in on itself, and the Yahi water storage pool was choked with dry leaves, its borders crumbled by time. Wind, rain, snow, and ice had done this, Ishi knew, for there was no evidence that any Saldu had come here since the forced breakup of his family. Only birds, mice, squirrels, and chipmunks had lived in Wowunupo since that fateful time. Ishi walked to the den where a grizzly bear had once slept, where not so long ago the ending people of a nation had hidden too.

> *Aiku tsub. When a few more moons of heat and harvest and cold have passed, what the people made here will be gone, just as the majapa asked that our marks go into the earth. The dawana mahde Saldu will not know on whose remains they walk. Pano Grizzly Bear will never come again to his den. Suwa!*

Inside the musty den, Ishi saw in the gloom a fragment from a colored basket on the floor. As he bent to pick it up, his heart beat painfully in his chest: the red-dyed piece of basket was one his own mother had made. Wanasi Ishi slipped it inside his carrying belt. There, on the lowest shelf of the cave, crusted with rust, was the metal pocketknife the Saldu had put there; beside the knife was the rotting sack of white man's tobacco. Ishi knocked the two gifts to the floor of his old home, watching the small satchel of tobacco spill its contents onto the dust. Then he went outside again into the heat and brightness.

Tired, hot, and no longer wishing to be among the living, Ishi walked his homeland of retreat aimlessly. His bare feet moved through dust and over hot rocks. He made the short climb, as if by accident, up to his old lookout point. The animals were hiding from the heat. Ishi saw no movement from his higher view, and heard only the low, sad call of a dove somewhere below in the canyon and the subdued rustle of dry summer leaves in the weak breeze.

Then he felt a quick tickle of movement across the top of his foot. A little lizard had streaked over his skin and, in an instant, was on a rock at the crest of the lookout point, sharing the sultry late afternoon with the last of the people. The gray skink pumped itself up and down on its short front legs, puffing out its blue chest, lord of its rock. Hunter Ishi, now the hunted, crept to the tiny creature slowly, then bent down and stroked this symbol of a god he once understood, using his forefinger. The skink lizard grew still.

"Su, you have not abandoned me, little one," Ishi said hoarsely, using his voice for the first time in many days. "You will be in the Center of the World long after I have gone. Aiku tsub."

He felt dizzy, flushed. Ishi lay down in the hot sun near the resting lizard, the two of them high above the muted sound of water moving slowly below in Banya Creek. Looking east, Ishi saw huge summer cumulus clouds surrounding the great volcano, and then he closed his eyes. In the intense heat, his head dizzy, it seemed that the tiny gray lizard, itself unconscious and dreaming, spoke to Ishi in the ancient intuitive language of animal and man.

> *Dambusa hisi, old man child of the gods, I will show you something. Kaltsuna has sent me. You are the last one, and it is right that you should know. Look east, look east with the vision of your Yana mind...*

Hunger seemed to awaken Ishi, painful hunger and a feeling of a gray mist around him charged with an unearthly light. He sat upright, ran the back of his hand across his clammy forehead, and looked out east at the barely visible windblown streamers of fog that danced across Waganupa's stony face. He felt as if he were actually inside an inchoate aurora of dancing lights. Ishi breathed deeply, got to his knees, and stood up. Steam now seemed to pour from the great volcano's crest, or were they bands of clouds sweeping over the high summit? He tried to remember if he had been dreaming, but he remembered no dreams, nothing coherent. Then, in that summer day of 1910, Coyote and his peers, Jupka and Kaltsuna, gave their native son a vision, a vision beyond the eyes of mortal men. Traveler Ishi saw further than he had ever seen.

Strands of vapor shifting endlessly, gyrating in dance, the wind making strange moaning sounds like a thousand doves, almost the same sounds as many people dying, wounded and bleeding, groaning, wailing...I see wild movement and am dizzy, yet there is a sensation of utter stillness. Haxa, over there at Waganupa comes new light, thrown from a distant source—faint violent tones of light gaining, gaining on me, flooding to intense crimson, the blood color of my people, flooding crimson and orange. The colors are coming at me!

Am I dreaming? I am dreaming with the little kaltsuna lizard. It must be so...

Flames, a wall of red fire. I am walking into it.

"Ishi, Tetna-Ishi." A voice in the fire calls my name. I am in the auna storm, a surging curtain of dawana twisting redness, but I feel no heat at all...

I am awake, standing on the lookout point in the Center of the World. Little skink lizard still sleeps on his hot stone, but someone else is close by. Dawana auna, who is with me? I feel someone here, an invisible presence, but where? You are real...Are you of the people?

"Dambusa Tetna-Ishi, I do not understand. How have I come back to my old home in the living world? How have I come back to my dearest one?"

Tushi? You are alive! I have searched all these moons for you, have heard your spirit call on Waganupa, but I have thought you were in the stars!

"I am here. Can't you see me, Ishi? I have chosen you to be mine, just as you have chosen me to be your marimi, though we could not break the laws of the old ways to marry in the Land of the Living. Here in the life beyond, Tetna-Ishi, all things are possible. I have chosen you for

my husband in the night stars above Waganupa, above the world. Will you choose me?"

You will be my dambusa marimi, little one. Even Coyote cannot stop us when we leave the earth. Come out of the red fire so I can hold you Tushi, and we will say prayers together. Some day we will have a child in the stars. Mother has seen it before she walked the star path to join you and Elder Uncle.

"Yes, Wanasi Ishi, she and Uncle are here and your father and grandparents too, but you must be patient now. The moons of six years must pass over your head before we may try to have a daana Yahi in the life beyond. Many things must come to pass before this can be true. You will walk among the Saldu, teach some Saldu to be good creatures, and live in their wowi to teach them the ways of the people. Aizuna Ishi, I tell you it is so. Before you leave the Saldu Village in the Land of the Living, Waganupa will explode again and again, and, when you are with us in the night sky stars, Coyote will make the great volcano at the Center of the World erupt anew. The Yana land will be covered by fire, and then the land and living creatures will be new, as it was long ago when our gods made the world. You cannot see me, Ishi, speaking to you?"

I feel you, little one. I see only red light and fire, but my heart grows glad that you have found me. Aizuna Tushi, I do not wish to live here any more. I do not want to go among our enemies. I wish only to come to you and the people at your firepit. Suwa, I will take my life today!

"No, my loved hunter, there are things you do not know. Your family wishes you to teach the Saldu what our people have learned. We want the white ones to know what they have destroyed, so they will learn that to kill the animals and the land is to kill themselves. Su. The Saldu must learn what you know. Coyote will send you friends among the white ones, and you will ride down the great Daha Valley

on the black creature's back and live by Outer Ocean. Tetna-Ishi, do not think to die now. I love you, and will wait for you in the bright stars. I may stay with you only a little longer now. Two worlds cannot rub for long or one will become the other."

Dambusa Tushi, do not leave me. Tell me of my mother and father, of Elder Uncle and Cousin; tell me of the old ones. How did you and the majapa pass from this world?

"When the Saldu came to us that morning, the majapa took me sliding down the trail to Banya Creek, to the crossing at the alder log. Elder Uncle pushed me up first, and when I slipped into the racing waters and lost the log, he dove to save me, but the waters were too strong. The majapa was too old and weak to pull us from the cold currents, and my robes pulled me down...Haxa, Ishi, I thought most of losing you, but I must go now."

Tell me, marimi Tushi. All these days I have searched! I have never forgotten what came between us at Wowunupo.

"Long after we had drowned, I seemed to have eyes to see and the coursing water was full of light. Our bodies traveled down the creek, and we caught on rocks and logs. Sometimes the fish nibbled on us, and sometimes we washed up on shallow banks until the strong water took Elder Uncle and I again downstream. Our journey was long. When Banya Creek joined the great Daha, I lost the majapa in muddy waters and currents, but we have met again since, and all is well. Our bodies floated in the great river separately for many days, meeting river sturgeon and many other fish, plants, snakes, and frogs of the Daha. Our flesh rotted. When we reached the great saltwater bay at the joining of rivers near Outer Ocean, my body washed up on a salt marsh. My bones began to show through the missing flesh of my arms and legs, but I felt nothing, aizuna Ishi. It was as if I were in a waking dream. Noisy seagulls came to pick at my flesh as I lay rotting for days; each day

the fog covered me and then left in the afternoons and came back at day's end. I saw lights across the bay, my love, shimmering lights like stars fallen to this distant earth, but no man came to me. One day when there was little left of me, a Jupka butterfly came and spoke to me. It said that I would have a visitor who would find Elder Uncle too and help us both to the hildaga path. That very night, a valley quail flew out of the salt marsh grasses to the brackish shore, climbed over my charnel of bones and torn skin, and she did not peck at me. She stayed the night through with me, and when the fog passed in the morning, the quail was gone and my body was gone. I had become a sigaga, flying back above the earth to the Center of the World, and the majapa was flying with me as a quail too."

I heard you calling, Tushi! I heard your two quail spirits call out to me, and I knew you were still halfway in this living world.

"We could see you, Tetna-Ishi, from high above when we came back to the Yahi world. It was us you heard in the canyons and high up on Waganupa's snows. We wanted to say goodbye to you. We wanted to tell you of our journey without taking you with us to the Land of the Dead. Elder Uncle and I flew up the great volcano the starry night you climbed after us. We flew beyond where there was air to breathe and found our places at the end of the star path, where the white-hot fires of all our Yana people light up the night. We live there still, Ishi. I will be waiting for you. I must go back to the life beyond now. It is dangerous for you if I stay any longer among the living."

Dambusa Tushi, little one, why can I not hold you, sing you my songs? Why can't I see you?

"You would die, my loved one. You must be patient."

I see only fire, Tushi, fire without heat. The fire is burning Wowunupo and Tuliyani and all our lands! The homes of our parents and grandparents are burning.

"It is the future, Ishi, the future for our Yana land. Our world will be cleansed by fire. I must go now."

I have saved the pieces of your shell necklace dambusa marimi. I will bring them to you in the night sky, but I do not with to wait the moons of six years... Will you still want me for your husband when I am old?

"We have no age, nor need of bodies, in the next life, aizuna Ishi. I must leave you, good son of Tetna Man. I have no power to remain...Remember your marimi Tushi waiting for you in the stars..."

Tushi, where have you gone? The flames close in around me, lap at my skin and face and sing my hair. Crimson tongues of fire lift me up from the lookout point and fling me through the flaming air, high up above the Center of the World, above the great volcanoes, Waganupa and Shasta, higher up toward the stars and on up into blackness. Absolute blackness, cold...and now I am among the stars! There are brilliant stars everywhere! They are all around me...

Falling. I am falling back to the earth through the red and orange flames. Stones and earth beneath my feet. Demons barking. Yellow eyes. I see yellow eyes around me. Tan fur and white fangs. These coyote and dog creatures wish to kill me: they howl and watch me with huge yellow eyes. I am in a strange Saldu place, Tushi. The demon coyote-dogs want to tear my flesh. I smell the blood of animals here. Shall I let the demons rip me with their fangs, marimi, and come to you now?

What is this? An animal voice is speaking. The tongues of red flame are dying away, and my feet are on a different earth.

"You wished to dream. Did you understand what you saw? It is dangerous to drift into the spirit world unless you are prepared. Su, I shall stay with you a moment longer."

The strange lizard voice stops speaking, waits for me to reply. Are you an animal person such as Grandfather said would sometimes talk to a human?

"For this moment, I speak for Kaltsuna. I am leaving now. The gods have things for me to do, just as you have been shown what you must do. Our fate is larger than ourselves, wanasi Ishi."

The gray skink does not move its mouth when it speaks to me! Tiny legs running...

Wait, little lizard! Before you run, tell me— did dambusa Tushi know the true way of things? Will we find each other again in the stars?

"Her name is different in the stars. There are things we cannot know..."

Chapter 21

Confused, changed almost completely in attitude by his amazing experience, Ishi stood on the overlook, staring to the east, trying hard to focus his blurred vision and slow his heart and breath. In the last of the twilight, everything he saw was gray, the color of the messenger Kaltsuna lizard which had vanished down these rocks without a trace. The distant top of Waganupa seemed suspended in strange and shifting mists, like a floating island caught somewhere in the nether lands between heaven and earth, between the gods and man. The last of the people felt himself shivering, though the hot summer day had turned only a little cooler at its end. Knowing darkness was not far away, he made his way shakily down the unused trail from the point, heading for his old home at Wowunupo. Ishi needed time and a safe place for the powerful fragments of what he had seen in his waking dream to make sense to his mind.

Back in the old bear's den, Ishi sat crouched on the dirt floor, cradling his knees, playing back possible reasons for what he had seen. His grandfather had told him stories long ago of animals who talked to people when the world was freshly made by the gods and men had not forgotten that forest creatures and people were made together. This remembered hope and the intense heat could have tricked him into imagining that the little gray lizard spoke. Tushi had appeared simply because he so deeply wanted her to appear. This was certainly not the first time he had dreamed about her in the long time apart. In the earlier dreams, he and his dambusa marimi always did the things of long ago, played as children, or later looked into each other's deep brown eyes, the eyes of adult forest deer, just as though that fateful day in the fall of 1908 had never come to pass. This dream, though, if it was a dream at all, was different. Ishi knew that he had not seen Tushi, but he had felt her presence and heard her soothing voice, like a river putting out the flames that grew around them.

The skink lizard said her name is different now?

Yes, of course, he knew it must be so. A Yahi woman first takes on a new and private name, never spoken outside her immediate family, when she leaves the lodge of the women to become a woman of her own. Tushi had done this long ago. Ishi, also, had taken on a private name when he had left the family house to enter the watgurwa house of men. But Ishi remembered his grandmother teaching him that a Yahi marimi or wanasi must also choose for themselves a new and sacred name at the time they enter the nighttime Land of the Dead. This last name of many names would live forever among the people in the stars. There, their night fires would burn without end, as they told stories and made up the words for things that are true. Tushi must have taken on another beautiful name. He would learn it soon among the night fires of his people.

But why had she told him of his destined journey to go among the Saldu, their enemies? Why had she told him of the years they had yet to spend apart, and of the great volcano spitting out molten fire again from deep below the Center of the World? Perhaps he was just tormenting himself in a self-induced dawana dream. Perhaps. But in his heart, with a pure legacy of thousands of years of man living with nature, Ishi knew that the vision had been genuine. Tushi had spoken to him, and spoken truly. His intuition told him it was so.

Ishi grew tired of thinking. He lay flat on the dirt floor of the Wowunupo den, naked except for his breechclout and the few small possessions tied to his makeshift belts. Normal dreams, the dreams of a man who has found a new reason for going on in life, took over him then.

He dreamed about Tushi—how he found her half-drowned by raging Banya Creek, lying there coughing up water, shivering uncontrollably. He lifted her lithe body and carried her—himself young again and powerful—to a secret cave mouth. There he built a fire and removed her clothing as she slept, mostly turning his eyes away from her full woman's body. He dried her off, trying not to stare at her loveliness, and then covered her with a blanket. In the light of morning, when she awoke, she looked at him with her huge, fathomless doe-brown eyes, and she knew what had happened and lighted up her round, smooth face with a glowing smile.

In another fleeting dream, coming to Ishi just before dawn, he and Tushi were together in a measureless ocean of space. They swam side by side among the tide pulls of near and farther stars, and neither wore any clothes. Then a piece of Ishi's power vision came back to him, and he was again on the lookout point near Wowunupo, staring east toward the great mountain. The strange mists were vanishing now, dispersed by warm winds. Ishi felt a crescent of light bending around and over the curve of the earth. The familiar horizon began to appear through the haze: closer mountains the whites would call Mt. Harkness, Mt. Hoffman, and Red Cinder Cone. The first bright plumes of the sun's sunrise headdress began to spread over black lava rocks. Ishi slept on. Waking would come hard to him in the old hiding place of his lost loved ones—like a powerful fist striking him in the stomach—but for now he slept the sleep of one who has a reason for all his tomorrows to be better than the long days that had gone before.

* * *

The last Yahi man stayed in Wowunupo for the remaining weeks of the summer of 1910, and he stayed on through the coming of the cooler fall breezes and the turning of colors of leaves. No Saldu came near the decaying village. Ishi had missed the signs of the university expedition from the year before, although subtle signs were there in broken branches, in the dust-covered footprints of Waterman and Hunt, and in the dirt-covered and hidden firepits.

He lived a strangely contented life in this village of so many memories, in this place where he had fallen in love. He made fire without the old apprehension, and he came and went to the creek without taking the old cares. Ishi had lived through torment and losses that would wreck most men, red or white, but now he had found an inner peace, and he was no longer afraid. He knew the unity of all living creatures, the inseparable ties that connect all things together beyond time and space. He knew his own spirit was immortal.

His brief closeness with Tushi's spirit and their shared vision of the past and the future had changed everything in Ishi's heart and mind. His purpose for living had returned. He could no longer lose more than he had already lost. If the nearby Saldu discovered him or tracked him down, so much the better. He could join his beloved Tushi that much sooner. If he somehow escaped discovery or was discovered but allowed to live, that was fine too. The gods had fated him to live nearly six more years before walking the star path, and, in living them, Ishi would be following the proper destiny laid out for him by Kaltsuna. For once, he could not lose, and Ishi came to the peace of those whose lives are free.

Ishi lived this quiet life near Banya Creek through the fall and into the winter that passed 1910 on to 1911. This difficult season came as cold and dangerous as many times before. The Yana wilderness again was covered deep in a shroud of snow, but Ishi lived the better life of one freed from tragedy by a purposeful future.

He began to raid abandoned Saldu cabins again, taking advantage of their owners' winter absence. In this way, he found a huge buffalo cape that had been brought by some white man from the distant plains. The thick cape served him well that winter and kept him warm.

* * *

In the spring of 1911, many white ranch hands, surveyors, and engineers began to return from Redding, Chico, Tehama, and Oroville to the Yana foothills. The grand migration of past decades over the difficult Peter Lassen trail had slowed to a trickle, for there was little gold to be found easily now, and there were easier ways to get to California's northern cities. Sometimes though, an archaic prospector would set off into the woods and hills to find his fortune. Mostly, riches lay in cattle and in companies like Oro Light and Power.

In April of 1911, a surveyor named H. H. Hume went back to work in the Deer Creek area, mapping out future sites for roads that would lead to yet another proposed dam. Hume knew the back-woods well, had some affinity for the natural world, and he looked forward to working in these woods again after spending a long, mostly house-bound winter in the Sacramento Valley.

One day Hume was in especially good spirits. The day was clear and warm, and he whistled while he sighted the markers he himself had set using his optical scope. Earlier that morning, he had been surprised to see a swarm of monarch butterflies resting on a large rock near the coursing creek. Awful early for butterflies to be hatching, he had thought.

Hume worked diligently. Twenty dollars a week was a lot to pay a man, and the company expected reliable data from him. He had not moved his whole family all the way up here from San Francisco just to get canned by the company in his third year in their employ. He sighted carefully through his glass and recorded numbers on a notepad while the warm breeze rustled the new green leaves around him and the fast-moving creek babbled below the ledge he surveyed. A loud stellar's jay protested Hume's thoroughness, hoping he would move on soon and get away from the nest where her chicks were waiting for the pulverized nightcrawler she held in her beak.

Hume paid no attention to the jay's high-pitched taunting; however, when his foot accidentally jostled the leg of the tripod on which his sight was mounted, knocking the glass off line, he saw something that startled him. There, in his accidental vision, appeared to be a satchel hanging high up in a nearby live oak tree. Hume left his tripod and tools behind him and walked toward the tree, searching the branches for what he thought he had seen through the magnifying instrument. There it was, in an upper branch, tied just at the height of a man's reach. Christ, Hume thought, who'd hide a burlap sack in an oak all the way out here?

When he was down out of the live oak, safely on the ground again, Hume saw that the secret bundle in his hands was really several old barley sacks and large fragments of canvas wrapped tightly around a lumpy collection of small goods. He looked over his shoulder, and, seeing nothing but trees and brilliant green chaparral, he untied the treasure satchel, hoping it held gold or something exotic and valuable enough that his family would be taken care of for a long time to come. The alluring cache, for so it was, held a tanned buckskin with the hair still on, a pair of worn out moccasins, some little bundles of pine tree pitch, and clumps of dried pine needles whose sheathed ends all pointed neatly in the same direction. What in the hell are these, Hume pondered. Could they be brushes or combs of some primitive kind? There was also a bar of unused lye soap, a cylinder of sweetened charcoal a few inches long, and a few rusty metal nails and screws tied separately in a rag, and, lastly, a sharp piece of steel with an eyehole at the wider end.

"Sweet Jeezus," Hume muttered under his rapid breath. "Somethin' strange is livin' up here. Somethin' strange..."

* * *

Wanasi Ishi, his eyes not so clouded that he could not see a Saldu invader on his own Wowunupo ledge, watched Hume pack up his strange three-footed tool and take Ishi's cache of prizes, things he had made himself or taken from Saldu cabins and hung safely out of any animal's reach. Ishi crouched high up in his gray pine lookout tree, watching this funny-looking white man pass within a few yards of the bear's den opening, none the wiser. When he heard the larger man's heavy steps fade away under the sound of the clean breeze and the sound of Banya Creek's timeless rippling, Ishi shinned down from his perch in the tall pine.

> *Su. These Saldu have no manners. They take even things they do not understand and have no use for. Su. It is just as well. This too must be for a purpose.*

Later that night, in the old bear's den, Ishi dreamed, his eyelids fluttering, his bare feet moving. He followed the gawky white man with the three-legged companion down the gentle green bends of the canyon to the west toward the wide valley. In his dream, Ishi always kept many yards behind him. They moved far past the dim trail leading from Wowunupo ledge to another broader, plainer trail far down the Banya Canyon. He walked after this Saldu for several hours until the two of them came to the Daha Valley floor and arrived, finally, at a large Saldu village full of many big wooden dwellings. From the outskirts of this Saldu village by one of the Daha's great tributaries, Ishi watched the man disappear into a big white house. He crept in closer, next to a wowi with a large fenced yard, to see better where the Saldu hiker had gone. The awful stench of butchered animals hung in the air. In his dream, Ishi's heart raced. Then, suddenly all around him, howling demon-dogs appeared, their white fangs showing, their lips snarling. Many tan fur shapes circled him and many pairs of fierce yellow eyes locked on him. When he awoke, perspiration was running down his broad forehead into his eyes. He was alone, as usual, in Grizzly Bear's Hiding Place.

He passed four final months at Wowunupo, living through the heat moons as well as he could, following the old and sacred ways of his ancestors. On August 28, 1911, Ishi made perhaps the most significant decision of his life. He started on the long journey of some thirty miles or so that would take him to Oroville and out of the Center of the World. Ishi walked all through that day, following the path of his dream down out of the brown hills toward the Daha Valley where he had seen coyote-dogs threaten him. He walked through the long night, half-consciously putting one foot in front of the other, until he was on flat ground and the dawn came.

Chapter 22

"We heared the dogs a little a'fore noon, Sheriff Webber. A hellatious noise they was makin'. O'Brady and me was workin', but we ain't no idigts so we done quit butcherin' and gone ta see what they's barkin' over. Up by the coral we seen the horses millin' and the dogs actin' moonstruck. He was a wileman and by the look of him almost a gone beaver.

"He was an Injun all right, but like nun we ever seen a'fore. Them eyes was what made him so strange. Fierce and furious glowin' eyes they was. Somethin' wile and frightened. This Injun was buck naked 'cept for a swath of ole canvas on his shoulder when we first seen him, Sheriff. He done stood there outside the corral with the horses goin' mad and them dogs yelpin' to beat the band, his cheek bones showin' strong. O'Brady and me seen them Maidu workin' the claims sometimes, usually way down south in El Dorado, and we seen lots of dead Injuns years back after rancher's raids, but never we seen one like this one. Honest to god, Sheriff Webber, this one was a sight.

"His belly was stickin' a way out, but the rest of him was lean and nut brown 'cause of sunburn, and his black hair looked like it was most burned off. Our wileman looked crazy scared of the dogs, and when we done showed up he slunk back to the corral fence, maybe seein' the cattle blood all over O'Brady and me's aprons, and then he starts up with wile idigt talk like we never heared a'fore, crazy talk like some strange wile creature just out of the forest."

Metal circles bind my wrists. Long guns and hand fires in the Saldu's hands. Shouting in strange tongues. Death fear inside me. Vomit muscles pulse in me but no food. It is better to die, to walk the star path. I am in darkness here but it is full daylight outside. They come in my sealed cave from time to time, the Saldu do, and suddenly there is sunlight in the cave room. A fat one wears metal on his breast, makes grunting sounds, uses his hands in the air in front of me; he stands tall above me, but I do not understand. Then they are gone and the bright light too, and it is darkness. There is sickness in my stomach. Need to get out of this cave like the one where the Yahi people die. Need to vomit. There is fire in my gut. Su, perhaps I am already in the world after! Coyote has sent his dogs to trap me. Jupka and Kaltsuna have abandoned their Tetna-Ishi.

Indian Enigma Is Study for Scientists

by Mary Ashe Miller, *San Francisco Call*, September 6, 1911.

Deciphering a human document, with the key to most of the hieroglyphics lost, is the baffling but absorbingly delightful task which Dr. A. L. Kroeber and T. T. Waterman of the University of California have set for themselves. The document is the Deer Creek Indian captured recently near Oroville, who should by every rule and reckoning be the loneliest man on earth. He is the last of his tribe; when he dies his language becomes dead also; he has feared people, both whites and Indians, to such an extent that he has wandered, alone, like a hunted animal, since the death of his tribal brothers and sisters.

The man is as aboriginal in his mode of life as though he inhabited the heart of an African jungle, all of his methods are those of primitive peoples. Hunting has been his only means of living and that has been done with a bow and arrow of his own manufacture, and with snares. Probably no more interesting individual could be found today than this nameless Indian.

Frightens his Discoverers

He was captured at the slaughter house about three miles out of Oroville, where he was trying to steal some meat. The dogs barked so ferociously one night that the men employed there went out to discover the cause of the trouble. They found the Indian, wearing a single shirt like garment made of a piece of canvas, crouched in a corner, frightened half to death.

His discoverers were as badly frightened as he was and telephoned to the sheriff in Oroville to come and get what they had found. The Indian was taken to town and lodged in the jail and a search for an interpreter began. Hundreds of Indians from all the surrounding country came and every Indian tongue was tried, but to no avail.

Finally Waterman, instructor in the anthropological department at the University of California, went to see him. He had a list of words of the North Yana speech and found that the unknown one recognized some of them with greatest delight. Sam Batwee, one of the oldest of the remaining score of Indians of the North Yana tribe was sent for from Redding. Batwee frightened the Indian more at first than did the white men, but now they have become very friendly.

Lived in Dense Jungle

The unknown is a South Yana, it is said, and Doctor Kroeber said the two languages were related probably as closely as Spanish and Portuguese, so that communication, while possible, is by no means easy.

It has been proved that the Indian is one of four who lived for some years in a patch of thickest brush in the heart of Tehama county. Practically on the great Stanford ranch, within two miles of a ranch house, these Indians lived without being discovered. The wooded bit was between a high cliff and a stream, Deer creek, and was about three miles long by one mile wide.

So dense was this jungle that not even cattle penetrated it, but in it was the Indian's camp. Two years ago a party of surveyors ran a line which passed through the camp and after the manner of surveyors they proceeded to chop their way through the brush primeval.

This frightened the Indians away; they fled to the mountains, and this man, the sole survivor, has probably lived by hunting, creeping up to ranch houses and stealing bits of food, finding deserted camps and foraging there and eating berries and roots. When he was captured he had a few manzanita berries and on those he had lived for some time, he said.

It is difficult to realize that he is absolutely aboriginal, yet seeing must be believing. He is without trace or taint of civilization, but he is learning fast and seems to enjoy the process.

Is Likable Old Indian

If he may be considered as a sample, man has not been invariably improved by the march of time. The Indian is wonderfully quick and intelligent, he has a delightful sense of humor, he is docile, cheerful and amiable, friendly, courageous, self controlled and reserved, and a great many other things that make him a very likable sort of person. Waterman says he has learned to sincerely admire and like the old fellow during their intercourse. Although he is probably about 60 or 65 years old, he doesn't look it by 15 or 20 years. In appearance he is far superior to the average California Indian. He is nearly six feet tall, well muscled, and not thin. His face is rather the pointed type, with a long chin and upper lip a straight nose. His eyes are large, very black, of course, and exceedingly bright and wideawake. His eyelashes are the variety that bring to mind the idea that he bought them by the yard and was rather extravagant about it. His thick hair is jet black and short, he having burned if off after the death of his family. His hands are long and narrow, with very long fingers. The palms show that he has never done manual labor of any kind, as they are as soft as a woman's.

His ears and inner cartilage of his nose are pierced, and this, Sam Batwee explains, is "what he b'lieve." It is "medicine" or religious faith that by this means he is saved from going to "bad place" and will certainly go to "good place" after death. Little knotted strings, apparently sinews of animals, are in the holes, which are of considerable size.

Coming down on the train from Oroville was a great ordeal for the Indian, but he showed his fear only in the tenseness of attitude maintained and by his closely clenched hands.

"Much To See Here"

Crossing the bay was a wonderful experience, and yesterday morning as he stood in front of the Affiliated colleges he asked Batwee as to the direction of where he crossed the big water. Batwee said: "First, yesterday, he frightened very much, now today he think all very funny. He like it, tickle him. He like this place here. Much to see, big water off there" and he waved his hand toward the ocean, "plenty houses, many things to see."

The first time that the unknown refused to obey orders was yesterday. He was to be photographed in a garment of skins, and when the dressing for the aboriginal part began he refused to remove his overalls.

"He say he not see any other people go without them," said Batwee, "and he say he never take them off no more."

Nor would he, so the overalls had to be rolled to the knees and the skins draped over them as best they might be. He was taken to the west end of the museum building and on the edge of the Sutro forest he was posed. The battery of half a dozen cameras focused upon him was a new experience and evidently a somewhat terrifying one. He stood with his head back and a half smile on his face, but his compressed lips and dilated nostrils showed that he was far from happy.

"Tell him, Batwee, white man just play," said Waterman, and the explanation seemed to reassure him.

After the camera men left he squatted in the sand and seemed happier than when in a chair under a roof. He was given a couple of sticks used by some tribe for fire making, taken from the museum, and he was delighted, showing at once that he knew what they were for. After a few seconds of twirling the sticks and making them smoke, he gave up and told Batwee that it was the wrong kind of wood.

Then he did some most delightful pantomime bits. Folding a leaf between his lips he sucked on it so strongly that a wailing sound, closely resembling the bleating of a fawn resulted. This was an illustration of his mode of deer hunting. When he hid himself and bleated the deer were sure to come. He was like a child "showing off" yesterday. Smiling delightedly he showed how, after he had called the deer, he drew back his bow to the farthest limit and let the arrow fly. Then he galloped away with his hands, indicating that the deer had escaped, making tracks in the sand with his two fingers.

He Has No Name

Then he bleated again and showed another deer approaching from the other side. Again he drew his bow, and that time the deer was his. Rabbits he hunted with a queer sound, resembling more the popping of gigantic corks than anything else. Queer tracks were made in the sand and strange gestures—all of which indicated rabbits. Bear he described by growls, more tracks in the sand, and finally by raising his arms high and lowering his head, bringing to mind by his mimicry the terrible "Truce of the Bear." He did not shoot the bear, but ran away and climbed a tree. Salmon fishing he illustrates, too, with prayers and the tossing of roots into the stream.

He talked to Batwee freely, but would tell little that was personal.

His name, if he knows it, he keeps to himself. It is considered bad form among aboriginal tribes, I am told, to ask any one's name, and it is seldom divulged until a firm basis of friendship is established.

The unknown, however, declares he has no name. In reply to Batwee's questions, he shows by a wandering forefinger that he has been all alone. There was no one, he says, to tell him his name and he has none.

He is so desirous of "doing as the Romans do" since he arrived in civilization that it was thought he might be induced to tell his name when he knew that all white men had them. Batwee told him it was customary in the best circles, or words to that effect, and in response he declared his entire willingness to have a name. He had none, he reiterated, but if any one had one to give him he would gladly receive it.

Batwee calls him John, but Doctor Kroeber declared that lacking in individuality.

"We must have a name for him, though," said Waterman. "We can't go on calling him 'Hay, there.'"

For the present his christening will be deferred, in the hope that some name may develop later.

All questions as to his wife he evades. He has a word, "maeela," which was at first mistaken for "mahala," which the Indians use for "wife," but that is not the meaning, Waterman says.

When he is asked anything about his wife, he begins to tell Indian myths or legends; how the coyotes stole the fire; bits of stories of women's work; imitations of a woman cooking mush, with bubbling sounds of boiling. This is perhaps because aboriginal tribes will never speak of the dead.

Waterman said yesterday: "It's as though you asked a man when he got his divorce and he began to tell you the story of 'Cinderella.'"

He will eat anything that is given him without much apparent preference. Sweets, however, he seems fond of, and doughnuts delight him. He knew nothing, of course, of eating with knives or forks, but he was taught in the Oroville jail to eat with a spoon. This habit he has adopted, and when given a peach proceeded to eat it with his spoon.

He has likewise learned to smoke cigarettes, and already his fingers are badly stained. When he was given chewing tobacco he ate it. Batwee remonstrated with him and asked if it did not make him sick. This the unknown denied, and said that it made him strong, did him good. When he was wandering, he used some sort of Indian wild tobacco, but his first taste of plug cut or its equivalent he received from the jailer at Oroville.

He told Batwee that this man, big man, all the same as chief, had given him tobacco and also the blue shirt and overalls which he was wearing.

Charles L. Davis of Washington, D.C., who is an Indian inspector, happened to be in San Francisco, and went out to see the Indian yesterday.

In parting, he presented the unknown with his knife, saying that he wanted him to remember him in case they ever met again. The Indian accepted it and seemed to know it use, opening the blades and finally putting it in his pocket. His newly acquired pockets, by the way, are as keen a delight to him as are those of a small boy, and he has a great collection of odds and ends in them already.

I thought I would give him a present, too, but found I had nothing either amusing or instructive with me save a white bone police whistle. This I blew for him, which seemed to please him greatly; then I gave it to him. He tried to blow it, but was afraid to put it between his lips at first. When he understood the method of manipulating it and found he must blow it hard, he blew a mighty blast. Nothing that he has had since he left the wilds has pleased him more, Waterman said. He would blow it with all his might, and then laugh heartily. Finally he fairly got the giggles, laughing out loud. Doctor Kroeber was away when he first whistled, and when the former returned the Indian became suddenly shy and wouldn't blow. At the noon hour a siren whistle, some place off across the city, sounded. He looked at me and smiled, and I nodded at the whistle in his hand. He laughed again and, with a sly look at Doctor Kroeber, blew with all his might and main.

All of this sounds as though the absolutely primitive state of the man's mind and life might be exaggerated. No one who sees him can doubt the statement of the anthropologists that he is the find of a lifetime on account of his lack of up-to-dateness.

What he can tell will be of the greatest value to them....

Part III:
At the Edge of the World

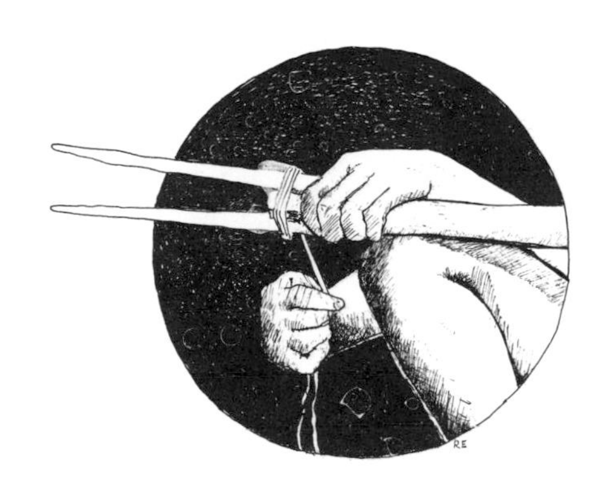

Chapter 23

I am assessing my life, because there is so little left of it, so little time. I want to tell you something. It's the most astonishing thing that ever happened to me. It's about a man I met and loved for five years. A man whose eyes held mysteries. Whose hands looked as though they were about to hand you all the gifts of human history.

My name is Saxton Pope, Jr., and I am an old man now, but when I met Ishi, I was a boy of only nine. He came to the Bay Area in 1911, and my father, for whom I am named, was Ishi's doctor at the University of California Medical Center. He worked with Professors Kroeber, Waterman, and Sapir, who studied Ishi and became his friends. I was the wide-eyed boy among the academics and the wild man, watching it all for five years. Now that I am nearing my own end and looking back on it all, I can honestly say that Ishi was my greatest teacher. More than that: he was the best friend a boy could have. Indeed, I can say he was the best friend I ever had. He gave me my true name, then helped me find my own identity. I'm eighty-seven now, but I was so young and alive then, in the time of Ishi.

Ishi came to us on a train from Oroville, where my father's friend Professor Waterman had rushed to liberate him. The sheriff there had brought in all kinds of interpreters who tried all sorts of Spanish and Indian dialects and even arranged for William Conway, a Bidwell Indian, to come to the Oroville jail to try to speak with Ishi, but it was clear from Ishi's blank expression that he understood none of the words tried on him. It was Thomas Waterman who began to crack the Yahi code, as soon as he arrived at the jail. I remember Ishi telling me that this powerful headman tried many strange words until he found a place to start. "Siwini! Haxa, yes," Ishi had said, "siwini pine wood," and for two days, off and on, they struggled to speak the tongue until the words flew from Ishi's mouth and the new Saldu majapa struggled to keep up.

When the two came to the museum in San Francisco to meet Alfred Kroeber, the head of the university's anthropological department, it was agreed that Ishi would live in his own room in the museum and help with keeping the exhibits and the building clean, while his new majapa, Waterman, and the other headman, Kroeber, would continue to learn Ishi's ways. After the first few days in his new watgurwa, Professor Kroeber asked my father to examine Ishi, and it was then that we met for the first time. This was the day I got my name.

My father and I came to the museum—I remember that I was proud to be trusted to carry his black doctor's bag—and found Ishi and Mr. Waterman in the bow exhibit room among the many Navajo, Algonquin, Comanche, and other rare bows. They were going over Yahi words, Professor Waterman's pen and paper at the ready, and I remember that Ishi looked up the instant my Dad and I walked in. His liquid-brown eyes searched our faces, as if looking for some clue to our souls. He was lean still, bedraggled almost, but something about his face suggested an immutable grace and kindness. I saw his broad forehead wrinkle a little as he studied us, and, when his deep, steady gaze locked lower on me, I saw his jet-black eyebrows shoot up in greeting. Ishi's face was so thin then, his cheeks so hollow, that his large aquiline nose seemed almost too big for his face, and, with his hair still burned short in mourning, he looked almost comical. But I was a little boy, and in spite of those warm brown eyes searching my face as if it were some topographic relief map, I was afraid.

Then Ishi smiled and looked back at my father. "Su, a good wanasi," he said in his new mix of Yahi and a few words of English. Those deer's eyes looked from my father's face to the big doctor's bag I was carrying. "He will be a wanasi hunter, or a kuwi?" he asked.

My father stepped forward, offering his hand, and Ishi's eyebrows went up again in recognition of this strange Saldu custom. Brown hand clasped white, and then my father smiled. "Who knows what this young man will be," my father said. "My son is a dreamer."

Thomas Waterman translated my father's words for Ishi, and, when he understood, Ishi turned his deep gaze back on me. "Aiku tsub to dream. Which is the path you wish to walk?"

When Mr. Waterman had translated again, I felt the eyes and heavy expectation of all three grown men upon me. I was all of nine. "I want to be a hunter before I am a doctor!" I said to Ishi with a little sideways glance to check my father's reaction. "Can you teach me to make a bow?"

"Haxa, yes, haxa!" Ishi spoke in his high, clear voice. "Together you and I will be Yahi wanasi, but we will hunt in the hills by the great ocean at the Edge of the World. You will be Maliwal—Wolf Boy—and we will be hunters for this museum watgurwa."

Before my father's friend had changed all of Ishi's words from language to language, from world to world, I knew what Ishi had said. Maliwal, I thought over and over to myself. I am Wolf Boy, son of wolves.

"Well, young Mister Wolf, would you like to stay with us while your father examines our friend?" Professor Waterman asked me.

I was busy trying my new name quietly again and again, wanting to hear it roll off other people's tongues. "I want to stay," I said, "but how did Mr. Ishi get his name?" I asked, still afraid to talk directly with this wild spirit from the Mt. Lassen forests.

"His name is our doing, I'm afraid," Professor Waterman explained to me. My father was gently opening his instrument bag and motioning for Ishi to remove his borrowed cotton shirt. "Indian names are private and are reserved for family and special friends like you two. Ishi wouldn't tell anybody his true name and the newspaper reporters kept pressing us and we couldn't call him, "hey you," so Professor Kroeber and I picked out the name "Ishi" for him, and he doesn't seem to mind. What do you think of it, Wolf Boy?"

My Dad had his stethoscope out and was ready to listen to Ishi's heart. I truly saw Professor Waterman for the first time, saw him as a man of great caring. Behind his mustache and his title, he was O.K.

"What does his name mean?" I asked him.

"It's Yahi. It means 'I am of the people.'"

"It is a good name for a wolf's hunting partner," I said proudly.

Mr. Waterman turned to Ishi. "This good kuwi wishes to be sure Ishi has no pains or sickness. Is this all right?"

Ishi nodded his assent in the universal language of gesture.

I remember that my father examined Ishi with the utmost care, using all the bedside manner that years of coping with all types of patients, some willing and some not, had taught him. It was as if my father was aware that Ishi was the patient of a lifetime, one so special and rare that Dad could never hope to find another in his career. Ishi no doubt was comparing my father's modern medical skills with those of a Yahi healer or shaman. Even at nine, I knew from the little Dad had told me that Ishi's people had suffered a gaping wound that no doctor, no matter how skilled, could heal.

Ishi sat passively, bare-chested and gaunt, while my father felt his pulse, listened to the beating of his heart, then heard his breath go in and out. My friend, the wanasi, stared at Dad's stethoscope as if it were a magical instrument. My father felt Ishi's glands, and, with a smile of reassurance, tested the reflex points in Ishi's knees and elbows.

As my father worked, it seemed that all of Ishi's uncertainty disappeared. I remember that the tightness in his face faded into gentler contours of forehead, of protruding cheekbones, and of a resolute but more trusting angle of jaw. It was as if Dad were earning more of Ishi's trust with each new examination, as if he were passing a test of ancient medical standards, proving himself wise in the ways of Yahi doctoring, a full-fledged kuwi.

When this check-up of two ages was finished, each one having judged the other as worthy, my father put down his stethoscope and closed his black instrument bag. He turned to Ishi, smiling: "This fine wanasi has no pains or aches or demons in him, but he could use a little fattening up."

With the help of Professor Waterman, my father continued speaking: "How does a Yahi kuwi stop the fever work of an evil mechi-kuwi or the bite of a snake?"

I remember that Ishi explained as best he could, with Waterman's help in translation, and I remember something else that happened then, something unique. I remember it even now that I am an old man as a special moment. Ishi asked my father if Saldu doctors had the magic to extract pains from the body and whether they had the power to make demon doctors flee. From years of watching my Dad work with children, trying to gain their trust, I had a young boy's suspicion about what my father would do.

"This kuwi has a little magic," he said, "that even a brave wanasi can see."

He opened his black bag, taking out a green glass bottle. My father, doctor, parent, hero, popped the cork out of the mysterious bottle and shook out a tiny capsule of some powerful medicine. He tucked it gently in Ishi's left ear, and, a second later, he pulled it out from under Ishi's right armpit.

Ishi's eyes opened wider in astonishment. His jaw hung open. Then my father laid the tiny capsule in the palm of his own hand. In a flash he closed his fist tightly and turned his hand over. He opened his palm again, but no medicine fell out. It was gone. Instead, my father motioned for Ishi to reach into the pocket of his cotton shirt. No translation was needed: Ishi reached deep into his pocket, and there was the medicine capsule!

Ishi's reddish brown face turned a shade redder in astonishment. Then he said: "Su! I can see that you have very good control over your medicine. You are a great kuwi majapa."

Chapter 24

Ishi made many friends that first year at the museum, but none better than Thomas Talbot Waterman, the first white man to talk with him, however basically, in Yahi Yana. Professor Waterman planned and shared Ishi's first train trip, and gave him his first view of San Francisco, the city on the huge bay at the Edge of the World. It was Waterman who introduced Ishi to his new home in the museum and first brought him to his own home, where Ishi was a frequent dinner guest, always appreciated by Professor Waterman's wife and children. Even though he was some twenty or more years younger than Ishi and much younger than my own father, Waterman was always "Majapa Watamany" to Ishi, the headman who had brought him into another world.

I remember in those first days, before Ishi and I became best friends, that Ishi christened Professor Kroeber as "Big Chiep" (the Yana language has no "f" sound). Even then, Ishi surmised that Watamany had his own boss, one who said yes or no to requests and who ran the museum watgurwa. Alfred Kroeber, some nine years senior to Waterman, was at least twelve years younger than Ishi. Nonetheless, it was clear to me, even as a boy, that Professor Kroeber held Ishi's acquiescence and respect. It was not that he ran the teaching and research programs in anthropology, for Ishi could hardly have fully understood that role. But Ishi knew that Kroeber set the limits on how far his new friends might take him from Parnassus Heights, and gave guidelines that Poyser, Warburton, Loud, and all the museum men had to follow. This powerful white man was not so much to be feared as respected. He clearly knew more than anyone else of the Yahi tongue and the Yahi ways, and he wanted to know more. Besides, while Majapa Watamany wore a mustache, Big Chiep wore a beard as well. Because all facial hair was taboo for Ishi, the older man's magic had to be very strong to survive with a mustache and a heavy beard. So it was.

My father, Dr. Saxton Pope, came to know Ishi in his role as Ishi's doctor, of course, but soon thereafter as his friend. Dad, or

"Popey" as Ishi called him, was the glue that cemented Ishi's and my friendship. Ishi had the run of "Popey's house"—the university hospital next to the museum. We wandered the wards together, visiting patients, sometimes watching my father work, but it was my father's passion for archery that really brought those two together. One day, my father looked out of his office window to see Ishi on the lawn below, fashioning a handmade bow. Still in his doctor's whites, he took me down to Ishi, where we could observe more closely. My father got Ishi to show him his shooting stance, his hold of the bow, and his method of release. I remember that Dad did no more work that afternoon. The three of us ended up on the open green grass at the edge of Sutro Forest, copying Ishi's straight vectors of arrow flight with feebler, wobblier flights of our own, until the sun bled down to purple twilight over the open ocean to the west.

From that day on, Ishi became our teacher. In that magical first year, he taught me not only how to shoot the bow but also how to make fire using a fire drill, and how to taste tobacco. My most important lesson, though, at the beginning of my apprenticeship as Wolf Boy, was the story that Ishi told me about where the world came from. One day, not long after Ishi had come to his new home at the museum, we sat together in his room talking.

Around us were Ishi's few, cherished possessions. A Yahi bow made of juniper wood that Professor Kroeber had given to Ishi from the exhibit room now sat on the table by his simple bed, and on his table in the corner lay five thin, straight arrows that Ishi had fashioned from hazel wood. Our conversation, still filled with gestures but much more understandable than in the first few weeks, came to a silence.

Ishi's face seemed troubled, his eyes dull, as if his mind had drifted far away. After a time, I felt uncomfortable.

"Hunter Ishi," I said, breaking the stillness in the room, "where did your people come from?"

I felt those deep brown eyes on me.

"From the land around the great mountain, Waganupa," Ishi responded quietly.

"Yes, but where did the first Yahi come from?" I asked. "Who made the people?"

I wanted to know more and more, in the way that children do, and I remember now, all these years later, what Ishi told me next. His eyes seemed to brighten, and he sat up straighter at the edge of his perfectly made bed.

"Back in the days before people, the great god Jupka, the butterfly, and the great god Kaltsuna, lizard one, were fishing in vast Outer Ocean. The two fished aimlessly for many days until one day Jupka threw out their longest line and watched it sink deeper and deeper into the dark waters until it could be seen no more."

Ishi stopped speaking for a moment. I heard his quiet breathing as I sat next to his bed.

"Then the great fishline caught fast on something very heavy, and the two gods, Jupka and Kaltsuna, labored mightily to bring it up from the darkness. Butterfly and Lizard tugged and pulled and tugged some more until they fished up the uncreated, blank world from the ocean bottom. They pulled so hard that Outer Ocean's floor now floated on top of the great dark waters, vast and flat and bare. There was no life on this new world yet, for these were the Old Times. The great gods looked out over the huge, flat world they had caught. Kaltsuna said: 'My friend, we have been foolish all this time.' Jupka asked: 'What is it we have done to foolishly squander our lives?' And Kaltsuna answered: 'We have been standing on the back of a whale while fishing for minnows.'"

Ishi looked directly at me. "Do you know what Jupka replied then?" he asked.

He could tell that I had no idea. I looked away from his intense eyes, and I watched sunlight from Ishi's window light up his bare white walls like an illuminated but empty artist's canvas.

"Jupka said: 'Let us throw back these other minnow worlds we have caught. We have fished up a better world. Aiku tsub.'"

I felt that I was no longer sitting next to Ishi's bed in his room at the museum. I was fishing in the great ocean too. I saw the wide, uncreated world floating before my eyes as Ishi's quiet voice became the voices of the gods.

"It was Jupka who dreamed of our race. 'I shall make some people,' he said, 'the First People. I will call them Yahi.'

"'Su! That is fine,' Kaltsuna answered. 'But how can these Yahi People live in a world without animals or creeks or trees or bushes?'

"'Suwa,' said Jupka, 'hmm. We shall cover this new world we have fished up with everything our People shall ever need.'"

I looked up at the bright electric bulb glowing at the center of the ceiling of Ishi's little room, but I did not blink my eyes. Bathed in the yellow light, I saw that Ishi was still staring intently at me from the bedside. His manner had changed: his hands were still folded across his lap, but he leaned forward at the edge of the bed now, leaning toward me. Ishi seemed more animated, as if recalling a time beyond his own, an earlier, beginning time that his grandfather had taught him of long ago, when Ishi was a boy in the watgurwa house of men. Something was definitely different.

When I looked away from the burning lightbulb, dark spots and strange amoeba-like shapes floated in my vision. I found myself returning to Ishi's wide-eyed stare as my sight began to clear. There was his kind, round face, his black eyebrows raised in expectation, and his dark hair growing back strongly in bristly tufts above his broad forehead. But I remember his liquid brown eyes most of all. Ishi's eyes danced with an inner light, merging with my own vision as he went on telling the story.

Su! This maliwal Saldu boy is as Tetna-Ishi once was long ago on Yuna Creek. Young wolf is as I was at the knees of my father, Tetna Man, but even a powerful Saldu kuwi like Maliwal's own father cannot teach him of the Way. This boy, like may other new friends, is a dambusa Saldu. I will teach him of the ways so he can preserve them when I am gone. Aiku tsub. Tetna Man left me when I was a boy, but Grandfather and Elder Uncle were there to continue the wanasi teaching. Haxa, so shall I be as a grandfather to young wolf. Aizuna Grandfather uses me even now to tell him the story of how the People came to be...I hear Grandfather's voice echoing in the Tuliyani watgurwa; I can almost see his face in the light from the smokehole as he speaks...

"The great mountain, Waganupa, burst up at the center of the uncreated, flat world, grew higher and higher still toward the World of Sky, so high that snows and great sheets of ice covered its top. Jupka and Kaltsuna blew their hot breath at Waganupa's snowy top, and some of the snows melted and flowed down the steep mountain in swift streams and waterfalls, taking boulders and rocks along with them, cutting the once flat land into many canyons and ridges, making many caves and hollows."

Haxa, that is what I was taught of how the land took shape.

"Kaltsuna and Jupka then made the first seeds, and Jupka dropped them from the air while the lizard god scurried over Waganupa spreading seeds with his tail and splayed feet. Tiny seedlings grew into tall trees and became siwini forests on the mountain; acorns that the butterfly god dropped became spreading oak trees; manzanita, the little apple bush, and chaparral covered the hills, while madrone trees, buckeyes, and alders took root on the canyon walls in the newly created world. Grass and clover bloomed all over the canyon floors and in the new meadows and on the ridges on the day the great gods made the world."

Suwa. This is Grandfather's lesson I learned as Tehna-Ishi, the bearcub boy.

"Even with this new green world to play with, the great ones were still lonely and fished in Outer Ocean beyond the world for something to give their lives more meaning. They created the First-Comers, other lesser gods and heroes, to keep them company. For a long time the great ones were happy living among the other gods on their new land, but after a while Jupka and Kaltsuna grew tired of the world as it was, grew restless. Lizard said: 'It is time for the world to change. The time of the other heroes and gods, the First-Comers, playing in the world, has ended. It is time for them to work. We must have living creatures moving upon our earth, under our water, and in our air.'"

This is what Grandfather has told me of the first times and the time after, the time of the Yahi. Suwa. Grandfather, your voice goes on.

"Some of the heroes, when they learned that a new time of mortal life was to come upon the world, did not want to help do the life-creating work, and so they went under the ground to hide. Two heroes, Ahalamila and Jikula, who were the first gods to ever fight over a woman and who sometimes squabble still, were banished to live deep inside Waganupa. There, they ignite the fires within the volcano to this very day. But most of the other gods and heroes were willing to do their work. They obeyed the great ones, the creators Jupka and Kaltsuna. These lesser gods turned themselves into First-animals, First-birds, and First-fish of the world. These are the ancestors of our deer and bear and smaller animals of the meadows and brush; they became the fathers and mothers of our ducks and wami geese which fly between the green earth and the blue sky world; they transformed themselves into our salmon and trout, which swim today in Yuna and Banya creeks.

"After the lesser gods had changed themselves into creatures of brushland, air, and water, each according to his wishes, Jupka and Kaltsuna climbed to the white top of Waganupa and looked down over the world they had fished up from Outer Ocean and given form. 'The world is finished,' Jupka said. Then Kaltsuna reminded him: 'It is time for you to make the People who will live in this good world.'"

I looked away from Ishi's face as he fell silent. With a boy's curiosity, I was impatient to hear the rest of the story, but Ishi's eyes were distant and not focused. His mind seemed very far away, as if working back over an old path that was for me unfathomable and impossible to follow. His hands were still folded peacefully on his lap; we sat so close together by his bed that I heard every breath he took. The ceiling light seemed to burn brighter now that the sun had dropped lower toward the horizon. I didn't fully understand what had been happening to me. I knew only that I had been Wolf Boy for many moments, as if Ishi and I were of one heart and mind, and now, suddenly, I was just Saxton Pope, Jr. again, waiting for Professor Kroeber and my father to come pick me up.

I looked at the ceiling light again, staring until salty tears trickled down my cheeks, and then the voice in my mind started anew. I looked at Ishi. A faint trace of a smile played on his lips, and I saw that his eyes were attentive and clear again, focused on my face.

Maliwal has a mind like a wakara moon shining bright over the land. His father, the kuwi, is right. This young Saldu wanasi dreams of the hildaga stars. Even now he asks to know more of the Way. Tell me more, his eyes say, tell me how the People began.

Suwa! I shall tell him more. With my grandfather's help, I shall tell him nize ah Yahi...

"Jupka had almost forgotten his promise to create the Yahi, so pleased was he with the new world as it had been

brought to life, but he knew that Kaltsuna was right. He had to create the chosen creatures, the People.

"The great god Jupka spread his orange wings and flew down to the green forest at the foot of Waganupa, where he cut down a buckeye tree and made many long, straight sticks from it. Jupka laid one stick on the ground pointing perfectly west and east, and then he lit his lava stone pipe. Jupka blew gray smoke over the buckeye stick and said: 'You will be the first Yahi. You are now hisi, man, the beginning of my People!'

"And the first red man stood up and said to Jupka: 'Nize ah Yahi, I am of the People.'

"The butterfly god then put a smaller buckeye stick on the ground, pointing perfectly north and south this time, and again he blew his thick pipesmoke over the stick of wood. This time he said: 'You are the second Yahi. You are dambusa marimi, woman, the first woman of my people!'

"This new woman arose too, and said: 'Nize ah Yahi' and stood with the first man.

"The great one broke one buckeye stick into two and put the two shorter sticks on the ground in the form of a cross, one running west to east and the other, across it, pointing north to south. Again he blew the creation smoke over them and spoke his commands. 'You are baby boy! You are baby girl! For every moon cycle, from this creation day forward, all Yahi children will have a father and a mother. In this way the siwini forests will always be full of children.'

"The two babies cried themselves awake on the forest pine-needle carpet, and the first mother and first father gathered them into their strong arms and said together: 'Aizuna daana Yahi, our own babies of the People.'

"Jupka cut many, many more sticks from the fallen buckeye tree as the sun moved through the sky. He did not look up from his work until the sun was hanging yellow and orange in the west. By then, Yahi people were in the steep canyons and in the green meadows and on the green hills and along the rushing streams of the new world."

Hexai-sa! How can I tell Wolf Boy that Jupka's promise is broken? There are no longer children in the Yana forests. Mechi-kuwi have allowed no daana Yahi in our land for years. Tushi, Boy Cousin, and I were the last daana hisi. I am the last of the People, the ending one. Perhaps Maliwal's father has told him that this is so. Jupka, Jupka, your promise is ended! How can you let the dambusa way of the Yahi disappear forever? But this young wolf wishes to know more of the old way. I see it in his eyes, those eyes dreaming of the hildaga path where Tushi and the old ones wait for me...

"Kaltsuna saw that these first people did not know what to do in the new land, so he decided to help his friend Jupka with the Yahi. Kaltsuna, the wise lizard, taught the People to make bows and harpoons from Waganupa's trees, to flake away arrowheads from Waganupa's black stones, and to build warm wowi of pine, bay, madrone, and hickory. For arrows, Kaltsuna told them to use hazel wood (humbola), buckeye (bahsi), or wild currant (wahsui), and to always make five arrows at a time, painting them with natural dyes: red from earth, green from wild onion lily (taka), and black from the eye of a salmon. From him the chosen people learned to fish and hunt, to create fire from a drill and to cook. Many times, Kaltsuna gathered the people of the forest together and said: 'Do these many important things just as I show you, and teach those Yahi children who come after you to do the same. In this way, you will have no need of gods to live one part of your lives, the part of survival in this real world, but you will still need us when you are troubled by this world and when you live

in the world after. Haxa. It is better to teach a man to fish than to catch his fish for him.'

"Jupka joined in again and taught the Yahi the signs of the moons and seasons and which dances, songs, and prayers belonged with each different moon. He taught them of the differences between women and men, and of the rules of the watgurwa and the family house. From Jupka the People learned about death and the Land of the Dead.

"Jupka, too, talked much with the first people. He said over and over: 'Listen to all I teach you now, and remember. Each of you in your turn will teach these sacred things to your children and your grandchildren. If you do this, then in the times to come the People will always live in warm houses; your baskets will stay full of salmon and deer meat; you will have peace in your village and inside the watgurwa, and with all your Yana neighbors up and down my streams, and you will be at peace with all of my creatures of the air, water, and brush too, for without them you cannot live in this world. The wild goose (wami) will feed you when he is flightless, and my squirrels (dadichu) will bark to warn you if a wildcat or fox is near. All of my creatures can act human parts at times, but you must listen and watch for them. The People must not forget their gods or our teachings or let any other people destroy the ways of our world. If this happens, I will cause the gods Ahalamila and Jikula to have a great fight within Waganupa, and the great mountain will spew out fire and destruction over all the Center of the World. But if my People keep to the Way in the moons to come, the world will be good, as it is now. Suwa! I say it is so.'"

Wolf Boy, the world is changing. The Way is dying even while we sit in this room near the Edge of the World. These are dawana times. Things may be left up to you, Maliwal, and to Watamany and Big Chiep and Popey. It is for you to say what you will of the Way and of the dambusa Yahi who once lived in and loved this good world. Grandfather's voice is weaker, but I still hear...

"Now Jupka and Kaltsuna's work was finished. The time had come for them, also, to transform themselves, to leave the Center of the World for the Yahi people to steward into the living future.

"Kaltsuna flicked his long red tongue in and out and said: 'I, Kaltsuna, Maker of Bows and Arrows, am now a tiny rock lizard. I will crawl among you as a reminder of where you came from. My skin shall always remind you of arrow point flint: gray flint on top, yellow, blue, and white flint on my underbelly. Remember that my little hands, the hands of a hisi man, once made bows and arrows. When I bob up and down on a sunny rock, I am reminding you it is your turn to work as I have. At night I may weave yellow tendrils of dodder vine to help you snare my deer, but you must work too. You must be makers of things. I will bask in the warm sun where the People do, and you must sometimes stroke me with a blade of sweetgrass to show that you remember who I am.'

"'Suwa! Thus it is,' Kaltsuna said, and then he was a gray skink lizard.

"Then Jupka spoke directly to the People for the last time. 'I, Jupka, am now a monarch butterfly of orange and black fringe and many other colors. Yahi women must weave the design of my wings into your finest baskets always. When I fly over Yuna and Banya creeks and over the meadows in the time of green clover each new year, you will remember who I am and where you came from, and the People will know that all is good in this world and that my way is a dambusa way.'

"'Suwa! I have spoken my last words,' Jupka said. Then his new wings opened and closed rhythmically, rehearsing

perfect flight, until he launched himself into the soft breeze and floated away in a slow blur of orange color over the green meadows."

Ishi's room in the university museum at Parnassus Heights in the city by the great bay at the Edge of the World was dark now, save for his burning overhead light. The walls that had been a painter's canvas were awash in a surreal glow of artificial light. The canvas that Ishi had painted with English and Yahi words was gone now, but I still saw its images in my head. We had been sitting together, side by side, for hours. Ishi sat on his narrow bed and plain wool blanket. I sat on his simple, straight-backed pine wood chair.

"So Maliwal, this is how our world came to be," Ishi said.

He stretched out his legs, looking oddly out of place in his white man's trousers and shirt, and stood up from the bed. Ishi was only five foot eight. I know, for my father took every measurement of him and looked after him with the care of a parent, but he towered over me like some god as I sat transfixed in his bedside chair. I know he was my hero then, to a boy of nine, and he still is to an old man of eighty-seven who still has the heart of that nine-year-old boy.

"Wanasi Maliwal," Ishi asked me, his black hair aglow with the electric light from the ceiling, "have you sometimes seen an orange butterfly in the city park where you and your father and I go to shoot the bow?"

I thought for a second. "I have seen many butterflies."

"Haxa, wanasi, but you have really seen just one."

I did not understand what Ishi meant.

"Have you ever seen a little lizard on a rock in the sunshine?"

"I have seen lizards many times," I answered.

"You have seen the one lizard Kaltsuna," he said. "Jupka and Kaltsuna are the good in this world, but sometimes their friend mechi-kuwi Coyote brings bad tricks with his good. Suwa! It is the way."

I nodded below my teacher's gaze. Ishi's shadowy outline above me was a silhouette ringed in yellow light. I felt his open hand touch the top of my head, his warm palm on my forehead and hair.

"If you hear many coyotes howling in the night, remember Maliwal, it is really just one."

Ever since, I have understood.

Chapter 25

As time passed, Ishi and I became closer and closer. Surely, he was my teacher, as his uncle, the majapa, had once been for him, but he was even more like the older brother I had never had. We went almost everywhere together. I got to see Ishi, this incredible man from the stone age, adapt to a new world of trolley cars, automobiles, electricity, and plumbing, and, most of all, to thousands upon thousands of Saldu crowded together in brick houses and on the sidewalks and streets of San Francisco. The crowds amazed him, for at most he had been used to seeing only a few people, his own little band at Tuliyani and Wowunupo, gathered together at one time. Sometimes, though, this new world at the edge of the earth seemed to be adapting to Ishi. I know my father, Professor Waterman's family, Professor Kroeber's family, and I were. We were learning as much of the Yahi way as Ishi was of our ways. That may have been one of the greatest differences between us. Ishi had one Way, taught to him by his grandfather and uncle when he was a boy. His belief was immutable and unshaken even when he found himself in a completely alien civilization. We, on the other hand, were far less sure of where the world came from and how to proceed sensibly in it, even less sure of what would happen to us when it became our time to die.

While the crowds of San Francisco awed Ishi whenever he ventured outside the University Museum or the Medical Center next door, he was not particularly impressed by tall buildings. These brick and mortar monsters, he informed us, were no bigger than the crags and cliffs near Wowunupo. The train he had come to the city on was the one he had seen and heard many times before. But to actually ride on the black demon that ran on rails was so far beyond his reckoning that Ishi concluded his friend Watamany's magic was the only thing that had allowed him to survive this encounter with the devil-driven beast.

When Professor Waterman, my father, and I took Ishi on his first trolley ride, he loved it. It, like the first automobile he rode in, was driven by some supernatural power, moved by one of Coyote's many tricks. But the trolley car was by far the most impressive to Ishi. It had a bell which sounded loudly, and a magic hiss like a snake's that blew the dust all around when the air-brakes were released. When he was not with us riding on one, Ishi would watch street cars by the hour from his upstairs window at the museum.

I remember that he never lost his fascination at turning electric lights off and on again. Once my father tried to show us how to type on the typewriter in his office. Ishi would not touch the machine, but he stood over my shoulder as I tried to type "thequickbrownfoxjumpedoverthelazydog" over and over again. He was childlike in his fascination, but I saw very clearly, even then, that Ishi was not a child, for he was completely at home within his realm and surely more at home in ours than we in his. Still, he found delight in things we take for granted: doorknobs were a great Saldu invention; safety pins were magic; and water faucets were miraculous—an instant running stream inside a wowi!

Miracles that were beyond understanding Ishi conceived as mechi-kuwi's work, or Coyote's tricks, or the workings of some Saldu god. Before 1911 was over, Professor Kroeber, Professor Waterman, and I took Ishi to Golden Gate Park to see the start of Harry Fowler's famous solo airplane trip across the continent. When the plane was ready and its engine started, Ishi was startled by its roar. After Fowler's fragile biplane launched itself into the air, it made a long circle, and then passed directly over our heads. Professor Kroeber pointed out the plane, high in the air. Ishi had been looking at the ground. When he looked a thousand feet skyward, he seemed only slightly interested. "Saldu?" he asked, nodding at the black speck against the sky. "Saldu man climbs up there?" When Kroeber said yes, Ishi laughed nervously. His eyes again searched the ground, where I noticed a little gray lizard making its way through the green grass near our feet.

Later on, Professor Kroeber tried to explain to my father that either Ishi had come to expect anything from the white man by this time, or else Ishi's amazement at seeing a man fly was too deep for him to show any outward expression. Like most people of nature, they reasoned, Ishi had tried to preserve his dignity in the face of the unfamiliar and overwhelming by refusing to express his shock. I knew differently. But I was a boy among learned men, so I never told them what I knew. You are better off letting some people believe what they want to believe.

I will never forget Ishi's first encounter with a window shade, though. It jarred him completely out of his equanimity and normal polite reserve. It was a day not long after my Dad had first taken me to the museum-watgurwa to help examine Ishi. Father and I arrived early that morning, just after sunrise. In those early days, Professor Waterman acquired the habit of coming to the museum early each morning to greet Ishi, to provide him with some continuity in his transition from one culture to another. We arrived at Ishi's door, only to find Waterman already standing in the hallway outside it with a big grin on his face. Putting one raised finger to his mouth, he motioned for us to stay silent, and then he pointed for us to look past the half open door. Inside, Ishi stood already dressed in his cuffed pants and borrowed blue suit coat, and a strangely tied bright red tie. I could just see Ishi standing by his one window, trying to raise the shade to let the new sunlight in. He tried to push the simple shade to one side, but it would not go. He pushed it up, revealing for a moment the pink morning light spreading across the city, but as soon as Ishi let the shade go, it fell shut again. We stood in the hallway, unobserved, smiling silently, sharing the odd realization that never in Ishi's experience had he grappled with the common roller shade.

We crept into the room, all three of us still smiling. Ishi turned around, his eyebrows going up as his perplexed expression changed over instantly to one of greeting. My father went to the shade and showed Ishi how to give it that practiced little jerk to make it run up. When we left his room about five minutes later, Ishi was standing at the window reflecting on what had happened, still trying to figure out where the shade had gone.

* * *

There were many memorable incidents for us that first magical year, some funny, some portents of things to come. But I didn't know what to feel the first time Ishi's culture and mine collided. To this day, I'm not sure what to think of that bizarre night.

Professor Kroeber and Professor Waterman had it in their minds that Ishi might enjoy some of our art, and they thought that I should go along too since I was fast becoming Ishi's sidekick.

In October 1911, Professor Kroeber accepted a local newspaperman's invitation to take Ishi to a vaudeville performance. Sam Batwee, the old northern Yana whom Kroeber had brought to the museum during Ishi's first weeks there to act as interpreter, asked Ishi whether he would like to see Saldu medicine men and women dance on a stage. Batwee, whose tribe had been only distantly related to the southern Yana, and who proved to be a poor interpreter before he was sent away, claimed that Ishi was overjoyed at the prospect of seeing the Saldu shamans perform as long as some of his friends went along. But I doubt Ishi had any idea what he was agreeing to. An eclectic group assembled. Mr. and Mrs. Kroeber, Mr. and Mrs. Waterman, Sam Batwee, Ishi, and I would meet the newspaperman, Grant Wallace, at a private box in San Francisco's Orpheum Theater. We had no idea that Mr. Wallace would later write up a highly exaggerated account of our evening in the *San Francisco Call.* It was the first of several lessons we would learn about some people's desire to exploit Ishi.

I sat next to Ishi to reassure him, while the others sat nearby. The crowd inside the theater was immense: there were probably two thousand people packed in for the show. Even before things got underway, I saw that Ishi was awestruck by the crowd. He sat at the front of our box in his finest clothes and red tie, his brown hands gripping the brass railing tightly, eyes scanning the many people in funny clothes below. When the great curtain went up, Ishi did not seem conscious of the stage or its players. His eyes stayed on the vast crowd, his eyelashes blinking in amazement, his breath coming hard. He turned to me.

"Hansi Saldu!" Ishi said.

"Yes," I answered, "there are many white people."

Even after the houselights dimmed and footlights lit the stage, Ishi kept his gaze on the crowd, which was larger than the entire Yana nation had been at its peak. The audience was clearly the show to Ishi, the show a diversion. To a man who had believed that the presence of even one white man meant danger, the sight of hundreds caused him to fight his natural fear. When, finally, I persuaded him to notice the stage and the glitter of the many costumed figures bathed in the colored footlights, Ishi's courage rose by degrees. A group of Brazilian dancers dressed in spangles and bright colors that caught and reflected the lights began whirling about the stage to the orchestra's loud music.

"See," I said. "Look how they hold each other over their heads and dance."

Ishi's grip relaxed a little on the brass railing. He hadn't understood all my words, but he knew that I had given him a sign that everything was safe.

Suddenly red lights snapped on, flooding the stage in crimson light as from a bloody moon. Ishi leaned backward in his seat and gripped Professor Kroeber's arm. Our friends in the back seats smiled to reassure him, but it was obvious that Ishi had been among us for too little time to have any idea of what was happening.

The first dance ended, and the troupe of dancers left the stage to thundering applause. Ishi turned to Sam Batwee and asked him in broken dialect whether these dancers were Saldu medicine men and women and whether the orchestra was designed to drive Coyote devils out of these sick people who grinned and clapped their hands when they were rid of Coyote's spirits.

"Him crazy-auna-tee. Him think the clapping scare our demons away," the old one-eyed interpreter said to us. "He say everybody run off stage when Saldu clapped their hands together. This one must think he at a movie picture."

The Brazilian leading man and woman returned to the red-lit stage, just the two of them, and the orchestra struck up a lively song. I patted him on the back, and some of Ishi's confidence returned. His wonderful, thick eyebrows went up as the couple began to cling, vault, and whirl wildly to the pulse of the music.

He watched the two dancers with more attention than any other act that night. His breathing quickened during their sensuous dance. At one point, Ishi half rose from his seat and hung over the side of our box for a moment. He spoke hurriedly to Sam Batwee in the mixed compromise dialect that neither of them fully understood.

"Too much he smokes," Batwee said with his usual curt disdain for his charge, who had drawn so much attention. "This Ishi whiskey-tee crazy-auna-tee. Him think these dancers try to tell the story of Lying Coyote, who tries to win the heart of a dancing maiden but she says him no good, says no to his suiting her.

"Lying Coyote him's smart. 'Wait you maiden,' he says. 'A powerful chief will come here. You must know him by his painted face. If you dance good for this great chief you may win his love.'"

The professors and their wives grinned at Batwee's speech, while the reporter was busy scribbling down notes, but Ishi, I am sure, had no idea he was the butt of the interpreter's harangue.

"So Lying Coyote sneaks away and paints and greases his own face, and when he comes back, this maiden smiles and dances with him, like these two dance. Then things like candy-tee. This beautiful dancing maiden she gets taken to wife by Lying Coyote. This Ishi crazy-tee."

The couple's dance ended, and again the echoing applause of two thousand people drove Ishi deeper into his upholstered seat. I put my hand on his knee for a minute, feeling the locked tension in his limbs. Even at nine, I knew this evening was a mistake. Ishi was resolutely trying to behave properly, trying to hide his fear and to make sense of the strange happenings on the stage in the only way he knew how, by relating them, however inappropriately, to his own inner compass, to his own world. But this was not his world. He was as out of place in this crowed vaudeville as would be someone first visiting earth from Mars. It was wrong to bring him here. Although Ishi knew we were his friends and could be trusted, he had no assurance that his life would not be taken at any moment by some crazy Saldu in the crowd. Ishi's own father and nearly all his people had been killed by whites. To be sitting with so many whites under these circumstances in the Orpheum Theater was heroic, I decided. Now that I am old, I think it was incredible.

The various acts went on. Australian wood choppers threw their heavy axes across the stage deep into an opposite log. A man named Stevens told some jokes, and Ishi laughed a few times, trying to fit in, but laughing too late, just after the crowd. When Stevens changed moods and told a sad soliloquy, Ishi laughed again mistakenly in a high unnatural giggle that carried like a young girl's voice over the silent crowd.

Beer-drinking Sam Mann drank what looked like a whole gallon of beer from his huge false-bottomed stein. I sat by Ishi, and the night wore on.

The stage lights changed to blue. Silvery-voiced Lily Lena from London took the stage in an iridescent Paris evening gown. She crooned "Have You Ever Loved Another Little Girl?" to scores of men in the crowd. Grant Wallace, the newspaper man, wrote that Ishi fell in love with Lily, the shining songbird from London, but I knew that was bunk even before my Dad gave me a speech about yellow journalism. Her gown did sparkle in many colors in the footlights, but I thought Grant Wallace and the professors were far more taken by Lily's warbling notes and dazzling appearance than Ishi or I.

Ishi seemed to be retreating within himself, away from the glitter and melody and horseplay on the stage. When Lily Lena stretched out her long white arms to Ishi in our box at the end of "Take it Nice and Easy," almost two thousand pairs of eyes turned upon him, and I saw Ishi blush bright red. He shrank down lower in his plush seat. His fingers grasped the crimson hangings around our box front, his hands trembling visibly. I reached out my hand and patted one of his. Already the crowd was turning its attention back to the stage and its calcium lights.

"Wanasi Ishi, you are braver than any one of them."

His deathgrip loosened, and then Ishi looked straight at me with those haunted brown eyes, the deep liquid eyes of a forest hunter.

> *Su. This young wolf wishes to make me feel safe in this mystery room of Saldu gods. This white marimi who sings is a great kuwi marimi to the Saldu, a dancing medicine goddess from their other world. Haxa. Perhaps my friends have brought me to see the heaven of the Saldu tonight, the place where hansi Saldu go when they are to die. Perhaps mechi-kuwi Coyote plays his tricks on me. Maliwal boy is not afraid.*

I felt Ishi's hand on mine, felt his trembling slowly pass away. Lily Lena had finished her set, and slipped blithely away from the stage. Again the applause rang out and echoed off the great walls of the Orpheum, but Ishi had his brave stoicism back or maybe he was depending on me.

A local comic singer named Harry Breen ran onstage, and the orchestra struck up again. Red-haired Breen must have seemed stranger yet to Ishi, but, if so, he made no sign. The singer began improvising his rapid fire songs, working in impromptu jokes on specific people in the audience. As Breen strutted about the stage, singing his satiric lyrics in the bright lights, I prayed silently that he wouldn't look up to our private box, for the city papers had already been full of Ishi's story, and even in his finest white man's clothes, Ishi was easily recognizable. After a few minutes, Breen seemed about to conclude his songs, and I relaxed.

Then it happened. Breen caught sight of Ishi and the professors. It was just what I had feared the most. Without pausing to take a breath, the singer's strong voice rang out through the vast room:

"The Indian caveman next I see
With the professors from the universitee;
He smokes a bad cigar and he hasn't any socks,
And he's laughing, although he's sure in a box."

Hexai-sa! He looks at me! The hansi Saldu turn in their seats and look too. Dawana Saldu sings at me, makes these ghost people laugh. The one on the stage is a mechi-kuwi. He casts his dawana spell over all these others, and all their eyes are upon Tetna-Ishi, and they laugh and clap their ghost hands together. There are too many Saldu in this ghost wowi, too many Saldu in this world. Suwa! These ghosts have no manners. They know nothing of the Way. They wear robes that cover all their bodies, and clothe their feet in shoes, but they know nothing of the ground they walk on. The ground of this huge Saldu village is all of stone. Su. These laughing hansi Saldu know nothing of the dambusa ways. They are like the mahde Saldu whose sticks of thunder killed Father and Sister long ago in the cave of endings. Suwa. I have come to my new friends out of the Center of the World and they have been kind almost as if they were of the people, but these other Saldu are mahde spirits of this city of stone. Hexai-sa, they laugh at me! Their kind have taken Tushi and Mother and Elder Uncle. They dare to make fun of me, the ending one, the last Yahi wanasi. Nize ah Yahi!

Fear was again upon Ishi, and anger too it seemed, for his face flushed even redder than it had before. The regiment of eyes was turned on him again, some in the audience even standing to get a better look at the wild man of Tehama County, while comedian Breen finished his clever song.

He let my hand go as frantic applause again filled the theater hall, clenching and unclenching the hand I had been touching. When Professor Kroeber reached forward to pat his back and reassure him, Ishi flinched as if being startled out of some hypnotic, angry dream. It was a mistake to have taken him so such a traumatic event so soon after Ishi came into our hands, and we all knew it. The ladies in our private box gathered their things, the men put out their cigars, and I stood beside Ishi, my face about level with his chest. The crowd's attention turned back toward a new diversion behind the colored footlights. We took our leave before the end of the third act.

I think, now that I am old and near to dying, that our night at vaudeville must have been the most nightmarish dream for Ishi, a calcium-lit irrational journey into a tunnel of pale faces all leering at his soul. I'm sorry, wanasi Ishi. I'm sorry for what my people are, what we can sometimes be. I hope I meet what lies beyond my own life, beyond everything I know and understand, with as much grace and bravery as you.

Chapter 26

The year 1912 came and went quickly for my friend and I. I turned ten and then eleven as the year 1913 came around. Always, I was learning the Yahi way from Ishi. There was talk among the adults in the Medical Center and museum of trouble in Europe, troubles around the world, but none of it touched us. We were too busy shooting our bows in the Sutro Forest, telling stories, and making up new myths for each other. School for me was just a bother. My real lessons all happened after classes where life with Ishi was a reality I felt I had always known.

I had heard Ishi talk to my father and the professors about the fact that there had been no wife for him among the last of his people, so it seemed natural to ask him if he had ever wanted to marry. One fine fall day in 1913, with the natural curiosity of an eleven-year-old, I put the question to him. I had no idea that my friend had so many thoughts on courtship. With his classic Yahi reticence, Ishi did not answer my question directly, preferring instead to use metaphor to get to the truth. The story he told me was a man's wish-fulfillment tale, the kind told to pass the time, yet also to reveal his heart and true feelings about a woman.

"U-Tut-Ne, Wood Duck Man, was a young wanasi," Ishi told me, as we sat on our favorite cliff above the ocean beach. We had taken the trolley through Golden Gate Park to the ocean as we had done so many times before, wanting to enjoy this perfect, sunny afternoon, one of the last warm days of the season.

"U-Tut-Ne was a high bred Yahi," he said, "a man of character and so great a hunter that he might let the tuihi [sun] rise and pass over the Sky World while he still lay in bed on his rabbitskin pallet and the others had to hunt. Wood Duck Man had no wife, but he had two sisters, U-Tut-Na and U-Tut-Ni, who lived with him in his wowi and obeyed his orders."

I looked down on the breakers, at the long, sandy beach studded with people walking in the sun's warmth and stretching miles away, past my vision. I looked at Ishi's sunlit face, and I saw that he was smiling. He was obviously enjoying Wood Duck's good fortune.

"U-Tut-Ne was happy," Ishi continued. "He hunted and sang and one day he told his loyal sisters, 'I believe many dambusa young women of the villages are talking of me and thinking that they would like to marry me.' He told his sisters to be prepared for visitors: 'Be sure to fill the baskets of all the young marimi who come to my house. Fill them with deer meat and with the meat of salmon.'

"Wood Duck Man was in no hurry to take a wife. He wanted to be the dallying, not the marrying kind of wanasi, until he found the perfect marimi. He wanted to have fun, and, sure enough, many dambusa marimi began to come to display their women's charms to him, to spend a long or short time in U-Tut-Ne's home, depending on his wishes. He sent each woman away, but always with full baskets of food."

As I listened, I watched the blue ocean and the lines of white waves breaking toward the shore below our cliff. A warm breeze blew on my face and in my hair. Ishi wore his black hair long now, tied back in a thick ponytail. A wisp of dark hair had fallen loose and blew about his cheek.

"Who were these many women who came to marry Wood Duck?"

"Ah, Maliwal, there were many. U-Tut-Ne sang his wino-tay wife hunting song over and over, and twenty marimi came to his house, each in her turn. Do you wish to hear of all of them?"

I looked at my friend sitting beside me. The sounds of the distant waves drifted up whenever he stopped speaking. "Wanasi Ishi," I said, "will you sing me some of the song which made all of the women love the Wood Duck and want him for their husband?"

The sound of his voice covered up the ocean. Ishi seemed sad for a time as he sang in high musical tones. "Wino-tay, wino-tay..."

he sang over and over, something plaintive in his voice. He hugged himself and rocked like a child there on the sea cliff at the Edge of the World, singing quietly into the whisper of the ocean breeze. "Wino-tay, wino-tay, wino-tay..."

"And the women?" I asked, after a long silence.

"First little striped skunk-woman, Ke-Tip-Ku, came out of the east to marry him. Wood Duck sent her away quickly because she did not smell right.

"U-Tut-Ne had a way of sniffing the air after he sang the wino-tay courting song. He would turn to the four corners of the earth, east and west, south and north, and he would sing his song in each direction, then wait to sniff the air. By this means, he could tell when a dambusa maiden was talking of him or thinking of him or starting to come to him, even if she were many day's walk away.

"He was always prepared, Maliwal. U-Tut-Ne would order his sisters up, sometimes in the middle of the night, and he would tell them to prepare food for the woman who was coming to marry him. U-Tut-Ne was a great hunter. Each day when he was courting, he would go out much later than the other wanasi to kill game in the woods, and his sisters would cook it. And he was a gentleman wanasi. Even though he had sniffed the air toward each corner of the earth and knew these dambusa marimi were coming, he always sent out his two sisters to greet them on their arrival and pretended that he didn't know who they were. When Wood Duck Man finally sent the disappointed maidens away, they always left with their baskets full of U-Tut-Ne's plentiful game.

"Flint woman, Kaka-Kina, was the next to visit Wood Duck, and he treated her with courtesy, but he quickly sent her away, for flint woman had no eyes."

"She had no eyeballs? Was she human or made of stone?" I asked.

"Haxa, Wolf Boy, she had no eyes. All of the maidens who came to U-Tut-Ne were related to the animals or to the elements of Jupka and Kaltsuna's earth.

"Beaver woman too came to his wowi and was welcomed until she spoke some Wintun and gave away that she was from another tribe. A full-blooded Yahi is forbidden to marry a Wintu or any other tribe's maiden, so Wood Duck Man sent beaver woman away, although she was very beautiful.

"Waterdog woman came. After her came Hop-Yu-Mu-Ku, the waterbug marimi, but neither was allowed to stay in U-Tut-Ne's fine house. Bat woman came and fishhook woman, and after them, chipmunk woman, shikepoke, and rainbow woman, but all of them left with full baskets and no husband."

"Didn't Wood Duck get interested in any of them?" I asked. I was growing tired of sitting on the cliff's rocky ground. "Weren't any of them pretty enough?"

"Mussel woman came next," Ishi continued, sensing my impatience. "And after her abalone woman, who was very pretty with skin like a pearl, but these marimi were from the faraway Pomo tribe by Outer Ocean where we now sit. The great wanasi U-Tut-Ne could not marry them.

"Fox woman and mountain quail girl, were from the Center of the World, but they were not beautiful enough. Brown bear woman brought sweet-smelling herbs and roots as gifts for Wood Duck, but even so, he sent her away.

"Dentalium woman, who was born from the money we Yahi traded other tribes for, came to U-Tut-Ne's village. She fell so in love with his courting song that she was determined to have Wood Duck Man as her husband. She wished to lie and sleep with him. During the whole time she was there, Duck Man's sisters and the entire village watched his house shake and rattle from their struggle, until exhausted Wood Duck was finally able to throw her out."

The late afternoon sun was over the blue water now, painting the rows of waves with yellow and orange.

"Didn't he ever find a good wife?"

Ishi looked over at me, a half smile playing at his lips. "You see beyond my story, don't you, young wolf?"

"I wish for Duck Man to be happy, to find his bride."

"Oh, Wood Duck finds the special one who is for him, Maliwal. That is the problem. Listen to the end of his story, so you will know the way this world can be. Suwa, his search will soon be over."

Ishi continued: "U-Tut-Ne began to feel sorry for the marimi he turned away. He gave magnesite woman rock beads as well as the usual deer and salmon meat. To pretty morning star woman, he gave beads and polished shell ornaments and much food. He must have been sorely tempted by the morning star one.

"Then something different happened. Blue crane woman, Giri-Giri, heard his singing and flew to U-Tut-Ne's house at twilight. All the Yahi of the village were talking of them when Wood Duck Man finally called his two sisters to take crane woman away in the full sunlight of the next day!

"Turtle woman was the next to last to visit. She was born from the nearby Maidu people and came wearing a fine elkhide skirt, but she said she had come from a college in the Saldu city by the great bay! U-Tut-Ne had no choice but to send this dawana turtle one away."

Ishi paused for a breath, and looked out faraway to the ocean's horizon where the world ended in a haze. He had been talking for a long time. The sound of waves breaking returned to my ears. Finally, he spoke again.

"When all of the maidens of the animals and of the earth had tried to win Wood Duck's hand and failed, a last marimi came to him, and she was born of the People, of human beings.

"Her name was Tushi. She was the most beautiful Yana woman that U-Tut-Ne had ever seen. Her eyes were brown and deep and clear; her hair like black feathers fluttered behind her lovely face. Her skin was the smoothest reddish hue, and she wore a buckskin dress of the finest making."

My friend paused, looking out at the ocean again. He seemed very sad.

"Wood Duck chose Tushi for his wife. He thought that this would be the end of all his days of searching."

"Did he marry his chosen one?" I asked. I wanted to know why my friend was not happy about this best of all possible endings.

"Another rival wanted the maiden too," Ishi said. "The great god Kaltsuna wished to marry dambusa Tushi also."

"Did Wood Duck fight Kaltsuna for her hand?"

"Yes, Maliwal," Ishi said, his voice growing quieter to an almost inaudible whisper. "Kaltsuna, the lizard god, cut Duck in two with one stinging whip of his tail. U-Tut-Ne's sisters restored him to life by sewing his two halves together, praying and wailing while they worked, but, by the time he was alive again, the great Lizard had already married Tushi and taken her off to live in the Sky World. Wood Duck was left alone for the rest of his life. Suwa! Maliwal. It is the way of this world."

I didn't know what to say to him then, and I don't know what I would say even now. I remember we sat side by side on the oceanside cliff for a long while, not saying anything, just watching the sun settle over the vast waters until an advancing fog bank came in from the ocean and obscured the remaining light. When we went home in the dusk, I knew I was not quite the same boy as when that afternoon had begun. There are some things that change you forever, and, once the change has occurred, you are not completely the same person. This had happened to Ishi years before, in the forest of his childhood, and, through his story, it had happened to me.

Now, all these years later, as I am assessing my life, I understand even more what Ishi was trying to tell me. Part of his Wood Duck story was telling me to delight in absurdity and in humor, even in self-irony. Under the strict Yana sex code, U-Tut-Ne's amorous adventures were the height of humorous exaggeration: no full-blooded Yahi would ever try out brides to find the best one. There were strict rules about sex, and most marriages were arranged. Ishi himself had probably never made love. His tiny, blood-related community provided no opportunity for that or many other simple pleasures. How ironic for Ishi, the lonely bachelor, to weave a tale where his character was wooed by twenty women whom he scorned, and a twenty-first who won his heart but who was taken away by the very god of creation.

I know now that the dentalium woman episode was a teacher's warning. Dentalium was Yahi money, but Yana land was bare of dentalium, so all the money that its people possessed had to be obtained from outside tribes, often at great cost of Yahi game and crafts. Dentalium woman was so aggressive precisely because she was not a Yana woman. But Ishi was also teaching me that wealth could mean abuse of power and the jaded habit of getting one's way; he showed me in metaphor that both are characteristics dangerous in life.

But the words that Ishi spoke about Tushi have lingered strongest in my mind. Ishi was telling me, with his masked confession, about his enduring love for Tushi, disguising his deepest feelings in Wood Duck's made-up character. He was telling me as forthrightly as he could that his heart had been broken and that it would only be whole again when he joined Tushi in the world beyond. This realization changed me as a boy and colored all my life as a man.

Chapter 27

My father and the professors were aware that Ishi was given to moments of deep depression. After all, he was a man who had lost nearly his whole basis for living: his cultural context, his people, his home. Ishi was happiest when he was working, when he had a clear purpose, and so Professor Waterman, Professor Kroeber, and my Dad kept him busy making things. Days at the museum found Ishi making bows and arrow shafts, feathering them or binding on their carefully flaked points with sinew. At nights he told stories and sang us his childhood songs. The professors recorded dozens of his stories, and Ishi knew and remembered some sixty Yahi songs. The stories he told were never so personal as the tale of Wood Duck he had given to me, and Ishi seemed to avoid stories that alluded to his recent, painful past, preferring instead to retell the myths and legends he had learned in his childhood. When not explaining where the world came from or how the People first got fire, he especially loved hunting and fishing stories. His heart was usually in the hunt or play. But sometimes even the work or storytelling was not enough to keep Ishi from falling into an inscrutable funk, no doubt caused by thinking back over his life which had seen loss after loss. At times like these, my father or the professors would make every effort to get Ishi out to do something unusual, some special diversion outside the museum walls. I, invariably, would tag along.

Toward the end of 1913, Ishi fell into one of his blue periods. Outwardly, he remained polite and mannerly, and if asked a question or for help with a project, he would gladly help. But it was clear to anyone who knew him that Ishi was suffering inside. Privately, I knew he missed Tushi with an ache that wouldn't go away.

It so happened that Buffalo Bill's Wild West Show was in San Francisco for two weeks that winter. My father was a doctor and a man of science, it is true, but he knew something about people's minds and spirits as well. He had won Ishi's confidence by his sleight of hand tricks. Now, he bought three tickets to Buffalo Bill's show, knowing that getting Ishi out for some less cultured entertainment might do him some good. Ishi had enjoyed the circus with its daredevil horseback feats and the antics of clowns, so my father guessed this new outing would be a natural. My father seldom guessed wrong.

We arrived at the huge indoor arena called the Cow Palace just before the show began. From the very first act, Ishi's somber mood seemed to melt away. He sat on his wooden bleacher seat among the multitudes, eyes transfixed, watching Buffalo Bill's cowboys rope Brahma bulls and herd trained buffalo. The cowboys did their best to make the creatures look wild and dangerous. Ishi loved the animals, especially the beautiful horses that Bill's skilled riders rode. He laughed with delight when Buffalo Bill's head rodeo clown called the children to come from the bleachers into the large arena, then turned loose several greased piglets, promising a prize for any child who could hang on to one. My father laughed too when the winner, a little blond girl, face streaked with grease and sawdust filling her hair from the tussle, trotted out to claim her ribbon and a promissory note for a year's supply of bacon.

Before the second half of the show, a small group of Plains Indians came out of the stalls nearby and walked directly in front of our row of seats to prepare for their upcoming performance. A dignified looking warrior, bedecked in bright paints and feathers, caught a glimpse of Ishi and immediately approached us. Ishi sat up straighter as this other native man, now a professional entertainer, made his way elegantly to our row of seats. When he reached us, Ishi rose from his seat. The two Indians stood face to face, and looked at each other in silence for several minutes. Some of the people near us left their seats, probably fearing a scuffle. The other Indians waited below to start their routine.

Su! This one looks at me. He is hisi, but he is not one of the people. Haxa, this tall dambusa one is not of the Center of the World or anywhere near, but there can be no doubt he is a wanasi. See how he looks at me. His eyes search my face, haxa, but his painted skin does not move. Somewhere he must have a watgurwa of the old ways to make such a fine headdress. Suwa. This one is a wakara hunter. He is hisi, not of the Saldu.

The Sioux warrior spoke in perfect English, breaking the silence.

"What tribe of Indian is this?"

My father stood up from his seat then and answered.

"He is Yana, from Northern California."

I watched, safe in my seat, while the three men from different cultures stood facing each other in a new silence. More long minutes passed.

Still this dambusa wanasi looks. He must be very wise to speak the Saldu tongue so well. Or perhaps he never learned the ways of his ancestors and has been among the ghost people since he was daana. Perhaps he is truly wise and knows the old way as well as the ways of the Saldu. Maliwal's father is wise too and knows the magic of a kuwi. Maliwal too has the mind of a Yahi, but most of these Saldu are not hisi. They have no knowledge of the earth, no manners, and wish to know things they should not know. Haxa, they are very smart, but in the ways of the gods and nature the Saldu are but children. This wanasi though has the face of a hisi who knows some things. Haxa. He has the eyes of a leader.

The continued silence made me feel like screaming out. I shifted around on the wooden slats of my seat, hoping for something to dissipate my pent-up tension. Then the Sioux warrior reached out to Ishi's impassive face and touched a wisp of Ishi's thick hair, rolling it gently between his fingers, staring searchingly into Ishi's expressionless face. The Sioux finally spoke again.

"This man is a very high grade Indian. Listen to all that he says."

With that, the buckskin-clad Sioux turned away and climbed gracefully down over the rows of seats to rejoin his friends and to put on their show.

Before the cowboys and Indians act was played out in the dust of the arena, I asked Ishi what he thought of the Sioux warrior.

"Him's a big chiep," Ishi said.

* * *

It was in 1914 that Ishi became most truly himself among us. He was an aboriginal man who brought a calm, a peace, and a grace to our new and civilized times. He was a magnificent creature, the best of animal and man. He had gotten his weight under perfect control after he recognized the dangers of eating too much sugary and rich white man's food. He loved, more than ever, to shoot his handmade bows with my father and I, still correcting us along the way, showing us new subtleties of native archery when we were ready for them and not before. We would go to Sutro Park together every weekend, the three of us, and shoot for hours while the sun made its way over our heads. He was my best friend. By the time I turned twelve, there could be no doubt of that. He was my teacher.

I believe it was Professor Kroeber who first suggested a trip back to Wowunupo. At first, Ishi refused to consider returning to the Center of the World. Why hunt, make fires, and fish for food when life was so easy at the museum watgurwa, he wanted to know. There were no houses on Mill and Deer creeks, no beds or chairs or electric lights. Camping there would be cold and uncomfortable. Besides, there were no trails into the remote canyons. The Yana homeland was a very long way from the nearest train. These things were no problem, Kroeber and Waterman answered. They would take food and blankets and could rent horses to carry men and baggage from the train into the Yana foothills, they said. Ishi could again smell the smell of pines on the slopes of Waganupa, could again taste fresh salmon and deer meat, could feel the canyon trails with his bare feet, could fill all his senses with the good familiar land at the Center of the World. He could swim the rapids of Deer Creek, they said; he could aim his best bow and throw his best spear to hunt food for his companions, not for an artificial demonstration in the museum house. Besides, they argued, it was precisely because they wanted to escape from the houses and the chairs of this big city that they wished to go to Yana country.

Still, Ishi was not completely convinced. He knew the matter had been decided, but he went around muttering "that treep, a dawana aunatee treep" in front of Gifford and Loud and Warburton, his friends and fellow employees at the museum. While the packing was being done and the preparations were being made, Ishi struggled with conflicting feelings. He knew that his friends would not abandon him in the old land, for Watamany and the Chiep had promised him that the museum watgurwa would always be his home, and they were both clearly men of their words. But to go back to his home of so many sad memories, to relive the pain of losing Tushi and the majapa would be difficult. The restless souls of his murdered Yahi people lingered there, some of them still wandering aimlessly in a limbo, searching for the right path to the stars. And what of Tushi and Elder Uncle's spirits? Even though he had spoken to her in the world beyond and Tushi had told him of their journey down the great Daha River and of their transformation into sigaga who flew back safely to the eastern star path, could he trust his vision? Perhaps his communication with Tushi's spirit was just another of Coyote's cruel tricks? The bones of the lost ones might still be somewhere below the great volcano, in a place he had not yet found in his many searches. If this were true, wouldn't it be better for him to go back, to search again in the new places he had thought of, and to perform the necessary cremation rites if he found them? No, he must not think like that, Ishi decided. He had truly heard what he had heard, truly felt what he had felt. His visions had never been wrong.

True, as his friends said, it would be good to be again in the land that Jupka and Kaltsuna had made and to teach young wolf more of the Yahi way in the people's home. It would be good to hunt for himself and the others and to live free for a while as he did when he was a child. The old memories flooded in, and for days Ishi's heart battled doubt and fear against nostalgic desire, while the others scurried about making their plans.

When the day of our departure came, my father, Professor Kroeber, Professor Waterman, and I were anxious to set off on our grand adventure, but I knew Ishi was the most excited one of our party. His longing to see the old places had worked its magic.

Part IV:
To the Stars

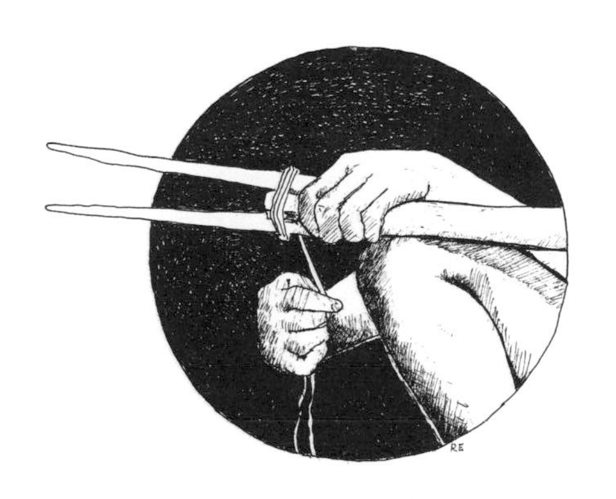

Chapter 28

The grand Yahi expedition got under way at the beginning of May in 1914. Spring was fully in the air, and classes at Dad's hospital next door to the museum were out, as were the two professors' classes across the bay at Berkeley, where most of the university was being built. I, too, was freed for the summer, never again to sit through the awkward trauma of seventh grade. Ishi was on furlough from his ceremonial job as a janitor at the museum. We were all free and glad to be on our way.

On the train to Vina, we had a special drawing room and sleeping compartment on board a Pullman car. As we rocked northward, fellow passengers and trainmen alike peered around our door for a look at the expedition party. We must have been quite a sight. I had a mop of blond hair then and was tall for my age, gawky; my father, dressed in his bow-hunting camouflage, looked as if he were ready to bring down a grizzly bear; Ishi sat moon-faced, anticipating, his black hair worn long and loose around his face in classic Yahi style; Professor Waterman's dramatic mustache twitched in daydreams as he napped; and Professor Kroeber took it all in, smiling sometimes behind his wonderful, well-kept beard. We were certainly an odd-looking crew. Battered tin cooking pots, bow cases, notebooks, quivers full of arrows, and rucksacks filled every corner of our Pullman car. Three sleeping bags lay opened out on the floor, for there were pull-down bunks for only two. Later that night, Ishi and I had fun trying to figure out how, exactly, to make those pull-down, pull-out, and flip-over beds work.

It was before dawn the next morning when we left the train at Vina, loaded with our gear. I remember that as we stepped from the smoking train, Ishi handed a quarter tip to a surprised porter, using all the cultured cool of a world traveler. It was money he had earned from his part-time work as a museum janitor, and he was proud to have it to give away. At Vina, the little town in the North Valley where Deer Creek empties into the Sacramento River, our two guides were waiting for us.

Ishi flinched when he recognized one of the two there in the half-light of the railroad platform. They were Merle Apperson, the man Ishi had fired an arrow at several years earlier, and Mr. Apperson's son, who had been with Waterman on his fruitless search for Ishi in 1909. I thought we had a problem on our hands.

Ishi hesitated when Merle Apperson held out his hand in greeting. Perhaps he was weighing out responsibility for the old wrongs. After all, here was one of the party who forced the break-up of Wowunupo, who contributed to the prompt deaths of Ishi's remaining family. Robbers and killers, the Saldu had wiped his people from the face of the earth. That was the final, incontrovertible, tragic truth. Yet this one among the others had spoken kindly to his mother, and he had brought small gifts back to Wowunupo when he realized the wrong the whites had done in rifling the little village. He had killed no one. Apperson, Sr. may never have seen Ishi before, or known it was Ishi who warned him back with an arrow, but Ishi had seen him. Perhaps he knew that one of the storehouses the Yahi had pilfered belonged to Apperson and his cattle herders. Perhaps in a desperate hour he had killed one of Apperson's sheep or cows. Perhaps the Ishi of 1914, now steeped in the white rules of ownership of property and land, felt tinges of guilt for having robbed and pillaged as well. I don't know. I do know that he shook the older Apperson's hand after the longest inward agony possible in a few seconds' time. Both Appersons were cordial to Ishi and were genuinely happy to meet him for the trip to his homeland. They had agreed to supply the pack horses and their services as guides for free, perhaps operating under their own natural desire to assuage the guilt of a whole race. But it would take Ishi a few wary days' time to warm up to them. Both Appersons would have to prove themselves through actions to show that in the earlier years they had meant no intentional harm to the Yahi people. Only then would Ishi forgive the older man's small part in those tragic events.

When the pack horses were loaded and all of us were safely on our own mounts, we rode off awkwardly, Ishi most awkward of all, toward the east and the new rising sun. We rode out of the valley as the sun's rays broke brightly over the horizon, back lighting the hulking silhouette of Mt. Lassen. We rode for several hours in single file into the Yana foothills, climbing upward among chaparral, loose rocks, and big boulders. In the afternoon, we arrived at an open meadow where Sulphur Creek flows into Deer Creek, and we decided to set up our base camp there. I remember this spot had everything we needed: good pasture grass for the horses, some felled logs for firewood, and an open, level area, sparsely timbered, where we could spread out our camp.

That first night something extraordinary happened. When all the many tasks for setting up camp were done and all the detailed unpackings were complete and the sun had set behind the coast range far over in the west, my father, the two professors, and the Appersons lay close to the fire in their sleeping bags, their bellies full, their muscles tired. Ishi and I spread our sleeping bags outside the campfire's diffuse orange circle of flickering light. We were soul mates, though separated by over forty years of age, and it seemed right to be a little apart from the rest. Close by the burning fire, the others in our party were soon asleep. Wide awake, Ishi and I talked, keeping our voices low. The only other sound was the tethered horses occasionally snorting or stamping their feet and the warm night breeze through the pines.

In whispers, Ishi told me the private story of how Tushi had come back to the Center of the World to speak with him in a fiery vision after her death. As we lay under the stars and constellations, he told me that for all these many months among his new friends he had been haunted by the nagging uncertainty that his vision had been false, that the bodies of his majapa uncle and Tushi still lay rotten and unsanctified, their souls imprisoned, near Banya Creek. He whispered to me that he had searched everywhere, over and over, but that in his time at the Edge of the World he had realized one place he had not searched. Keefer Ridge on Rock Creek, far south of Wowunupo. He and Tushi had once talked of going there for a better look at the strange black creature as it smoked its way up the Daha Valley. The ridge the whites called Keefer would have been a good place for the two lost ones to hide, he said. It was true they had never hiked there, but Tushi and he had spoken of it several times as they saw the ridge in the hazy distance to their south. Perhaps she had led their majapa there to hide and to wait for him to come. Perhaps they had starved to death or had been killed by a bear, he worried. True, he had found some of Tushi's necklace below the treacherous log-crossing at Banya Creek, he said, and true she had come to him from the world beyond to explain what had happened, but Ishi had to know for sure. The idea haunted him.

Under the bowl of the dark, wide-open sky, he told me that he did not intend to sleep until he had searched this one last place where the lost ones still might lie. I was to say nothing of his going. He would be back before the sunrise. Barefoot, Ishi noiselessly disappeared into the shadows beyond the faint yellow circle of our firelight.

I spent the long night nervously turning in my sleeping bag on the hard ground. Several times the sound of the horses snorting, or the far-off screech of an owl, or the pop of sappy wood in our slowly dying fire brought me half-awake, thinking that Ishi had come back with an answer, but each time I was mistaken and drifted back into fitful sleep. At last, I slept the sleep of a twelve-year-old whose body was too tired to keep fighting itself awake while his hero was out searching for his heart somewhere in the darkness.

Something intuitive, not sound, awoke me from my dreams. It was just before dawn. Our fire was dead. Ishi lay beside me in his sleeping bag, awake, studying my face. I heard the call of quail far off in the half-darkness.

"It is well, Maliwal," he whispered. "I have not found the bones of the two lost ones. I have looked in the new place I worried about, and dambusa Tushi and Elder Uncle are not there or anywhere on this earth. Aiku tsub. I will not doubt my true vision again."

* * *

The first few days of our expedition into Ishi's past went quickly. The weather was perfect, providing us with sun warmed afternoons and nights cool enough to keep our supper fires burning into night campfires. Jupka and Kaltsuna must have been watching over us, for, even though we took to native undress in camp, none of our party got poison oak, sunburn, or cut our bare feet. Only Ishi and the Appersons remained modest. The father and son pair kept their clothes on throughout the trip, and Ishi chose to keep at least his breechclout on.

We quickly settled into an easy routine. We shared the cooking, cleaning, and dishwashing without complaint. Within a day or two, Ishi warmed visibly to both our guides. In truth, the Appersons were unnecessary: Ishi knew every foot of Deer Creek Canyon. These volcanic tablelands dressed in timber were his home, a canyon homeland of basaltic rock eroded into naked spires, hill-sides thick with manzanita, and a swift but wadable stream flowing down from deep springs in the volcanic honeycomb south and west of Mt. Lassen.

All of us swam daily in the cold water; we ate fish and meat that our three hunters, father and Ishi and I, took with spears or with bows and arrows and broiled fresh on sticks over our cooking fires. Each night we sat around the fire eating the pumpkin seeds, per-simmons, and pine nuts we had brought along, or Ishi's peppery watercress, or his little apple-colored manzanita berries that tasted of citrus on my tongue. He showed me how to shampoo my hair with soaproot he had dug up, and it worked. Late spring was all around us, providing us with everything we needed.

Nights before bed found us still around the fire singing to my father's guitar or along with Ishi's Yahi songs and shaking rattle. We of San Francisco and Berkeley learned how to dance the simple stamping steps of the Yana circle dance while the Appersons clapped their hands rhythmically in the flicker of firelight. It was a long way from the Sunset District in our own city by the bay. Most entertaining of all were the stories. Professor Kroeber and Profes-sor Waterman matched Ishi's creation tales with those of other tribes, and my father and the Appersons swapped bear hunting, deer hunting, and fishing stories deep into the clear nights.

If Ishi had any lingering terrible associations from being back in his vanished people's land, he did not show them after our secret first night conversation. In fact, he seemed to be having the time of his life. For once, he didn't have to struggle with broken English, pantomime, and half-understood Yana. He could show us the techniques of climbing up and down perpendicular rock walls with hemp ropes, the ways of swimming in deep swift waters, the manner of spearing a salmon or stalking a blacktail buck. I suspect he felt liberated by this warm reliving and redoing of the old familiar ways. Perhaps Ishi knew that in teaching us these things, he was keeping his tribe alive, not merely as history but as part of the living, unfolding story of mankind. I think he knew that everything he told us of his people's technology, religion, and culture would be passed on through us to new generations. Great men always find a way to leave their mark on the world. I know Ishi left his hand on me.

When Professor Kroeber asked him whether he might take us to Wowunupo, I took it as a sure sign of Ishi's psychological health that he agreed. We set off from base camp early one morning, leaving Merle Apperson and his son to tend their horses and mind our gear until we returned. Professor Waterman explained to us that the three-mile trek had taken him a long time when here on his previous search, but I had no idea how difficult the way would be.

We moved downstream slowly, Ishi in the lead, picking our way through the almost impenetrable brush as the sun climbed higher. Ishi could have moved along much faster, but he hung back patiently while we four city slickers walked and crawled through the tough manzanita and over tangled lattices of wild grape. Sometimes my Dad and I had to use our machetes to clear the bushes. It was easy to see how the last four Yahi had stayed hidden so well for so long. I saw manzanita as I had never seen it before, from every angle and in every direction. The smooth trunks of the larger bushes were exactly the color of dried blood. We all had scratches on our hands and faces and tracks of sweat on our skin before the sun climbed halfway into the branch-punctuated sky. All but Ishi, that is.

While we approached Wowunupo, Deer Creek sang in its ancient babbling language, just as it still does today. When our faint trail kept dying out, we had to cross and recross the stream several times. Where the water was treacherous, Ishi made us use a rope link to keep any single one of us from being caught in a roaring whirlpool and battered against the many boulders that rest in Deer Creek's bed. Once, at a crossing where the stream was wider and quieter, we all dove in to ford it, Ishi swimming in the lead. I remember that he slowed up in the middle and told me to hold onto his long hair. He then piloted us both through the sparkling ripples to the other side.

We came at last to the high, narrow ledge above the creek where Pano, the first grizzly, sent his bears to hide. The sun was high and hot, and the cool of the water on our skin quickly dried away. When every trail, structure site, and free-drifting association had been recorded, I felt Ishi had closed a definite chapter of his life. Now the white people's history books would be able to tell something of the people who once lived on and loved this land. Now his friends knew something more of how it once had been.

By the time we hollered out our safe return to the Appersons back at base camp, they had a fire going, and the full moon had assumed sentry duty in the darkness above our heads.

Chapter 29

Ishi offered to take us to Mill Creek, so we broke up our first base camp, leaving little trace that we had ever been there, and made our way over the lofty, pine-smothered ridge that separated the two Yahi home canyons. It was hard for me to imagine that Ishi's little band had managed to stay hidden for so long, for the difficult ridge we crossed was plainly marked on top by old wagon and horse ruts, the remnants of the white pioneers' hand-hewn Lassen Trail. This very ridge had been the settlers' main artery into the Sacramento Valley, and it bisected the Yahi's ancient and newer homes in Mill and Deer Creek canyons.

Our expedition spent a week at Mill Creek, making camp at the old Yahi villages, exploring, learning more of the Yana lands as they had been when Ishi's people were free to roam as they wished. He took us to village sites he had known from his first years, but which had been abandoned forever because of the pressing in of white gold seekers and ranchers. Ishi had left some of these homes when he was too young to remember more than their place names and who some of the important village people had been. We went into the caves of Mill Creek, even the wet, dark places where the bones of the ancestral Yahi dead had been buried long before, undisturbed by any living Yahi, undisturbed by us. Once, our party passed an odd pile of stones and Ishi stopped in his tracks.

"Popey, now we will see who is a great hunter," Ishi told my father.

He began moving the big rocks, and, when they were all off the hidden ground, he began digging up the dry earth. After a few minutes of this, and with me helping, Ishi pulled a large fur of some hide up out of the depression the stones had covered. He shook the big, dried hide in the air over his head, great clouds of dust billowing out of the hairy skin and dispersing, falling like specks of fool's gold all over his black mane and all around us.

"He is a cinnamon bear," Ishi smiled at my father and the others. "Boy cousin and I brought him down years ago with only our arrows and obsidian knives. You are a powerful kuwi, but have you done this, Popey?"

I remember that my father and his friends were astounded. I just stood with a smile spread wide across my grubby face as Ishi explained how he and his cousin had taken the bear, brought its tasty meat to the village, and cured the hide by smoking it until the skin was coated with preserving creosote. He had hidden the great pelt, Ishi explained, in the hope that he might someday give it to his bride's family as a dowry.

He turned to me then in the bright sunlight, dust coating his shoulders and long black hair. His expression became suddenly more serious, and the playful smile left his lips.

"It is yours, young wolf. Take it as a gift from the son of Tetna Man."

I still have the cinnamon bear's robe. I wear it now in my most comfortable chair, in the winter of my life, and I remember.

When the professors' notebooks were full of more than two hundred place names, maps of all the ancient, old, and modern hunting and burial sites, and records of an equal number of herbs and plants used as food or medicine, our month was nearly gone. Ishi took us for a final week to camp at Black Rock. It was there that he seemed as happy as I had ever known him, almost as if this trip were an emotional adventure, like psychoanalysis, for him, and that now he had finally faced his private demons and had survived. It was there, at Black Rock, that Ishi gave me my final lessons. This would be the last and most heightened time we would all be together.

We spread out our last camp below Ishi's Black Rock, a crumbly dark tooth of columnar basalt that juts hundreds of feet up from the valley floor. I remember spending the days playing chase games with Ishi among the digger pines and elbowy black oaks on the dry slopes above camp, resting in the shade of bay laurels, buckeyes, and lattices of wild grape when the sun got too hot, telling each other stories. We were two wild creatures playing below the omnipotent snow-capped mountain that dominated the eastern horizon. Dad even let Ishi tattoo my chin with nutmeg needles. I wore those marks proudly back to school in the fall of 1914 before they completely faded.

One morning, Ishi awoke me before the others. Dew still covered all our sleeping bags, and the fire from the night before was out.

"Maliwal, look," he said. "Waganupa is waking up."

There in the new light to the northeast of camp, I saw what looked like the silhouette of steam clouds coming from Mt. Lassen's stony crest. The sun was only then rising, so I couldn't be sure. Perhaps the shapes were only streamers of windblown fog dancing across the top of the mountain. There was not enough light to tell.

"Should we wake up the others?"

"What is to be will happen anyway without us," he said. "What could the Chiep and Watamany do anyway?"

A few nights later found us singing around our new firepit below the spire of Black Rock. Dad played requests on his guitar for us and whenever Ishi's turn came that night he always asked for his two favorites: dramatic renditions of "Gunga Din" and "Mandalay." We sang into the warm May night while Merle Apperson's horses sometimes joined in with a neigh or whinny. Ishi, himself, was in an expansive mood, singing high and loud in his hybrid English and Yana.

After a while, a brilliant, nearly full moon rose on the horizon. The water rippled on in Mill Creek, and we sang, while the moon climbed higher overhead, sometimes pausing to throw new wood on our crackling fire. The moonlight began to light our camp. By day, I knew we were surrounded by stout ponderosa, bay, black oak, and alder trees, but now the moonlight was throwing strange tree shadows on the ground outside the circle of firelight.

"Grandfather taught me that deer move when the moon is bright or wakara," Ishi said to no one in particular.

"Banya deer are restless on such nights when they can see. The time to hunt is with a bright moon, Grandfather and Elder Uncle used to say. When the moon is nearly full and looks like a bow fully drawn, Kaltsuna is telling us it is a time to hunt."

I had a feeling that this was to be one of Ishi's best storytelling nights. I think the others did too. We all stopped singing, and for a while the only sounds were of the horses and the song of the creek.

"How about a new story?" Professor Kroeber asked.

"Yea, give us another myth," the younger Apperson said.

Ishi's face was lit now from above, as were all of ours, as the fire burned less brightly for a time.

"I will tell you the story of how the People got First Fire. Aiku tsub. I will tell it as Grandfather and the majapa taught it to me.

"In the beginning time, Jupka's people had no fire," Ishi began, obviously enjoying the prospect of his friendly audience and the telling. We settled in for a long tale.

"The world's Fire-god had the fire in his house far away in the east, and he wouldn't let any humans get hold of it. Fire-god was a huge round fellow with a face that burned; later on the People called him Tuihi.

"Fire-god kept a close eye on his fire. Each day he traveled across the wide sky, spreading his light to the world, always watching below for people who might be on their way to take his fire. He flew all day. As he got to Outer Ocean at the end of each day, Fire-god turned around, leaving a dambusa color splash over the waves, and he went back to his watgurwa, traveling under the belly of the earth so no one could see him. He had to move quickly under the ground, because when he got home he could only sleep by his fire for a few hours before it was time to get up and to go on his travels again."

Su. The lost ones' voices speak through me as I tell the story of Stealing Fire. Haxa, I hear Grandfather's voice especially as it was here on Yuna Creek when I was aizuna Tehna-Ishi. Grandfather is speaking...

"Clever Coyote had a den at the Edge of the World. He thought it would be good for humans to have fire, but even better for him to have fire, too, in his lair by Outer Ocean. He was tired of eating raw rabbits and raw mice, and he didn't like raw clams or raw abalone either. Besides, in the winter moons the wind off Outer Ocean was quite cold.

"So Coyote went running up and down the Edge of the World, trying to find fire. Everywhere he went, he asked about it, and finally Seagull told him about Fire-god, the strong tuihi creature who lived behind Waganupa, far away in the eastern corner of the world. Seagull warned Coyote that if he tried to fight this one, he would surely lose and get his fur singed and his haunches roasted. Seagull said if he wanted to steal fire, Coyote would have to use his tricks on Fire-god.

"Trickster Coyote gathered all his money and his friends, Otter and Pelican, and set off running east, clear over the coastal mountains and beyond Waganupa to Fire-god's home. It was dark when they got there.

"Pelican and Coyote went inside, while Otter hid outside by the Fire-god's door. There was the round old god, lying by his fire, fast asleep.

"'Say, Fire-god, are you alive or dead?' Coyote howled. 'We came all this way from Outer Ocean to gamble with you.'

"The Fire-god jolted up with a start, rubbing his eyes.

"'Okay,' he said sleepily. 'We'll play the guessing game. We may bet with dentalium shells.'

"'All right,' Coyote answered. 'We will play until someone falls asleep. The first one of us who sleeps loses the game. The winner takes all the bets.'

"Fire-god said 'Deal.'

"So they played on and on, singing to each other then guessing, moving the game along endlessly. They played long enough for five moons to pass overhead. Fire-god got nervous. He hadn't been making his daily rounds for a long while. The sky was black the whole time while they played, and all the people in the world wondered what was going on. It was very cold outside the watgurwa. Outer Ocean was freezing up, and, inland, the Yana people huddled together to stay warm.

"Finally, Fire-god's head nodded down a little bit. Trickster Coyote leapt up and howled, 'I won! I won!'

"Fire-god's head jerked up suddenly. 'Hey, wait a minute!' he hollered. 'I wasn't really asleep! It's not fair.'

"It was too late. Pelican had already seized the tuihi fire in his big bill and flown out the door. He passed the burning fire to Otter who was still waiting there, and Otter took off running toward the Edge of the World.

"Fire-god went running after them lickity-split, but Otter chewed a hole in a big cedar tree and tossed the fire in it. Then Otter disappeared into a cold stream.

"Fire-god went angrily across the sky, lighting the world for day after day, his anger melting ice everywhere as he looked for his missing fire.

"Coyote laughed and howled. He told all the people: 'Keep this tuihi fire hidden in the tree until this mad fellow cools down a little. If you need some fire, take a cedar drill

from Otter's tree and make only what fire you need. Just watch out that Fire-god isn't watching you.'

"After that, Coyote spent many happy days eating cooked mice and rabbits by Outer Ocean. He went around grinning and singing to himself, 'Good trick, Coyote, good trick.'

"When he got tired of sitting around on his smug haunches, Coyote went poking his nose up and down the Edge of the World, all along the Klamath and Eel rivers, looking to make more mischief and fate in the world."

Suwa. That is how Grandfather taught me the story of First Fire when I was a young wanasi.

Ishi stopped speaking. The seven of us became aware again of Mill Creek running nearby, the quiet fire in front of us, and the luminous moon overhead. I felt as if I was coming out of a trance, only beginning to focus on the weird shapes that the trees cast outside the circle of our firepit.

I saw my father look at me and smile a wry, knowing smile. Then Ishi spoke again.

"So you see my friends, Coyote does not always do evil in the world. If it fits his mood, he uses his tricks to help Jupka and Kaltsuna's people."

We sat for a while under the gaze of that searchlight moon that hung above the looming cusp of Black Rock. When I got up, finally, to grab more wood for our fire, I saw that Mars too had taken up night sentry duty above the rock. Then, just before I headed back to join the others, a meteor slashed across the dark fabric of the sky.

Chapter 30

Suddenly my dreams were interrupted by screaming horses, by something moving, something strange. I leapt out of my sleeping bag to find Ishi already standing, wearing only his breechclout. The ground shook all around us. My father, the professors, and the Appersons struggled to their feet half-naked, shedding their sleeping sacks like five startled moths. The fire was out, but burnt embers from the night before shook in the circle of stones until the rock wall fell away in places as some of the blackened stones tumbled apart. Ishi pointed to Black Rock, which seemed to sway and tremble a little even as the earth around us shook.

Then, just as suddenly as it had come, the jolting quit. Merle Apperson's horses settled down. Professor Kroeber looked around, surveying the mess in our new camp. The tarpaulin sun shade we had built on sticks had fallen and pots and pans were scattered about.

"Good morning, friends," he said.

He stood there in his long knit underwear, stroking his beard quizzically.

"Does anyone else find it strange to have an earthquake so far from the nearest faults?"

Nearby, Mill Creek's waters tumbled over rocks and boulders, whispering its old song in the cool morning. We set about putting things back in order as the sun started its journey up behind the dark mountain to the east. Lassen peak loomed conical and perfect, busting up the morning sky.

When things were back in place and we had all dressed and eaten, deciding that everything was obviously safe again, my father let me go with Ishi up Black Rock. We climbed what trail there was and shinned up the rest. From the top of this black pinnacle, Ishi and I saw far out over the green Yana land. We saw Mill Creek running like a white snake down from Lassen's base toward the

Sacramento Valley. Ishi pointed out the little slice of view where he had kept his eyes on the comings and goings of the smoking black creature so long ago. We waved to the grown-ups down below, who looked like midgets from our height. He and I sat down in the smooth hollow at the top of the big rock outcropping. Once comfortable, we started to talk. I had some things I wanted to know.

"Wanasi Ishi," I asked, "now that you are home in the Center of the World, will you want to go back to Big Chiep and Watamany's museum and Popey's hospital?"

"Maliwal, this is no longer my aizuna home. Yuna and Banya creeks are dead, except in the marks our friends make on paper, and except in our hearts. The museum watgurwa at the Edge of the World is now my home."

I looked around at the view of the horizon, saw Lassen first, then McGee peak, then the distant hulk of Mt. Shasta shining in the north. I looked northwest toward the raw backbone of the Trinity Alps, and west toward the green and shadowy coast range, beyond which lay virgin forests of redwoods and fog and then the whole Pacific Ocean, invisible to my eyes but alive in my mind.

"But it is so beautiful here," I said. "How could you ever want to leave?"

Ishi looked straight at me.

"It is beautiful, Wolf Boy, but it is not enough. A wanasi must have someone to hunt for. Nize ah Yahi. I am of the people, but I need someone to share the ways with. I need a young wolf and some friends to love."

His words left me feeling warm but awkward, as any twelve-year-old boy would feel when confronted by the truth that he is loved, wanted, and appreciated. I felt my face flush red. I didn't know what to say.

Ishi seemed to sense this, to read my mind and my mood, as he was often able to do.

"Haxa. Now if the young wolf with hair of no color could only darken it, he might be almost Yahi!"

He got us laughing, giggling like two lunatics, hundreds of feet above the ground.

I found a new subject, one that had also been preying on my mind.

"Father, Big Chiep, and Watamany have been talking of the war that is beginning across the other Outer Ocean. These Saldu wanasi are fighting with guns and cannons."

Ishi looked directly at me again. His broad forehead wrinkled, his grin disappearing.

"These Saldu are not wanasi, Maliwal. I have seen the firesticks they kill with. It is not of the Way.

> *Tetna Man, my own father, they have killed you with their deadly magic. All the last ones huddled together in the damp cave. Claps of thunder. The little ones screaming.*

"Why is it that they fight?" Ishi asked me.

"Father says a country called Belgium was attacked by an enemy. Her neighbors are helping her fight, but the enemy country is strong. Dad, Watamany, and Big Chiep are afraid our people may have to go across this other ocean to help the Belgium ones fight."

> *All of us going back in the cave. Some of the people knocked down by flying stones from the firesticks. Their flesh ripped open, torn. Old ones screaming. Smell of blood in the dark.*

"Hexai-sa, Maliwal, the Belgium ones are as we Yahi were when the Saldu came among us and took away the land. Perhaps those ones will not all be killed if the neighbor ones help fight the mechi-kuwi too. Perhaps the Belgium gods will be kinder to their people..."

"Father says this help may not be enough," I interrupted. "This enemy has powerful auna guns, ones that shoot the quick-fire again and again, and they have many warriors. Some of our wanasi may have to go to that fighting world."

Harsh voices outside. They cannot be people these demons with sticks of fire. Smell of blood. More Yahi going down. These demons cannot be animal ones. Marimi sobbing. Thunder sounds. Flying stones bouncing in the cave. What mechi-kuwi demons do this?

"Wolf, this war, the across-the-other-ocean war, can it come to our museum watgurwa?"

"My father says not this time, but he worries that he will have to leave Mother to go across the ocean to fight in this war."

The people going down. Yahi blood and dambusa twitching bodies on the cave floor. My people going down. Father dead. My sister gone. Jupka, where are you? Running. I am splashing through Yuna Creek, rocks stabbing my feet. Thunder noises. Darkness. It is all darkness around me.

"Would Big Chiep go, Maliwal? He does not even hunt, does not wish to kill."

The late May sun was high above us as we sat talking on top of Black Rock. We were bathed in the warm sunshine, but our minds were far away, on dark thoughts, on the great lie of killing fellow human beings.

"I don't know what the Chiep will do," I said. "But I have heard Watamany say the Saldu wanasi may have no choice but to go."

My friend looked at me. There was so much sadness in his eyes, the dark eyes of a wild buck who had been badly wounded, and who had been healed, but who could never be wholly the same again.

"Your father has asked me many times what I think of the Saldu, young wolf. I have told him what I think after having lived among you at the Edge of the World. I have said that there are too many Saldu crowding each other in the streets and too many wowi crowded on the land. Often I have seen your people fight.

"But I told Popey that there are many kinds of Saldu. Suwa! It is just as there were some good Yahi and a few dawana Yahi too. I am like an older brother to you, Maliwal, and Popey, Watamany, and the Chiep are my new family too.

"I will tell you this, my youngest brother. A Yahi wanasi can never understand the Saldu gods. Haxa, the ones you speak to in Saldu churches are smarter, much smarter gods than Jupka, Kaltsuna, and Coyote. These Saldu gods have given your people many, many more gifts of magic than the Butterfly and Lizard gave to us in the old world. The black train creature and many other things are good things. But your Saldu gods do not seem to care if their people should be wise. Your gods have not set a Way to live in this world, a simple and unchanging path for you Saldu to walk. Your people are very clever, Maliwal, but most of them are not wise. Su. You have much wonderful magic, but you also have magic that kills."

"Maybe you are right, big brother wanasi," I said. "I am glad you are here to always teach me of the way of things."

Ishi looked at me differently now. The sun overhead made my eyes smart and fill up with moisture. Or were they tears?

"I will not always be here with you, my wolf with the hair of no color. But you are already wise."

He stood up and stretched his arms and legs in the warm sun, as a lizard might.

"Come, little brother," he continued. "The others will be missing us. I promised them a Yana sweat bath today and a story if they still wish."

As we made our way down the rough, steep rock, I remember that my eyes kept filling with salty moisture. I have had lots of time to think about it since then, and I have decided they were tears of joy. Years ago, my father had a Latin word, *patria*, that he loved to use. It's the real name for your home—not for country or causes—but for the ground that is yours, that makes you who you are, that has in its every pebble and stone feelings, memories, and associations that all add up to you. Patria, dear father. That is what Ishi and I found up on our tower of dark basalt. That is what you and I will have when I join you in the next world. Patria.

By the time we had joined the others by the rushing creek, eaten some fresh early-run salmon steak for lunch and cleaned up from our meal, it was late afternoon. The Appersons' free-ranging horses were grazing and rooting in the new clover that grew everywhere around. Ishi, true to his word, set about gathering rocks from the creek and placed them in our cooking fire to heat for a sweat bath.

As the fire burned down to coals, he showed us how to build a simple wood bough shelter over the firepit and beyond its circle. That done, all seven of us lay down, crowding together under the makeshift red alder roof. The heat began to build. Lying there, Ishi sang a ritual song in his quiet voice, then said a purification prayer, speaking almost in an inaudible whisper.

The heat kept building. I began to feel an odd sense of nothingness, as if there were nothing in the world but this place, this sweatbath house, and these people. Sweat began to drip down my shoulders and the end of my nose. Our faces, hair, and naked bodies began to steam from the heat, and still the rocks glowed next to us.

"Aiku tsub," Ishi said finally. "It is almost evening. Do any of my Saldu friends wish to hear the story of why the ground shakes, as we lie on it now and sweat?"

He didn't need much encouragement.

The strong, cleansing heat made my mind drift freely as Ishi spoke. The others lay there sweating, listening to his words, lost in their own private reveries.

"This is why the world shakes," he began in his high, melodic voice. "It is because of a battle between two old heroes. Long ago, two old heroes, Ahalamila and Jikula had the first fight in the world. I think they were still fighting inside Waganupa this morning as we slept.

"Su, long ago the two of them got along, but then they saw the dambusa daughter of Moon. Both heroes wished to marry her, and began collecting a dowry to offer her father, wakara Moon. The dambusa marimi chose Ahalamila, however. They built a warm wowi in father Moon's village, and the daughter of Moon bore a fine son to the hero. They called him Topuna.

"But the scorned hero, Jikula, did not rest or forget. He was dawana for revenge. Su, he came up with a plan. Jikula knew that Ahalamila led the Yahi hunters in the spring to hunt deer and to bring some of their tasty venison to Jupka as a gift. Jikula decided to use his kuwi magic to make all the deer invisible. For weeks Ahalamila and his hunters tracked in the Yana meadows and brush with their bows and arrows, but they did not take a single deer. They heard them, but they could not see the forest creatures to send their arrows flying straight. As they turned home empty handed, there was much complaining among Ahalamila's wanasi."

I forgot the heat. Ishi had me hooked again, and I listened intently as evening approached. Swallows swept the air noiselessly, hunting for invisible bugs, and I focused on Ishi's voice rising and falling above the sound of the rushing creek.

"One day soon thereafter, Jikula bragged of his revenge, and Ahalamila learned what his former friend had done. Suwa, what happened then was terrible.

"Ahalamila and his frustrated wanasi began a great battle with Jikula and his men. It was the first war in the world, and many wanasi in the two long lines of fighting men fell to arrows and spears. Jikula was still dawana over revenge, and he killed Ahalamila with an arrow. It was the first time any of the gods or heroes had been killed. This bloody battle would have gone on until the two lines of Yahi warriors were dead, but Jupka heard the screams of dying men and flew down from Waganupa's summit to the field of battle.

"Landing between the lines of angry warriors, he commanded: 'Stop now! It is enough. Go home, all of you, to your families and think long of what you have done in my good world!' Then Jupka flew off with Ahalamila's body, and the battle was ended."

"Is that the end of the story?" Mr. Apperson wanted to know. "It's getting damn hot lying in here and I've got to tend to my horses. No offense, Mr. Ishi..."

Professor Kroeber interrupted him. "We'll all need to cool off and get some supper soon, but what about the Yahi warriors, Ishi? Did the People learn anything from their war?"

"Haxa, Big Chiep," he said. "All the fighting ones prayed to Jupka not to take their bows and spears away and the grieving marimi made them promise to use their weapons only to hunt for food. The People never again turned their bows on any of their Yana brothers, that is except for one boy."

"What happened to Jikula?" Professor Waterman asked from somewhere in the thick blanket of rising steam.

"The mahde boy Topuna could not stand to hear the endless tears of his mother, the daughter of Moon. He took up his dead father's best bow, and broke free of his mother's arms when she tried to hold him back. Topuna went out after Jikula with vengeance in his heart.

"He found the old hero crouching in the brush, hunting sigaga. Unseen by Jikula, Topuna crept behind a bay tree. He was invisible to Jikula, and he began making the call of the yellowhammer woodpecker. Tap, tap, tap. Then he made the whirr of quail wings and the call of the sigaga—ra raa ra, ra raa ra, ra raa ra. Jikula moved out of the underbrush, his bow drawn to shoot.

"Topuna leapt out from his bay tree. Before Jikula could react, Ahalamila's son shot him in the foot with an arrow. Jikula could not move or run away.

"Topuna readied his father's bow with another arrow while Jikula begged for mercy. Topuna almost found it in his heart to let this wicked one live, but he thought of his mother's endless tears and of his father's lifeless body carried off by Jupka's orange wings.

"The last Yahi boy to raise his bow against another of his kind sent his arrow deep into Jikula's heart.

"'Go deal with Jupka's judgment for you,' Topuna said."

Night was on us now. The shining, nearly full moon had again tracked its way above us. Its pale light pierced the open cracks in our tree bough roof, mixing with the gray steam atmosphere we lay breathing. In between Ishi's flow of words, I heard a lonesome chorus of animals in the canyon. Some owls hooted far off in the upper branches of a dead tree. Toads croaked in the heavy underbrush, and some frogs croaked back from the nearby stream. Close by, our horses stamped around wanting their nighttime treat of oats.

"What did the butterfly god do with Jikula?" my father asked from where he lay beside me.

"Yea," Merle Apperson said, "how come the ground shook this morning? Hurry it along, Mr. Ishi. I've got chores to do and I'm about to pass out."

"When Jikula was dead, he did not go to the world after," Ishi continued. Jupka sent him deep into the mountain Waganupa as punishment for fighting, where Ahalamila had already been sent upon his death, and Jupka commanded them both to get along in peace forever in their new underground home.

"For most of the time since, these two banished heroes have been able to get along, but sometimes they still fight over the old wound of the beautiful marimi who was the daughter of Moon. Butterfly spared Topuna, for he was only a boy. Topuna lived on many years happily without hearing his father fight with Jikula about his dambusa mother, but since those old days the heroes have not always been silent. When Waganupa smokes and trembles and the ground at the Center of the World shakes, the Yahi people know their quarreling heroes have not kept their promise to Jupka. Those auna two are a reminder to us to always get along in this good world."

"Women! See all the trouble they can cause," my father said, and everyone laughed. Ishi most of all.

"Come on, smelly friends," he said. "It is time for a cold night-time swim. We should be grateful that fiery Jikula and Ahalamila have not caused great Waganupa to cook us all."

Somewhere out in the darkness, I heard the lonesome cry of a sigaga quail. Ra, ra raa. Ra, ra raa.

Aiku tsub, aizuna marimi Tushi. Soon I will be with you in the stars. Aizuna dambusa marimi. It will be soon. Aiku tsub, aiku tsub. Tetna-Ishi will be with you soon...

Chapter 31

One morning before we left our camp at Mill Creek, the sun rose pale and muted in the east. We thought nothing of the odd, weak sunrise light as we went about the morning business of the camp: washing the previous night's pots and pans and preparing our breakfast. We just assumed thick clouds had come in over the night. But as the eastern sky lit up at least enough to see, it became clear that something was different. Something was wrong.

Ishi was the first to notice it.

"Maliwal, Popey, come see Waganupa!" he called excitedly, his reedy voice rising even an octave higher. "Big Chiep and Watamany, look," he screamed, pointing to the northeast.

There, the rising sun had turned the low clouds blood red, and above them Lassen's peak itself was visible, but a massive tangle of eruption clouds was rising from the summit to two or three times the mountain's height. Dozens of vents and fumeroles must have been spewing molten ash and steam. From our distant camp, Mt. Lassen looked like it had a huge stick of black cotton candy rising from its center. Ishi was right: Jikula and Ahalamila had turned the great mountain into a volcano.

We all dropped our mundane tasks to follow Ishi as he raced for the trail at the bottom of Black Rock. Clearly, my friend had decided that this was the place to watch his people's gods at work. He raced ahead of us fluidly like some young buck, not frightened or afraid, but excited beyond words, grace exhibited in his every contour.

On top of the big column of rock, we all stood panting, out of breath from our sudden pell-mell exertion. Our seven pairs of eyes were on the primal spectacle looming on the eastern horizon. There in front of us, almost close enough to touch it seemed, was the angry volcano. Hissing steam and spit ash hurled upward out of the peak. The black eruption cloud grew higher, rising to three, four times the height of the mountain.

"Jikula and Ahalamila must be fighting fiercely," Ishi said in a quick, high-pitched burst of words. "Or maybe someone has done something to anger the great god Jupka."

I felt my father's hand reach out and touch my head. Then he spoke. "Perhaps it is the war across the Atlantic that makes our world tremble even here."

"Or maybe now Jupka is avenging the killing of his chosen people," Professor Waterman added.

We didn't have time to figure it out. Ishi's gaze was locked on the eastern horizon, and his mouth fell open.

"Look!" he shouted.

There above the lower, crimson sunlit clouds, the dark eruption cloud was rapidly changing its form.

> *Su! Waganupa is forming a face in its smoke. The great black cloud is making a face out of itself.*

"Sweet Jesus," Merle Apperson muttered under his breath. All of our eyes were on the huge amorphous cloud, watching something form out of the black chaos second by second.

> *It is the face of one of the people! Jupka and Kaltsuna are telling me that they still watch over the people in the world to come.*

An outline was taking shape out of the massive cloud, vague at first, then defining itself. Suddenly, its form was clear and unmistakable. The eruption cloud had become a profile: a face with a broad forehead, a wide set eye socket, a nose, aquiline and strong, above an open mouth with full lips, and then a strong jawline and neck. What looked like long dark hair and billowing plumes of crow feathers flowed from behind the upraised head. The face seemed to look upward toward the east and far off into the strange ashen sky.

"Are you seeing what I'm seeing?" Professor Kroeber asked, his a voice stunned, unbelieving whisper.

None of us had the words to answer.

> *Su! It is the face of my own father, Tetna Man, in a full Yahi headdress of clouds! He has not forgotten me. He looks away at the sky world where he and the other dear ones are waiting for me to join them. Jupka has given me this magic sign.*

Then, as suddenly as it had taken shape, the face was gone, leaving dark, jumbled, and puffy randomness in its place. The billowing jet clouds of ash and steam seemed to have reached their peak. Waganupa was beginning to quiet down.

There could be no denying. All of us had seen the face, and none of us would ever forget it. It was the face of an Indian.

We made our way down Black Rock in awed silence that morning. We talked little of our adventure as the day passed, but it dominated our thoughts. A new day came and then another. The volcano became silent again by degrees, becoming a sleeping giant. We watched it constantly, but two days after our running march up Black Rock, not even one cloud of steam hung over Lassen's stony summit.

Just as quickly as our trip had begun, it was over. May turned into June, and it was time to go, time to break up our good Mill Creek camp.

On our last full day at Mill Creek, I went off along the stream, and tried to have my own power dream. At twelve, I had all kinds of notions about my future and thought that a dream like the ones Ishi spoke of might help me choose. Was I Wolf Boy? Was I a white physician's son? I needed to know. Should I grow up to be a doctor? Should I be a writer and put Ishi's stories down on paper? Should I be a hunter for my friends and family and live open and free in a forest of my own choosing?

I did not get my vision that last day at Mill Creek in June 1914. I still wait for it all these seventy-five years later, but when it comes, and I believe it shall come, I will be ready, if not in this world, then in the next.

Mt. Lassen began erupting during the year of our grand, crazy trip. The great volcano continued a cycle of large explosions up through 1916, and it went on erupting, to a lesser extent, for five years thereafter. World War I was fought and I grew to be a man while Jupka's volcano rocked the ground at the Center of the World. I will take those memories to the grave with me, but the great mountain will never die. Mt. Lassen is only sleeping now as I write these words, wrapped in Ishi's old warm bearskin, rocking in my chair.

* * *

Ishi and I spent the remainder of that perfect year of 1914 almost constantly in each other's company. Back at the Edge of the World, the summer faded slowly into fall. School began again and interrupted our routine somewhat, but there were still the many afternoons of Indian summer we spent together when the air was still warm enough for long walks outside. Often, we would go to the little patch of forest left undeveloped directly behind the Medical Center and Museum of Anthropology on Parnassus Heights.

Ishi and I built a trail there that fall, our gentle path through a tiny portion of the city that had remained California wilderness. Our path is still there, although it is now even more hemmed in by concrete and buildings. It is still well kept, but I'm not sure by whom. I know because I still walk it whenever I go south from Redding to visit San Francisco.

We walked behind "Popey's house" and "Big Chiep's museum" for many hours that fall of 1914. We hid out from the world among stands of eucalyptus trees, the thick patches of green miner's lettuce, blackberry brambles, and reddish green poison oak at our feet. Sometimes, we sat together huddled and bent in our tiny secret cave. Near the end of fall, we would look out of its small, open mouth at the rich gold of the few aspen trees and the fiery, low-growing bush maples mixed among the eucalyptus. Sometimes it seemed as if we were looking out of the eye of the earth itself, not from a small cave. We imagined together that we could see across the entire continent. Sadly, like the trees' colors, all of that play of the mind could not last.

Ishi developed a hacking cough in December 1914, and my father checked him into the hospital for tests and treatment.

Chapter 32

When January of 1915 was nearly gone, my father let Ishi go home from the hospital to his own room in the museum. Ishi appeared to have recovered from his mild respiratory infection: his temperature was normal and Dad could find no evidence of tuberculosis. Although Father and the professors were very concerned, there seemed no reason to keep Ishi in a hospital room. I saw him every day after school, but I knew my friend was not completely well. He still loved working, making arrow shafts or flaking arrow points on the museum floor while his audiences watched, but his endurance was down. He needed more breaks and went to bed early many nights, often without telling one of his ritual evening stories. All that winter, Ishi and I stayed off our private hideaway trail among the eucalyptus and aspen trees.

When spring came, when his native hills were growing green with new clover and Waganupa sometimes steamed, Ishi reentered the hospital. My father could find no tubercle bacilli in his lungs, but Ishi's tuberculin test was positive. Professor Waterman and Professor Kroeber came to visit Ishi often, and my Dad brought me by to see him every day. All the doctors in "Popey's house" were interested in getting Ishi well, and my father himself, Ishi's private kuwi, gave him more attention than any of his other patients. By the end of that spring, Ishi's lung disease seemed to be in remission, and he went back, eagerly, to his museum watgurwa room.

We were all confident enough about our friend's health that plans were drawn up for the remainder of the year. Ishi would spend the summer across the bay at Berkeley with Professor Waterman and his family, taking life easy, eating and sleeping well, sometimes working with the great linguist Edward Sapir, who would spend the summer in Berkeley too and who would come to Waterman's house to record the Yahi tongue and ways in his notebooks when Ishi had the energy. Professor Kroeber would leave for Europe for the year on his sabbatical, but he would stay in close contact with Ishi through the mails and would resume his work with my friend upon his return. All this was the way we thought things would be.

That summer of 1915 began well enough for Ishi, although he and I were separated, sometimes for days, until my father could make time to take me across the bay on a ferry to see him. He loved being a part of the Waterman family in Berkeley. Whenever Dad and I were lucky enough to be invited to stay for dinner at the Waterman's, it was obvious that Ishi fit right in.

He was shy around Mrs. Waterman, and would speak to her only in response to a direct question, but it was clear that Ishi liked her. He imitated her every motion with a knife, fork, or spoon perfectly, and his table etiquette was always a graceful mimic of hers. Although he never looked directly at Mrs. Waterman, I often saw him studying her with demure sideways glances. I think he was quite awed by this tall, gentle Saldu woman, the dambusa marimi of his friend Watamany. For her part, Mrs. Waterman adored Ishi and often held his neat habits up as an example for her husband to follow. I remember that once, in July I think, Ishi was in the Waterman's bathtub when Father and I arrived for a visit. Outside the bathroom, we could hear much splashing, singing, and commotion going on. Professor Waterman teased his wife about the high tide she would find when Ishi's bath was over, but, when he emerged, cleanly scrubbed and perfectly dressed, we all peeked behind Ishi into the bathroom to find every towel and every washcloth folded and in its place, and not one drop of water on the floor.

In August, my father and Professor Waterman noticed that Ishi's appetite had fallen off. Professor Sapir's notebooks of Yana words and phrases had been filling all summer as the two worked together several hours each day, but now Ishi tired easily and did not always want to repeat his beloved words and stories. By the end of August, my father and Professor Waterman agreed that Ishi needed to return to the hospital across the bay.

September came and went and my friend's tuberculosis did not advance or disappear. Dad kept a constant watch on his moderate cough and made sure that Ishi had plenty of rest and good food. All the while, Professor Kroeber was in constant touch from Germany and then England. He kept up frequent correspondence with my father and the museum staff, always enclosing a note or a trinket for Ishi and asking the rest of us about his health.

By October, it was agreed that Ishi should be returned to live somewhere near his homeland when he was strong enough to travel. We knew that he would not want to give up his home at the Edge of the World, but, with no natural immunity to the diseases of civilization, my father and the professors felt this might be Ishi's only hope of a full recovery. Professor Kroeber suggested contacting Merle Apperson at his Tehama County ranch. He was sure the Apperson's would be glad to make a home for Ishi there in the uncontaminated north. The grown-ups' plan was to put Ishi back into the museum for a few months while he regained his strength, and then to move him to the country. If the plan was put into effect, I already had my own romantic ideas of quitting school and running away to the Apperson ranch. Before November came, Ishi was once again out of the hospital and back in the museum.

All through November and December, I came to see Ishi every day in the sunny, well-ventilated room which had been used for the museum's finest exhibits until Waterman and the others had cleared it out and turned it into a temporary home. There, Ishi had every care, but he did not get better.

By January 1916, when I should have been starting out the new year with the boundless enthusiasm of a new teenager, my friend developed a persistent fever, grew weaker, and began to spend most of his time in bed. Some afternoons after school, I would sit with him as he lay motionless in his room looking out the window for hours. On good days, we would talk or make fun of the monkey-like antics of the construction workers on the steel cage of the new university hospital being built just across the street. The papers were carrying the news of Waganupa's continuing activity back in the Center of the World. When he had energy, Ishi always wanted to know whether the great volcano was still shaking the earth. On his bad days, Ishi would lie silent for hours, or else sing his old Yana songs, quietly, inwardly, as if he had almost forgotten that I was in the room.

Weekly letters came from Professor Kroeber, who had arrived in New York City for the last part of his year off. He wanted to know Ishi's daily temperatures, his weight, his state of mind, and whether Ishi was willing to return to the Center of the World until he was once again the vital forest wanasi he had been. We had no idea those two soul mates were never to see each other again, at least among the living.

By March 1916, my father had to put Ishi back in the hospital for the last time. He needed alimentary feeding and was extremely weak. At fourteen, I was losing the best friend I ever had in my life.

* * *

It is early spring, the ending time for the Yahi in my dream. Great Waganupa is exploding at the Center of the World. Su. I see a dark cloud rising out of the volcano's red fire. I am rising too, rising up somewhere. Waganupa's smoke is taking form and shape again, as it was when Wolf Boy and my friends and I felt the whole world shake. Haxa. I see Tetna Man's face again in the black swirling clouds. I am rising upward toward the star path, to Tushi, and to all the other lost ones on my father's headdress of rising smoke and glowing ash that pours ever upward into gray sky, then higher still into blackness and stars. Haxa, I see the white hot stars coming closer. I am floating on my father's headdress of fiery ash and smoke to the stars. They are close around me and far ahead too, larger and smaller and shining through the blackness. I see them moving at me through Waganupa's billowing clouds, coming faster and faster. I hear winds blowing, and I am surrounded by the most beautiful stars! There are people's fires everywhere in the dark night. Glowing points of light are everywhere. Something white is ahead of me. Haxa, it comes closer. I see a shifting cloud opening up in front of me. Su, it is so bright it stings my eyes to look deeply into it. This white cloud is spreading open all around me, Kaltsuna. I rise into it! There is brightness everywhere here in the dark. In the wind and light, I hear a far-off voice. Suwa! A face is forming in front of me. Tushi's face comes out of this cloud! There is brightness all around her, a circle of light, and stars stream in blurred streaks through her face and hair toward me. Dambusa marimi, I see your beautiful eyes, brown and deep and clear, dancing with the inner light of stars. I see your hair like streaming black feathers full of starlight behind your smooth face, and I see your beautiful face glowing. Out of the powerful wind, your voice grows nearer. I pray to Jupka that all I see and hear is real. Your soft voice is nearer in the warm wind, nearer. What is it you say to me?

"We are all waiting for you in these stars, Tetna-Ishi. Your own mother and father, your grandmother and grandfather, Boy Cousin, Elder Uncle, and I, too, are all gathered around our glowing fire here in the Sky World. There is love in the world after, my husband. There is love."

Afterward: The Face in the Clouds

When Ishi died on March 25, 1916, the last of the Yahi people vanished into the night sky forever. After that, his friends T. T. Waterman, A. L. Kroeber, and Saxton Pope, Sr. did their best to keep the memory of the Yahi alive. Following their deaths, Saxton Pope, Jr., the wolf boy, and, especially, Mrs. Theodora Kroeber have done their best to keep Ishi with us, to honor what he was and to remember a lost way of life. Now, they too are gone, and it is up to us to tell the story to our children, to keep alive what once was.

Mt. Lassen, elevation 10, 457 ft., is the southernmost of the Cascade volcanic peaks. Like her northern sister Mt. St. Helens, Lassen is an active volcano, and did, indeed, erupt repeatedly during Ishi's life among the whites. From May of 1914 through 1917, there were nearly three hundred significant explosions. During one of these, on August 19, 1914, to be exact, the eruption cloud assumed the form of an Indian face and was photographed by a forest ranger. This phenomenon happened during the summer that Ishi, the university professors, and the Popes made their epic month-long trip back to Ishi's homeland. While the forest ranger reported that the strange face in the cloud lingered only a few seconds before it vanished, his photograph has been permanently preserved and was later included in the B. F. Loomis private collection of historic prints. Loomis' widow left his collection to the public. The original face-in-the-clouds print may be seen at the Lowie Museum of Anthropology, University of California at Berkeley. The original glass negative is housed at the Loomis Museum Association in Mineral, CA, 96063, and multiple print copies may be seen at that address too.

The area around Mt. Lassen is now Lassen Volcanic Park, probably our nation's least visited parkland. Lassen peak at the center of the park is a relatively young mountain, as little as five thousand years old, and there is no doubt that the volcano figured extensively in Yahi mythology, especially their creation myths. Just south of the peak lies the huge fragmented caldera of what was called Mt. Tehama, a mountain that was far larger than Lassen

peak. Geologists tell us that Mt. Tehama blew up in the not-too-distant past, giving birth to Mt. Lassen and the numerous vents, steam jets, and hot springs that remain active in the Lassen park area. Ishi's ancient ancestors may well have witnessed the primordial destruction of the greatest mountain in California and fashioned their myths to make sense of it. The answer lies in the stars, with those who have already walked the eastward path of more than a hundred thousand lights. Aiku tsub.

Photo: Mt Lassen and Manzanita Lake

On August 19, 1914, Mt. Lassen's eruption cloud assumed a profile form of a human face and was photographed by a forest ranger. Within seconds the 'face' vanished.

Lassen Volcanic National Park Photograph